ALEX REACHED THE EDGE OF THE AIR SHAFT.

The ground had opened up beneath him and he lay, stretched out on his stomach, gazing down into nothingness. The beam of his headlamp was nowhere near powerful enough to reach the bottom and simply stopped in midair, illuminating the metal circle around it. The height of the Gherkin. It was as if he were lying on the roof of a London skyscraper, thinking about throwing himself off. Smithers had assured him that he had a plan and that it would work, but Alex could only take his word for it. Was he reliable?

Well, there was only one way to find out. Alex swallowed hard, then reached behind him and found a cable poking out of his backpack. It had a jack plug that clicked into a socket built into one of the shoulders of his combat suit. He turned it and heard the safety lock engage. Then he waited for the computer that he had carried all this distance to boot up and do its work. Smithers had said it would only take five seconds, but he waited half a minute just to be sure.

This was worse than the snake. What he was about to do went against every instinct. It was like committing suicide. But there was no other way.

Alex swung himself around and threw himself into the void.

>—<

ALEX RIDER MISSIONS:

ALSO BY ANTHONY HOROWITZ

THE DIAMOND BROTHERS MYSTERIES

ALEX RIDER

SECRET WEAPON

SEVEN UNTOLD ADVENTURES
FROM THE LIFE OF A TEENAGED SPY

ANTHONY HOROWITZ

PUFFIN BOOKS

PUFFIN BOOKS
An imprint of Penguin Random House LLC, New York

First published in the United States of America by Philomel Books,
an imprint of Penguin Random House LLC, 2019.
Published by Puffin Books, an imprint of Penguin Random House LLC, 2020.

Visit us online at penguinrandomhouse.com

THE LIBRARY OF CONGRESS HAS CATALOGED THE PHILOMEL BOOKS EDITION AS FOLLOWS:
Names: Horowitz, Anthony, 1955– author.
Title: Alex Rider, secret weapon : seven untold adventures from the life of a teenaged spy /
Anthony Horowitz.
Description: New York, NY : Philomel Books, [2019] | Series: Alex Rider |
Summary: "A short story collection that expands the universe of teen spy Alex Rider from
author Anthony Horowitz"—Provided by publisher.
Identifiers: LCCN 2018053724 | ISBN 9781524739331 (hardback) |
ISBN 9781524739348 (ebook)
Subjects: | CYAC: Spies—Fiction. | Adventure and adventurers—Fiction. | Short stories. |
BISAC: JUVENILE FICTION / Action & Adventure / Survival Stories. |
JUVENILE FICTION / Law & Crime.
Classification: LCC PZ7.H7875 Ale 2019 | DDC [Fic]—dc23
LC record available at https://lccn.loc.gov/2018053724

Puffin Books ISBN 9780525515784

Printed in the United States of America

1 3 5 7 9 10 8 6 4 2

American edition edited by Michael Green and Cheryl Eissing.
American edition designed by Angelie Yap.
Text set in 11.5-point Life LT Std.

CONTENTS

ALEX IN
AFGHANISTAN

33.9391°N,
67.7100°E

FALCON'S EDGE

THERE WERE FIVE MEN sitting around the fire, huddled together in the Herat Mountains in the northwest corner of Afghanistan. Although it was May and the plains were already dotted with spring flowers, up here, five thousand feet above sea level, the winds still came rushing around the corners in icy blasts and the temperature tumbled toward freezing after the sun had set. The men had erected a tent made from woven goat hair and tied down with long ropes nailed into the hard ground. They had rested here for three hours and now squatted down with their backs to it, waiting for their meal to cook. The horses that had brought them here were tethered nearby.

Five men and a boy.

Alex Rider came out of the tent and took his place on the rough piece of carpet that had been set down for him. He examined the food that was bubbling away in the metal cauldron in the middle of the fire. It was some sort of lamb stew, and he had to admit that it smelled delicious. The men had barely spoken to him since they had picked him up at the rendezvous point, a day's ride away on the other side of Afghanistan's border. He knew that they were Kochis—Afghan nomads—and that they were loyal only to themselves. They would have been paid to bring him this far . . . gold, weapons, food, or all three. He wasn't sure if he trusted them. Certainly, from the moment they had set eyes on him, they hadn't trusted him.

They had not been told why it was necessary to escort a fourteen-year-old English boy into a landscape that really could be described as the middle of nowhere. They knew only that he was important. He had been brought to them in a Lynx Mk9A, the British army's primary battlefield utility helicopter, said to be the fastest in the world. It had landed on the outskirts of the town of Yazdan, in Iran, and that had told them something at once. It could not have been there without the permission of the Iranians. The British and the Iranian government working together! This was serious.

The food was ready. The leader of the Kochis, a man Alex knew only as Rafiq, unwrapped a piece of cloth and laid out several pieces of flatbread, which they would use as plates. There were no knives or forks. He scooped out some of the meat and vegetables and handed it to Alex.

"*Mamnoon*," Alex said. It was the Farsi word for "thank you."

The other men served themselves and they all began to eat. The moon had come out, giving them enough light to see what they were doing, and the sky was also crowded with hundreds of stars, shimmering over the mountains with a silver glow. Holding the flatbread in both hands, Alex tore into it with his teeth. The lamb was cooked in yogurt, lotus roots, chickpeas, and garlic. After the long journey, he would have eaten anything, but it was even better than he'd expected. As he ate, he glanced at his companions. They were hunched together, somehow looking relaxed on the hard, stony ground, occasionally examining him with dark, intelligent eyes. They were dressed in loose-fitting clothes in neutral colors, with either turbans or the soft, round-topped berets that were known as *pakols*. Rafiq had a velvet waistcoat that might have been green and gold when his grandfather wore it but was now threadbare and faded. It was impossible to tell the age of the men. They could have been twenty. They could have been fifty. They had all been hollowed out by the sun and the wind.

And what did they think of him? Alex wondered. He had seen their astonishment when he climbed out of the helicopter, and as they had traveled together toward the mountains, they kept glancing at him as if they still couldn't believe he was there. He couldn't have looked more different from them. He was half their size, fair-haired, European. He was wearing a black combat suit with hiking boots and a backpack. It was unfortunate that horse riding was one of the few outdoor activities he had never fully mastered. They had given him a sleek black Egyptian colt with a white blaze on its chest, but he was barely able to control it, bouncing along helplessly.

He was very glad to dismount and have a rest. The lower parts of his body felt like they'd been mangled.

"English boy!" It was Faisal, the second in command, who had spoken. Alex didn't like him. He had an ugly, crooked smile, and a cataract had turned one of his eyes a milky white.

Alex looked up.

"You living in London?"

Alex nodded. He didn't want to pass on any information, but there was no point denying it.

"Big Ben! The Queen! Chelsea soccer!" Faisal roared with laughter as if he had said something hilarious.

Rafiq muttered something in Farsi, but Faisal snapped back angrily, then turned to Alex once again. "Why you come here?" he demanded.

Alex shrugged. "There's no school at the moment," he said. "And I didn't know what else to do."

Faisal, who had only half understood, frowned. "You go to Falcon's Edge," he said.

A gust of wind tugged at the flames, and Faisal's face seemed to become distorted. The other men were waiting to hear what Alex said. Even Rafiq was gazing at him intently. Once again, Alex didn't want to reply. But they knew anyway. They had been paid to take him there. "Yes," he said simply.

"Why?"

Alex ignored him. But then another of the men spoke. His name was Usman. As well as a rifle strapped across his shoulders, he had an ornate dagger with a curved blade hanging from his waist. "You no go there, English boy," he said. "You enter Falcon's Edge, you no come out." The others nodded in agreement.

"Nice lamb," Alex said, holding up his food. "What's for pudding?"

Falcon's Edge. Alex had never heard the name until a few days before, and suddenly he was four thousand miles away, back home in Chelsea, relaxing in the comfort of his bedroom. The sun was shining. It was going to be a warm day. Alex had schoolwork to do—but no school. A large part of Brookland had burned down and all the students had been sent home while the police investigated what had happened. Alex could have told them, of course. He had been there when the fire began. He was lucky he hadn't died in the flames.

The doorbell rang.

Alex waited for Jack Starbright to answer it, then remembered that she had gone out shopping. He swung himself off the bed and padded downstairs with no shoes on. This was the house that his uncle had bought. All his life, while Alex was growing up, Ian Rider had pretended to be a banker, but it was only after his death—he had been killed in Cornwall—that Alex had discovered the truth. He was a spy, working for the Special Operations Division of MI6. As Alex had unraveled all the lies, there had been a part of him that had wanted to sell the house, to move out of London, to start living a life that was actually real. In fact, the exact opposite had happened. MI6 had come for Alex, sucking him into their world, sending him on two missions—first to Cornwall and then to a private academy in the French Alps. He had been lucky to escape from Point Blanc. He had even been invited to his own funeral.

He reached the front door and opened it. Who had he been expecting? The postman? Of course it wasn't as easy as that. Mrs. Jones, the deputy chief executive and number two to Alan Blunt, was standing there, wearing a light raincoat, with her hands in her pockets. Alex recognized the man who was with her, dressed as always in a cheap suit with what looked like an old school tie. This was John Crawley. "Crawley from personnel"—that was how he had described himself after Ian's death.

"Can we come in, Alex?" Mrs. Jones asked.

"Maybe you should wait for Jack to get back," Alex said.

"Actually, we waited until she'd left."

Alex didn't remember opening the door for them, but somehow the two agents had made their way past him and entered the house. Alex led them into the kitchen. He didn't offer them coffee.

"You're not at school," Mrs. Jones began.

"You know very well. School burned down," Alex said.

"Yes. That was very unfortunate. We should have realized that one of Dr. Grief's clones was still on the loose."

Alex had been chased around the building by a boy who was an exact replica of himself. It was like being attacked by his own reflection. He remembered the last moment, seeing the boy falling through a crater in the roof, disappearing into the smoke and flames. "What happened to him?" he asked.

"We're looking after him," Mrs. Jones said. Alex didn't even want to think about what that might mean. "How are you?"

"I'm still alive. No thanks to you."

Mrs. Jones smiled thinly. She took out a packet of mints and, without offering one to Alex, slipped one into her mouth. She always sucked peppermint when she was about to deliver bad news. Behind her, Crawley was perched on a kitchen chair with his hands on his knees. He somehow reminded Alex of a ventriloquist's dummy. "We need your help again," Mrs. Jones said.

"I'm afraid I'm not interested," Alex said. "I've got math homework."

"I know."

"And science homework, history homework, geography homework, French homework. I'm still trying to catch up from last term."

"Mr. Blunt asked me to come and see you. Something's come up, and from what we understand, Brookland won't be open for at least another week. That gives you plenty of time to do what we have in mind and to be back without anyone noticing."

"You'd think most young people would jump at a chance to visit Afghanistan," Crawley said, speaking for the first time.

"Afghani . . ." Alex's head swam. "No!" he exclaimed.

"Forget it! You've got to be joking! Why do you keep asking me? Why can't you leave me alone?"

"Because you're very good, Alex," Mrs. Jones replied. "Ian Rider trained you for this. All your life you were prepared for it and you've already proven yourself twice. That business with Dr. Grief really was spectacular."

"You forced me into all that," Alex reminded her. "Why should I be interested now?"

"I'll explain." Mrs. Jones turned to Crawley. "John, would you mind making us some coffee?"

"Certainly, Mrs. Jones." Crawley swung off the stool and busied himself in the kitchen.

Alex watched him in disbelief. "Do you know where the milk is?" he asked.

"Oh yes." Crawley smiled. "I know everything."

Mrs. Jones looked back at Alex and began to explain. "I'm sure I don't need to tell you, Alex, that terrorism is now the greatest threat to world peace. You've read about the horrible incidents in New York, in London, and in Paris. The whole of the Middle East is a cauldron, and for the security services, it's a situation that's almost impossible to control . . . not when you have so many tiny groups that are ready to strike at any time with no overall plan.

"Imagine how much worse it would become if those groups were able to get their hands on the most advanced weapons . . . by which I mean nuclear or biochemical technology. That's our biggest nightmare—a terrorist with a nuclear bomb—and intelligence services all over the world have been working together to make sure it never happens."

"Caffeinated or decaffeinated?" Crawley asked. He had filled the kettle and flicked it on.

"I don't really mind, thank you." Mrs. Jones hadn't taken her eyes off Alex. "It could be about to happen," she went on. "And all because of a man named Darcus Drake."

"Who is he?" Alex had to ask.

"He's a very interesting person. For many years, he was a photographer working for the international press. He lived in London. He was wealthy. He won a great many awards. Darcus traveled the world, taking photographs of war zones. That was his specialty. When bombs went off, when children were hurt, when the hospitals began to fill up, somehow he'd be there. He didn't care about his own safety. He made it his mission to show people what was happening in places like Syria, Yemen, Iraq, Sudan, and Ethiopia. The strange thing is, Alex, there was something almost beautiful about the images he took. He had a way of capturing horror that made you want to look."

"He sounds like a good guy," Alex said.

"He was. There's no doubt about that. But somewhere along the way, he changed. I suppose it's impossible to keep witnessing so much pain and suffering and just click away with your camera as if it's got nothing to do with you. Darcus Drake came to believe that the West was responsible for everything that he was seeing. He became more and more interested in terrorism until the inevitable happened and he became a terrorist himself.

"The thing is, he had traveled all over the Middle East. He had made hundreds of contacts. He knew journalists, intelligence officers, field agents, local tribesmen . . . He'd even met some of the terrorist groups. He spoke four languages, including Arabic and Farsi. There's no question that he had a brilliant mind. I don't know exactly what happened. I don't know if there was a light bulb moment. But suddenly he realized he was in a perfect position to take control, to form his own terrorist group, fighting against the West. And that is what he did."

"What's all this got to do with me?" Alex asked.

"I'm coming to that, Alex. For the last two years, Darcus Drake dropped out of sight, but he recently emerged again in Afghanistan. We've received intelligence that he's holed up in the Herat Mountains, quite close to the border with Iran. He's occupying an ancient citadel that was built around 330 BC by Alexander the Great. It's been rebuilt many times since then. In the nineteenth century, British soldiers fighting in Afghanistan gave it a name: Falcon's Edge. That's how it's been known ever since.

"It's a fantastic place. It looks out over an empty plain with Iran just to the west. The entrance to the citadel is very high up. There's a wide stone platform open to the elements, with a three-hundred-yard drop. During the First Anglo-Afghan War, the local tribesmen used to tie up their prisoners and throw them to their deaths. Only one track winds up through the mountains to this entrance and it's heavily guarded. It would be impossible to approach without being seen. And there's more to Falcon's Edge than meets the eye. It's perched on the edge of the mountain, but more recently it's been extended into the mountain itself. There's a network of tunnels and chambers. It has electricity and advanced telecommunications. But there's worse. According to our latest reports, the citadel is hiding a terrible secret."

"Here you are!" Crawley brought a tray over to the counter. He had set out three cups and a small jug of milk. He glanced at Alex reproachfully. "You don't have any cookies."

"I try not to eat them," Alex growled. He was annoyed. He had allowed himself to be drawn into this story. Despite himself, he wanted to know more. "What secret?" he asked.

"For the answer to that, you have to go back to 1979," Mrs. Jones replied. "That was when the Soviets occupied Afghanistan at the start of what turned out to be a disastrous nine-year war. While they were there, for their own reasons, they decided to build something called a calutron. I don't suppose you know what that is."

"It's a giant particle accelerator," Alex said. "It produces uranium 235, which you need to make a bomb. We covered it last term in science and humanities." He sighed. "I was actually there for that lesson . . ."

"Well . . . yes." Mrs. Jones blinked. "A calutron is used to produce small quantities of pure uranium. For what it's worth, it needs a huge amount of electrical power to run it and an equally huge cooling system to stop it from blowing up." Crawley handed her a cup of coffee and she took it. "We've learned that there's a Soviet-built calutron inside Falcon's Edge and Darcus Drake is trying to get it working. He's planning to produce uranium, and basically what he's going to do is open a nuclear supermarket. He's offering to arm every terrorist group in the Middle East with nuclear weapons."

She paused. Was it Alex's imagination or had it suddenly gotten very quiet outside?

"Can you imagine it, Alex?" Crawley muttered. "A nuclear explosion in London or Paris . . ."

"Go on," Alex said.

"To begin with, we didn't believe it," Mrs. Jones said. "A plant that size would have to show up. We've had planes over the country looking for heat signatures. Satellite photography. Nothing. But then, two weeks ago, we were contacted by a Russian scientist who had worked on the project. He confirmed that the calutron is there, buried deep in the mountain, invisible to the world outside. And very soon it's going to start production."

"So why don't you bomb it?" Alex asked.

"Because it's too well protected. The walls of the citadel are far too thick and the mountains make it almost impossible for an air-to-ground missile to get a proper sighting on the target. Anyway, these days you can't fly bombing missions without evidence that you can show the world. Photographic evidence. That's what we need now. Someone has to get into the mountain and prove that the calutron is really there. Then we can go to the United Nations and persuade them to take action."

There were many questions Alex could have asked, but in the end, he knew it boiled down to two words. "Why me?"

"We've managed to look at some blueprints, and as far as we can see, there's only one way into Falcon's Edge. As I've explained, the front entrance is impossible. But if you were to climb through the mountains and go in the back way, there is a possibility. The Soviets built a network of pipes and ventilation shafts and there's an access panel that could be opened. It's the one weak link in their security, and the reason it's been overlooked is simple. Some of the pipework is very narrow. Too narrow for a man . . ."

But not too narrow for a boy.

Alex found himself staring into the flames of the bonfire, the cold breeze tugging at his hair, as he remembered the conversation with Mrs. Jones. The man called Usman had brewed mint tea. He handed Alex a tiny bowl that burned his fingers. He raised it to his lips and sipped. The tea was hot and sweet. The other men had lit cigarettes. They were talking among themselves in low voices, ignoring him now. How had he allowed MI6 to talk him into this? It seemed to Alex that everything had happened in a whirl. He had been driven to the seventeen-story building near Liverpool Street Station that pretended to be a bank and where Special Operations was based. There had been further briefings. He had been provided with all the equipment he would need. And then, finally, a Royal Navy Jetstream T3 aircraft had flown him halfway across the world. He had transferred to the Lynx Mk9A helicopter in Cyprus and then—after refueling on an aircraft carrier in the south Mediterranean—he had been dropped on the edge of a dusty town in Iran. And now he was here.

Why him? There was no answer to that question and, anyway, it was already far too late to ask.

2

IN THE PIPELINE

THE KOCHIS KNEW WHAT they were looking for, but even so, Alex was amazed that they had been able to find it without GPS or highly detailed maps. The entrance to the pipe network was a round hole set in a block of concrete, covered with thick steel wire. The whole thing was built into the side of a hill and half covered by rubble and wild grass. Even in broad daylight they could have walked past without seeing it, but they had come here in the middle of the night and they hadn't even hesitated. The man called Usman cried out and beckoned them over. They set to work at once.

They had brought with them an oxy-acetylene torch and gas cylinder, strapped to one of the horses, and now they used it to burn through the wire. Alex watched the heavy strands as they glowed red and then peeled away. Part of him was afraid that the brilliant light of the cutter would alert someone that they were there, but as with the bonfire, the tribesmen showed no concern. They were surrounded by the great bulk of the mountains with nobody in sight. Falcon's Edge itself was half a mile away and below them, tucked away in its own rockface. A passing satellite might notice the sudden glare, but by the time it had communicated the information to whichever intelligence agency controlled it, they would have been long gone. It was probably safe enough.

Alex found himself staring into the black, round hole that could have been the barrel of a gun, pointing straight at his head. He could just make out the curve of the pipe itself as it burrowed into the hillside, and the thought of crawling into it filled him with horror. Mrs. Jones had been right about one thing. Alex was slim and small for his age, but still, his shoulders would barely pass through and certainly no adult would be able to follow. He realized that once he began, it would be impossible to turn around. If the plans that he had been shown were wrong, if he came to a dead end, he would be trapped. Effectively, he was being asked to bury himself alive.

"Tomorrow." Rafiq, the leader of the group who had brought him here, hadn't dismounted from his horse. Glancing down at Alex, his face was full of doubt. "We meet . . . the Shuja cemetery."

"Midday," Alex said. Mrs. Jones had described the operation while he was in London. Getting out of Falcon's Edge was going to be easier than getting in. If all went well, in less than twelve hours' time, Alex's work would be done and he would be escorted back across the border into Iran. If not . . . Alex didn't like to think about the possibility of failure—and why should he? There were only about a hundred things that could go wrong.

Rafiq nodded. He took one look at the mad English

boy who seemed determined to kill himself, then wheeled his horse around and rode away. The others followed him. Faisal, the man who was blind in one eye, twisted in his saddle and spat at the ground. It was as if that summed up everything he had to say about the adventure. He rode off, leading Alex's horse behind him.

Alex was alone. Suddenly he felt very lonely, lost in the mountains. The wind was still gusting over his shoulders. He ran a hand through his hair, clearing it out of his eyes. Well, there was no point standing here having second thoughts. Right now, there was only one way back home.

He gathered his things together. Nothing that he was wearing was quite what it seemed. Derek Smithers, the ever cheerful, overweight science officer at MI6, had supplied Alex with all the gadgets he had needed on his last two missions, and he had equipped him for this one too. First, Alex checked the belt he was wearing around his waist. It was divided into various pockets, each one containing different items—weapons, medical supplies, maps, food, water—that he might need. The belt also had what looked like four suction cups, surrounding his body like points on a compass. Alex would need those later.

He had taken off the backpack. It would be impossible to fit into the pipe while he was wearing it. The backpack contained two batteries and a miniature computer, which would control all the equipment concealed in the combat suit. This extended to his hiking boots, which looked ordinary when seen from above but had two small glass plates concealed in the instep, in front of each heel. Finally, Alex slipped on a charcoal-gray helmet made out of some sort of impacted plastic. It wasn't just there to protect his head. It housed a miniature digital camera, barely larger than a matchbox, that would record his journey through an opening one-sixteenth of an inch wide. Alex had been given a professional camera to photograph the calutron when he found it, but the helmet camera would act as backup. The helmet was also fitted with a Speleo Ultra Vario headlamp, powered by a built-in lithium ion battery. It was the lightweight, state-of-the-art flashlight favored by cavers.

He flicked it on and the beam shot out ahead of him. Alex directed it into the yawning mouth that waited to devour him. "The first part's the worst part," he muttered to himself. It was something Ian Rider had often said . . . helping him with his homework or teaching him to climb mountains. It was a joke between them because they both knew that the first part never was. It just got worse as it went along. Alex lowered himself onto his knees. He grabbed the backpack in both hands, took a deep breath, and plunged in.

The wind was cut off as if by a giant blade. The stars disappeared. He was completely surrounded by the smooth metal surface of the pipe. He could feel it pressing down on his shoulders, rubbing against his arms and legs. It seemed to go on forever. Looking ahead of him, he saw the light from his helmet cutting through the darkness, illuminating . . . nothing. There was just the pipe, a perfect circle glinting in the light, and him, the insect who had been foolish enough to crawl into it. He would have to worm his way along, pushing the backpack ahead of him. And suppose the diagrams that Mrs. Jones had shown him were wrong? Suppose the pipe narrowed? Alex put the thought to one side. There was no point wasting energy on problems until they became real.

He crawled forward, following the beam. It would be impossible to tell how far he had traveled, not when every section of the pipeline looked the same. Nor did he waste time checking his watch. He only knew that the farther he went, the more his elbows and knees, unused to bearing his weight, began to hurt. He also had to fight to stop himself from panicking. His brain was screaming at him to stand up, to turn around, to go back. But that was out of the question, he reminded himself. He had a job to do. He just had to focus on that. What would he do if the light went out? No. The lithium battery would last eleven hours and, in case of an emergency, he had a spare in his belt. Stop worrying about nothing. Alex knew perfectly well that the real danger was still to come.

A whole hour passed. At least, it felt like an hour. The pipe seemed to be getting narrower. Alex was sure he could feel it closing in on him. Was he imagining it or was it getting harder to breathe? He must have been about a quarter of a mile into the mountain and he could only imagine the thousands of tons of soil and rock bearing down on him from above. He stopped and forced himself to relax. A trickle of sweat slid down his face, finding its way through the crack between his helmet and the side of his head. It had been cold outside, but as he penetrated farther into the ventilation system, he began to feel the warm air being blasted up from somewhere far below. The deeper he went, the closer it seemed to get. He was also aware of a strange smell. It was mechanical, a mixture of oil and electricity.

He came to a T-junction. He had arrived before he knew it, almost hypnotized by the single beam of light. The second pipe, running left and right, was twice the size of the one he was in and he squeezed himself into it, feeling like toothpaste coming out of a tube. It was still pitch-dark but at least he no longer had the feeling of being trapped.

"You'll be starting in one of the auxiliary outlets. It feeds into the main air shaft—and all I can say is that I'm glad they didn't send me. I'm not sure I'd have gotten very far!"

It was Smithers speaking, his hands resting on his enormous stomach. Suddenly Alex was back at MI6, studying the charts and diagrams that were spread out in front of him. Mrs. Jones was in the room and there was another, thin-faced man who had been introduced as Orlov. He was the scientist who had worked on the calutrons and had come to British intelligence with the information.

"Once you get to the junction, you turn right. You'll be able to move a little more easily. That's the good news. But I'm afraid this is where your problems begin, old chap. You're going to have to get through the exhaust fan."

Alex could already hear it. The fan was whirring at high speed about fifty yards away. He felt the warm air rushing into his face. Alex grabbed the backpack and strapped it onto his shoulders. He was glad to have it behind him, out of the way. Then he started moving toward the next obstacle, supporting himself now with the palms of his hands. It was good to feel the space between his shoulders and the pipe as it curved over him. Briefly he wondered what had happened to Rafiq and the other Kochis. By now they should have worked their way around the mountains and onto the track leading down from Falcon's Edge. Another two hours would bring them to the Shuja cemetery, named after a famous shah but in fact built by the British two hundred years ago for the soldiers who had died in the Anglo-Afghan War. Their instructions were to wait for him there, but Alex wondered if he would ever see them again. He hoped they were still owed money. Then they might stay.

Something flickered ahead of him. There were two silver struts coming down from the ceiling, joining together in a V, and they had reflected the light from the headlamp. The struts were part of a larger machine, a fan sucking up the stale air from below. It was blocking the entire passageway, turning so fast that the blades had become no more than a blur. The engine that controlled it was set behind the struts with a cable looping around. Even at a distance Alex could feel the power of the contraption. There was no way he would be able to stop it with his hand. He would simply lose the hand.

He continued forward until he was right up close, the breeze now battering his face and making it difficult to see. Automatically, he reached up to a special pocket, built into the breast of his jacket, and unzipped it. He drew out a rectangular box, black metal, about the size of a TV remote control. It had an antenna, which he unfolded, and a simple on/off switch. Alex pointed it in front of him, wondering even now if it would actually work.

The technology was simple even if it was still top secret. It had been developed by the US Air Force as part of CHAMP: the Counter-electronics High-powered-microwave Advanced Missile Project. How Smithers had gotten his hands on it, he preferred not to say. The box was a radar transmitter. Alex directed it toward the engine management system that turned the fan. He flicked it on. Instantly, the machine sent a series of magnetic pulses that traveled through the wiring loom of the fan system, confusing the electrics and causing the entire engine to shut down.

The fan came to an immediate halt. Alex was impressed, despite himself. Smithers had told him that one day the same technology could shut down an entire city, and now he believed it. Now he could clearly see each of the four blades, spaced out with enough of a gap for him to crawl through. He reached out to rotate them around so he could do just that.

If the creature hadn't moved, he wouldn't have seen it, and seconds later, he would have been finished. As it was, the beam of his headlamp reflected off some of its scales as they briefly twisted and that was what alerted him. He froze, his hand still outstretched, his mouth dry, his heart thudding against his chest. It was a snake and not just any snake. Crawley had shown him a picture during his briefing, just in case he happened to see one when he was crossing the desert. Alex recognized the ugly brown diamond shapes on its skin, the pear-shaped head, the oversized eyes. It was about twenty inches long . . . medium sized. Its Latin name was *Echis carinatus*, but it was better known as the saw-scaled viper. It was one of the most dangerous snakes in the world.

How had it gotten here? If the fan had been turning, it couldn't have crawled through. Either the engine had been turned off, perhaps for general maintenance, or it had reached this section of the pipe from another direction. It had been asleep, but Alex had disturbed it and already it was uncoiling itself. It was making a loud hissing noise that didn't in fact come from its mouth. It was rubbing its scales together to make the sound, preparing to strike. When it did so, it could travel three times farther than its own length. The fan wouldn't stop it. The blades were too far apart. Even if Alex began to back away, it would still reach him. If it bit him, he would die. The saw-scaled viper has killed more people than any other species of snake, and he could already imagine it lunging at his throat, its fangs burying themselves in his flesh. After that, there would be a long, agonizing death. It might be months before his body was found.

How could he get past it? That was the next question. Alex knew that there was no other way around. If he turned back the way he had come, he would find himself alone in the Herat Mountains, and it was unlikely he would make it out of the country. But nor could he sit here hoping that the snake would simply go away. There didn't seem to be any chance of that. The viper was angry, hissing louder, waiting for him to make his move. Alex remained perfectly still. One hand was on the propeller. The other, he realized, was still cradling the radar transmitter, and suddenly he knew what he had to do. It was all a question of timing. There really were going to be just microseconds between life and death.

Very carefully, he adjusted his hand, feeling for the on/off switch. All the time, he kept his eyes on the snake, almost willing it not to move. For its part, the snake stared at him with all the evil in the world. The hissing was more insistent, approaching the point of no return. It was about to strike. There could be no doubt of it. Alex weighed the transmitter in one hand. Then, quite deliberately, he slammed his fist into the side of the blade.

The snake believed it was threatened and leapt. It

would have reached Alex before he could so much as blink, but it had to maneuver its way through the gap between the blades, and that slowed it enough for Alex to do two things. He threw himself backward, putting as much distance between himself and the snake as he could. At the same time, he flicked the switch that deactivated the transmitter, allowing the fan to start again.

The next two seconds disappeared in a chaos of hope and fear. The fan restarted, the blades reaching maximum speed almost at once. Alex felt the breath being knocked out of him as his back and shoulders slammed into the pipe. Out of the corner of his eye, he saw the viper above him, its eyes blazing, its mouth stretched open to reveal its curved fangs. The snake landed on him, its head on his chest, and Alex squirmed, barely able to stop himself from crying out in horror. Something splashed into his face. It tasted foul on his lips. He waited for the snake to bite him, but it had twisted away, as if more interested in something else. Another two seconds passed and in that time he saw that his plan had worked, that he hadn't been bitten. The fan had cut the saw-scaled viper in half. More accurately, about five inches had made it through. The other fifteen had been left behind. Some sort of signal must have reached whatever brain it had, but it had lost interest in Alex, staring back at its own remains. Alex backed away, moving like a crab on the palms of his hands and the soles of his feet. He was feeling sick. He reached up with one arm and used his sleeve to wipe the snake's blood off his face. The viper was no longer moving. Finally, Alex reached for his water bottle and emptied it in three large gulps.

Snakes—and spiders—have a power that's hard to define. It's primal. When one comes close, human beings will react in the same way as any animal, and that was what had happened to Alex. He had been submerged in pure, instinctive terror, and it took him several minutes to recover, all the time staring at the severed head and the red, bleeding stub, wondering if the creature was really dead. Only when his heart was beating normally did he turn the transmitter back on, deactivating the fan once again. Then, carefully, he made his way through, trying to ignore the blood splatter on the pipe all around him.

After that, he moved as quickly as possible—both to make up time and to put the nightmare far behind him.

"When you get through the exhaust fan, there's about a hundred yards. It's pretty level and you should have nothing to worry about until you get to the main air shaft. That's when things begin to get interesting."

Smithers's voice guided Alex as he continued forward. The pipe was large enough to allow him to move freely, but he still felt the weight of the mountain, the intense darkness, the loneliness, and he had to fight to stay focused, to breathe normally. He had remembered to turn the fan back on before he left. He didn't want a maintenance engineer turning up to see what was wrong.

Ahead of him he was aware of a soft beating sound, some sort of machinery. He knew that he was getting close to the end.

"The plans show that the air shaft drops vertically— six hundred feet. That's about the height of the Gherkin in London. It's one hell of a drop, but unfortunately it's polished steel, so you can't climb down. It's too far to lower you on a rope. And I'm afraid it's not quite wide enough for a parachute."

"So what do I do?"

"That's a very good question, Alex."

Alex reached the edge of the air shaft. The ground had opened up beneath him and he lay, stretched out on his stomach, gazing down into nothingness. The beam of his headlamp was nowhere near powerful enough to reach the bottom and simply stopped in midair, illuminating the metal circle around it. The height of the Gherkin. It was as if he were lying on the roof of a London skyscraper, thinking about throwing himself off. Smithers had assured him that he had a plan and that it would work, but Alex could only take his word for it. Was he reliable?

Well, there was only one way to find out. Alex swallowed hard, then reached behind him and found a cable poking out of his backpack. It had a jack plug that clicked into a socket built into one of the shoulders of his combat suit. He turned it and heard the safety lock engage. Then he waited for the computer that he had carried all this distance to boot up and do its work. Smithers had said it would only take five seconds, but he waited half a minute just to be sure.

This was worse than the snake. What he was about to do went against every instinct. It was like committing suicide. But there was no other way.

Alex swung himself around and threw himself into the void.

3

A LONG WAY DOWN

ALEX FELL, FEETFIRST, HURTLING to what felt like certain death. He couldn't see. The light was spinning uselessly around him, bouncing off the walls of the shaft and turning them into a dazzling blur. He could feel the wind punching up at him. He wanted to scream but iron bands had fastened themselves around his chest and his throat and no sound came. How fast was he falling? A hundred miles per hour? Two hundred? If he hit the ground at this velocity, every bone in his body would shatter. Everything depended on the equipment he had been given, but even Smithers had sounded uncertain.

"Of course it'll work! I mean, I hope it'll work. But it is a prototype, you know . . ."

And now its moment had come. There was nothing for Alex to do. It all worked automatically.

First, the shoes. There were two miniature echo sounders built into the soles, behind the glass panels. They worked in much the same way as a depth finder on a boat. As Alex fell, they transmitted sound pulses that bounced back off the floor. The exact time of each pulse was recorded by the computer in Alex's backpack and—if

Smithers had done his job—it would know exactly how far he had fallen.

Just three and a half seconds after Alex had launched himself over the edge, they registered that the end of the pipe was exactly one hundred yards away. One second later, the distance was just sixty yards. Instantly, the computer activated four tiny explosive devices in Alex's belt. Alex felt the suction pads being released, exploding outward, trailing four lightweight cords. These were made out of the same superstrength nylon that Smithers had built into the yo-yo that Alex had taken with him on his first mission in Cornwall. The pads slammed into the metal wall and instantly stuck in place. The cords led back into a spool system concealed in the backpack, and as they unraveled, they slowed down the rate of Alex's descent. He heard the gears turning and felt a lurch in his stomach as the cords took up more and more of his weight. Fifty yards, forty yards, thirty yards . . . He was like a spider dropping out of a web. At ten yards, the rushing wind had stopped and Alex finally felt able to look down. He could see the floor below him. The cords lowered him the last few yards. His feet gently came to a rest against the bottom of the next horizontal pipe.

He had arrived.

He took a deep breath. He felt as if he had left his stomach somewhere behind him, and his head was throbbing, if only because of the change of pressure. With a shaking hand, he released the cords, which remained dangling from the edge of the pipe. Good old Smithers! He would be delighted to know that his invention had worked perfectly . . . assuming, of course, that Alex got back in one piece to tell him.

The new pipe offered him a choice of two directions. Trusting his instincts, Alex crawled forward and a moment later he arrived at a maintenance hatch, locked from the outside. But once again, Smithers had prepared him. Alex drew a short black cylinder out of his belt and weighed it in his hand. It looked like a flashlight, but in fact it was a metal vapor torch fueled by a mixture of copper oxide and magnesium to produce an astonishingly powerful flame burning at 4,500 degrees Fahrenheit. He flicked it on and the flame leapt out, the carbon fiber nozzle turning it into a blade, which cut through the metal in a matter of seconds. Alex glanced at his watch. It was half past four in the morning. Everything had been timed so that he would arrive at Falcon's Edge when almost all the personnel would be asleep and security would be at its weakest. He waited until the metal had cooled, then pushed the hatch open and climbed through.

He found himself on the edge of a vast chamber the size of an aircraft hangar—and there was indeed a burned-out helicopter abandoned on one side. The place was like nothing he had ever seen before, nothing he could have imagined. It was as if the entire mountain had been hollowed out to make room for storage, weapons, ammunition, and machinery. A night lighting system had been set in place, a series of neon tubes that cast a soft glow over everything, and looking around him, Alex saw half a dozen jeeps and other military vehicles parked in rows, some with anti-aircraft guns mounted on the roof. There were great piles of wooden crates, metal cylinders, half-dismantled pieces of machinery, and, everywhere, a fantastic array of weapons, including rocket launchers, bazookas, hand grenades, and AK-47 machine guns—enough to supply a small army. Alex began to creep forward, then ducked down, burying himself in the shadows, as something moved. A moment later, he relaxed. It wasn't a guard. There were three horses tethered to a rail. One of them had stamped its hoof on the stone floor.

The far end of the chamber was open to the night air. Keeping his distance from the horses—he was afraid of disturbing them and alerting any guards who might be passing—he made his way outside and found himself on a huge platform. He had plummeted two hundred yards down the pipe, but he was still another three hundred yards above ground level. Now he knew how Falcon's Edge had gotten its name. The fortress was built into the side of the mountain, far above the empty plain that stretched out below, washed over by the silver light of the stars. Standing on the edge of the platform, Alex was surrounded by giant walls, ramparts, and battlements. If he took one step forward, there would be nothing to stop him from falling to his death. It would be like stepping off a cliff. This was where the tribesmen had once executed their prisoners, throwing them into the abyss. Looking down at the ground, far away, he could imagine the terror they must have felt.

A massive archway stood to one side, with a gate, a portcullis, that was closed and locked. The gate looked ancient, but the security camera mounted in the stonework was brand-new, and Alex made sure he kept out of its range. A rough track ran down the mountainside behind it, but he couldn't possibly have entered that way. He would have been seen at once. Even so, if all went well, that was how he would be leaving in a little over two hours' time. Somewhere, out in the darkness, the Shuja cemetery was waiting for him. It suddenly occurred to him what a grim meeting place Mrs. Jones had arranged. He just hoped he wouldn't be needing it for all the wrong reasons.

He went back into the main body of the fortress, once again passing the horses. They were still restless, sensing his presence, but there didn't seem to be anyone else around. He had a job to do. Mrs. Jones needed evidence that the calutron was there and that it was close to working. Back in England, he had studied the plans and he knew where he had to go—it meant crossing back through the storage area. He had gotten about halfway when he heard the unmistakable sound of boots on stone. Instantly, he crouched down behind one of the crates, noticing an expanse of white silk draped over the top. That was interesting. It was a parachute. Quite a lot of these supplies must have been dropped in by air, suggesting that Drake had friends in neighboring countries. Pakistan, perhaps? Or China? Alex knew that Middle East politics were enormously complicated, but it still might be in somebody's interest to support the new terrorist group, and he made a mental note to mention it to MI6.

Two soldiers walked past without seeing him. They were dressed in loose-fitting olive-green jackets and trousers with heavy boots, the uniform of ragtag armies all over the world. Both were dark, bearded, and young. They carried machine guns slung over their backs. Alex waited until they had gone, then continued through the hangar, past the jeeps, making sure there were no cameras. Looking up, he saw iron gantries crisscrossing the ceiling with dozens of arc lamps hanging down. Huge fans were slowly turning, circulating the air. There didn't seem to be any closed-circuit cameras.

He reached a staircase that he knew led up to the living quarters, contained within the fortress itself. Ahead of him, there was a corridor. It was exactly where he knew it would be. He followed it to the end. Five metal steps led into a second chamber. The calutron was right in front of him.

He had been shown photographs and knew what to expect, but even so, the size of it and its sheer ugliness surprised him. It was housed in a sort of cradle made up of concrete pillars, steel girders, walkways, and ladders. It had the oval shape of an athletics stadium but it was about one-tenth of the size, with a wall of ceramic tiles and, above it, a platform and handrail that went all the way around. Alex guessed it would have taken him about five minutes to walk the complete circuit if he had wanted to. The whole thing looked strangely old-fashioned, but then, it had been built back in the eighties. It looked dead and neglected. Smithers had given him a lecture about how the calutron worked—something to do with magnetic fields, ions colliding, uranium isotopes, and all the rest of it. Was it actually working? It was making no sound at all. The truth was that Alex didn't really care. That wasn't his concern. He just wanted to take his pictures and get out of here.

He unzipped the backpack one last time and took out the camera he had been given. It was a Leica S 007 (the number had made him smile), one of the most advanced medium-format digital cameras in the world. Alex had been quite surprised that MI6 had provided him with such a stylish—and expensive—piece of equipment. He knew that it was incredibly fast and responsive, with a capture rate of 3.5 frames per second. He also knew that it would have cost him $25,000 if he'd gone out to buy one. Why did he need it? He wasn't out to win a photography competition. He was just here to take pictures of a lump of machinery. The camera concealed in his helmet would have done the job just as well.

Still, he wasn't going to argue. Quickly, he began photographing the chamber, the machine, the various wires and pipes, the dials and the gauges. Mrs. Jones had asked him to capture everything he could.

"Take a thousand pictures if you have to. I want to know everything that's in that room."

Of course, it would all be useless if he couldn't get out himself. That was the problem. The great mass of the Herat Mountains had prevented satellites from picking up any evidence of the calutron, and for the same reason, Alex was unable to send his images over the internet. He would carry them with him, physically, when he left.

And that had all been arranged. He took some photographs of one of the control panels, then glanced at his watch. Quarter past five. At seven o'clock, three supply vehicles would be arriving at Falcon's Edge, delivering fresh food from the market. One of the drivers had been bribed. Alex would be smuggled out in a crate and driven through the archway he had seen, then taken to the cemetery. When Mrs. Jones had outlined the plan, it had seemed unlikely, but she had been confident.

"You don't need to worry, Alex. They're only worried about people breaking into the complex, not breaking out. No one will have any idea you're there. The driver's name is Farshad and he'll be in a truck with a green cross on it. Just make sure you're not seen by anyone else . . ."

He had taken enough pictures. Alex had decided that, for once, Mrs. Jones had gotten her intelligence wrong. None of the gauges that he had photographed had shown anything but zero. Some of the cables were disconnected. If Darcus Drake was planning to manufacture uranium, he wasn't going to start anytime soon. Part of him was annoyed. Of course he was glad that Drake wouldn't be able to supply terrorist groups with nuclear material. But after all the effort of getting here, Alex was beginning to think it had all been a waste of time. Couldn't Mrs. Jones have found out the truth before he left?

The camera was still hanging around his neck and he was just reaching up to turn it off when something metallic touched the back of his head and a voice, speaking with an Irish accent, said, "Please raise your hands very slowly, Alex, and don't try anything stupid or I really will blow your brains out."

Alex did as he was told. Without turning around, he lifted both hands, at the same time asking himself not how he had been caught, but how the man with the gun knew his name.

4

THE AWAKENING

"ALL RIGHT, ALEX. YOU can turn around now."

Keeping his hands above his head, Alex did just that. He felt the gun move away from the back of his skull, but as he turned full circle, he saw it pointing directly between his eyes, a silver TT-33 self-loading pistol—made in Russia, like the calutron. One twitch of a finger, and it would fire a 7.62 mm bullet, traveling at four hundred yards per second, into his head.

The man whose finger was now curled between life and death was smiling. He had only just been roused from his bed. Alex could tell that from the stubble on his cheeks, the untidy silver hair, and the gray eyes that hadn't quite shaken off their sleep. He was in his mid-thirties and reminded Alex of a long-distance runner, very slim and light on his feet. He was wearing a loose-fitting black tracksuit with a T-shirt. This had to be Darcus Drake. As Drake stood facing him, Alex's first thought was that this was an unusually handsome and very confident man. It was only as the seconds ticked past that he realized something was wrong. Drake was still smiling. His expression hadn't changed, as if the photographer had been photographed himself. And the smile was only on his mouth, not in his eyes. There was nothing friendly about it, nothing humorous. It was simply there.

He was not alone. There were three soldiers surrounding him, watching Alex with deeply hostile eyes.

"You must be Alex Rider," Drake said.

"Yes." There seemed to be little point denying it.

"And you got in through the ventilation system?" He laughed softly, but the smile remained the same. "I have to say, I really hadn't seen that one coming. It must have been a tight squeeze, even for you. Anyway, it's very early and you must be hungry. Why don't we have breakfast together?" He glanced at the guards and spoke to them rapidly in Farsi. Then he turned back to Alex. "I've told them to take everything you've brought with you and to give you a new set of clothes. I'm afraid we may not have anything very stylish, but I'm not taking any chances, not when you've been equipped by MI6. Once they've done that, they'll bring you to me."

"How did you know I was here?" Alex didn't expect Drake to answer, but he had to know if he had made a mistake.

To his surprise, Drake seemed to be amused by the question. At least, his eyes lit up even if the rest of his face refused to move. "Well, I suppose you deserve to know that, after all your effort," he said in his lilting Irish accent. He gestured with one hand and a fifth man appeared, coming down the metal steps. Alex recognized him at once: the unpleasant white eye, the beard, the turban. It was Faisal, the tribesman who had ridden with him into the mountains.

"You should be careful whom you choose to trust," Drake said. "That's the trouble with the Kochis, Alex. They've been fighting so many different people, they don't really care which side they're on. Whoever's got the money, that's all that interests them."

"Alex Rider. England spy," Faisal muttered, as if there could still be any doubt of it.

"I'll see you very shortly for breakfast," Drake continued, still addressing Alex. "And don't worry. I won't be inviting your friend. In fact, now that I think about it, he probably isn't your friend anymore. Take it easy. If you try to fight with my men, they'll break your arms, and we wouldn't want that."

He turned and left. The soldiers closed in.

An hour later, escorted by two guards and wearing a dark green uniform that was one size too large for him, Alex was taken back through the great cavern beneath the citadel. His backpack, his belt, his camera, his shoes . . . everything that he had brought with him had been removed. He had no socks, and there were rough leather sandals on his feet. He missed his combat boots more than anything else. He might get a chance to make a break for it—but there was no way he could make any fast moves the way he was dressed now.

Everything was very different. Sunlight was streaming in through the opening and the whole place had woken up, with soldiers everywhere, many of them training on the outer platform, others carrying crates, cleaning weapons.

Alex saw that the three supply vans had arrived. One of them was white with a green cross, and he saw the driver, a dark, hooded man, staring in his direction. This must be Farshad, the man who was supposed to smuggle him out of here. Well, it wasn't going to happen. There was no way the two of them were going to make contact. More soldiers were helping to empty the vehicles, carrying fresh provisions—meat, vegetables, sacks of grain—into the compound. The horses were kicking impatiently, anxious to be on the move.

The guards led him toward a stone staircase on the other side of the burned-out helicopter. Alex hadn't noticed the staircase when he was there before. A hand shoved him hard in the back and he staggered up, climbing about fifty steps and emerging in a vaulted hallway with brick walls and chandeliers filled with candles. The citadel was a strange mix of ancient and modern. As Alex continued down a long, windowless corridor, electric light bulbs lit the way, but the flagstones under his feet could have been medieval. They came to a curved wooden door and one of the guards knocked, then entered without waiting for an answer.

Darcus Drake had living quarters directly above the open terrace looking out over the plain. The room was huge and austere with a very old, solid table and twelve chairs, a stone fireplace, and rough afghan rugs laid out on the floor. A fire had been lit but the room was cold. Alex noticed that there was no glass in the windows, and although the sun was now well up in the sky, he could still feel the chill of the night. There were maps on the wall: the local area, the country, the whole Middle East. This was the sort of room where wars were planned. He wondered who had sat around this table and what horrors they had discussed.

The two guards waited by the door. Alex stepped forward.

Drake was alone, waiting for him. Breakfast had already been brought up, and despite everything, Alex had to admit it looked good. There were eggs cooked with vegetables, sweet bread, pastries, cheese, dried fruit, and black tea—or chai, as it was called. Less welcome was the sight of his backpack with the contents scattered over the rugs. The computer, the vapor torch, the belt, the boots were all there. Drake was turning over the Leica camera in his hands. The smile was still on his face, exactly as before.

"This is a really fantastic camera," he said, and Alex remembered what Mrs. Jones had told him. Before he had become a terrorist, Drake had been a professional photographer. "I'm quite surprised, MI6 giving it to a kid like you. No offense."

"They wanted good photographs," Alex said.

"Of the calutron?" Drake sneered at him. "Well, that's a waste of time, Alex. I can't get the bloody thing to work. Not that I need it. I've got much bigger plans." He set the camera down in front of him. "I'll keep this, if you don't mind. It'll be something to remember you by."

Alex didn't like the sound of that. "If you want to steal the camera, I can't stop you," he said. "And if it makes you smile . . ."

The gibe struck home. Drake's eyes darkened. "You've noticed that, have you?" He pointed to his mouth. "It's called Möbius syndrome. It's a very rare nervous disease, a sort of facial paralysis. I was born with it. It's funny, really. I've been smiling all my life, even though I've never found very much to smile about."

"A bit like the Joker in Batman," Alex said. He was being deliberately offensive. He didn't want Drake to think he was scared.

"And who does that make you? Robin?" Drake shook his head. "I don't think so . . ." He gestured at the table. "Why don't you sit down? I promised you breakfast and you might as well enjoy it. It's going to be your last meal."

Alex felt a hollowing in his stomach as he took his place at the table. He had been threatened with death before. The last time, it had been Dr. Grief who had wanted to cut him up in a biology class at the Point Blanc Academy. But now he was thousands of miles away from home. He had been betrayed. MI6 had no way of knowing what was happening. This wasn't looking good.

"I have to ask you some questions," Drake said. "I already know most of the answers. Faisal has told me everything. So if you lie to me, I'll know at once, and then, I'm afraid, I'll give you to my men, who will do horrible things to you. This is Afghanistan, Alex. These people can be terribly cruel."

"What do you want to know?" Alex asked. He helped himself to some bread and cheese. He didn't feel like eating but was determined to try.

"You know, I'd heard a whisper that MI6 had employed a teenager. Was it you who took out Herod Sayle?"

"Yes." Alex muttered the single word. The first time he had worked for MI6, he had been sent to Cornwall, where the Stormbreaker computers were being manufactured, and in the end Herod Sayle had died. But he wasn't going to add any details if he could help it.

"That's very impressive. How many times have you worked for them since then?"

"This is the third time."

"Third time unlucky. You should have said no."

"They didn't give me much choice."

"That's a shame. Why did they pick on you?"

"They wanted photographs of the calutron. The only way in was through the pipes."

"And the pipes are too narrow for a fully grown man?"

"Yes."

"What were they going to do with the photographs?"

"They wanted to show them to the United Nations. They needed authorization. To bomb you."

Drake laughed delightedly. "It's very difficult to bomb me, Alex. First they have to find me, and I move around a lot. You've done well, so far. I've got just one more question. Did they tell you I would be here?"

Alex hesitated. He didn't want to help Drake, but neither did he want to be tortured. In the end, he decided that he had no choice. It probably wouldn't be that important anyway. "Yes," he said. "They thought you might be here."

"I'm surprised they didn't send you in to kill me."

"I wish they had," Alex said.

Drake laughed a second time. "You're a boy with spirit. I'll give you that! I'm very sorry it's had to end this way, Alex. For you, I mean. But I've got no more questions. You can eat your breakfast now, and while we're together, I'm going to tell you what's going to happen, although I doubt that you'll like it. What do you say?"

"I'll have some tea, if you don't mind."

"Of course." Drake poured. Then he began to talk. "You were wasting your time, Alex. They can't bomb me, whatever they may have told you. The walls of Falcon's Edge are too thick and the caverns are too deep. They'd need to send a smart bomb in through the window, but I'm not sure they've got a bomb that's smart enough for that. What other options are there? A drone? I have two hundred men surrounding me, my own personal bodyguard. They'd shoot it down before it got anywhere near me. There's only one track that climbs up from the valley and I make sure it's well protected. And anyway, like I told you, I'm not here very often. I move around. That's what keeps me safe.

"I want you to understand who I am. I used to be a newspaper photographer. I'm sure they told you that. I was born in Dublin and I spent five years working for the Irish *Times* before I moved to London. After that, I was sent to villages all over the Middle East, taking pictures after they'd been targeted by the British and the French and the Americans. Do you know what it does to you, after a while, recording all that misery? Dead people. Destruction. It gets to your head, Alex, and in the end, I realized that I couldn't do it anymore, supplying nice people like you or your mom and dad with pictures to look at while you're having breakfast."

"I don't have a mom or a dad," Alex said. "You don't know anything about me."

Drake ignored him. "I'm doing something amazing. I'm organizing an army. You see, the whole of the Middle East is crawling with freedom fighters—but there are too many of them, too many different groups. Every country has got half a dozen different factions and they're all too busy fighting each other to see that the real enemy is laughing at them. The West! The billionaires who sell the weapons and buy the oil. That's who they should be fighting. And here's the funny thing. They're listening to me. I speak their language and I understand their needs. They've accepted me as their leader, and quite soon, they'll come together in a new organization that will stretch from here to Iran, Iraq, Libya, Pakistan, and Syria. I've called it the Awakening. It has weapons. It has money. And quite soon it will launch a campaign of terror that will be unlike anything that has gone before."

"Why do you think killing people will make any difference?" Alex asked. "Don't you think enough people have been hurt already?"

"You're just a kid. You don't understand." Drake scowled but only with his eyes. His smile remained frozen in place. "I can see I'm wasting my time talking to you, which is a shame because, you know, I'd heard so much about you. But you can still be useful to me."

He picked up a pastry and tore it in half.

"Here's what I'm going to do," he went on. "We'll wait until sunset. It'll be more dramatic then, with a red sky. And then we'll take you outside and put you in front of a firing squad. We're going to execute you as a spy, Alex. And we'll film the whole thing. You'll be on the news. Your friends at school will watch you die. And the film will remind the whole world of the sort of dirty tricks that the intelligence services play, sending schoolboys to do their work for them. It'll also show them that the Awakening is here and that we're in business. It's a win-win situation for us, Alex, although I suppose it's a lose-lose situation for you. Do you want some more breakfast?"

Alex said nothing. Drake gestured and the two guards came forward and grabbed hold of him. As Alex was led out, Drake picked up the camera and took a couple of shots of him. As always, Drake was smiling.

BREAKOUT

ALEX KNEW THERE WAS no way out of the cell. It was buried as deep in the mountain as it was possible to be. There was no window. But for the single bulb burning over his head, he would have been in the pitch-dark. The door was a piece of solid wood, ten inches thick. Alex had measured it when he was led in. He had also noticed the two iron bars that would slide across on the outside. If he'd somehow gotten his hands on a pile driver or a battering ram, it wouldn't have done any good. And Alex had nothing. All his equipment had been taken away from him. He was dressed in loose army combats and sandals. The cell had a bunk, a table bolted to the floor, and a plastic jug of water. Darcus Drake was taking no chances.

At sunset, he was going to be tied to a stake and shot. Alex tried to force the image out of his mind. He was scared but he wasn't going to let fear weaken him. They still had to lead him from this cell, up two flights of stairs, and through the main chamber to the stone platform outside, and somewhere along the way, an opportunity would arise. All it needed was one guard to make one mistake. Perhaps the man in the white van—Farshad—was looking for him. After all, he had seen Alex taken prisoner. And what of Rafiq and the other tribesmen waiting for him in the cemetery? They would soon realize that something had gone wrong and they might try to help. Something would turn up. And Alex would be ready.

That was what he thought, but as the day wore on and he was left alone for hour after hour, he had to fight for control. He had no watch. He had no idea how much time was passing, how close he was to sunset. He kept himself active with push-ups, counting to fifty before he allowed himself a rest. He paced from one wall to the other—six paces there and back—until he could do it blindfolded. He sipped a little of the water. Nobody came with any lunch. He guessed that Drake was doing this on purpose. He wanted Alex to look worn-out and defeated when he was taken to his execution. It would look better on film.

Three hours, four hours, five hours . . . Alex guessed it was close to midday when he heard a sound outside the door, metal scraping against wood. He had been resting, lying on the bunk, when it happened, and his eyes flicked open, instantly alert. Someone was drawing back the bars. Had they come for him already? He expected the door to open. It stayed shut, but Alex was already on his feet, crouching down beside the wood, listening for any sound in the corridor outside. He heard soldiers march past, their boots stamping on the ground. Then silence. He reached up and grabbed hold of the iron ring that served as a door handle. He pulled. The door opened.

Looking out, he saw that the corridor was empty. Alex

was puzzled. What was going on? Was this some sort of test? Was Drake playing a trick on him? He wasn't going to waste time wondering about it. This was the opportunity he had been waiting for. He slipped outside and found himself in a dungeon area with stone walls and doors. He watched the soldiers—there had been four of them—disappearing into the distance and tried to work out his next move. He already knew that even if he was out of the cell, he wasn't out of trouble. Drake had told him there were two hundred men at the citadel. He was high up in the Herat Mountains with a dizzying fall from the edge of the stone platform. The only way out was through the portcullis with the track beyond, but that would be heavily guarded. And if he did make it out of Falcon's Edge, where would he go next? The Shuja cemetery was about twenty miles away, the Iranian border a lot farther. He was on his own. As relieved as he was to be out of the cell, Alex knew that his position was almost hopeless.

He watched the guards go, then went in the opposite direction. There were just a few steps until the passageway came to a corner, and as Alex reached it, a man suddenly appeared, walking toward him. With a shock, Alex recognized Faisal, the Kochi tribesman who had betrayed him in the first place. Faisal opened his mouth, about to call out, but Alex was already moving, running forward and lashing out with the front kick—*mae geri*—that was one of the first moves he had learned at karate. Alex was half the size of the man he was attacking, but that didn't matter . . . He had chosen his target carefully. The ball of his foot slammed into Faisal's solar plexus, knocking the wind out of him in one sharp breath. He followed through with a vicious back fist strike, targeting the man's throat. Faisal crumpled. Both his eyes had gone white, although, of course, one of them had been that way already.

Which way? Before Alex took off, he reached down and removed the *shemagh*—the Afghan scarf—that Faisal had been wearing, winding it over his head and around the lower part of his face. In a way, Drake had done him a favor. By making him change his clothes, he had made him invisible . . . Now he looked like everyone else. He continued forward, leaving the unconscious man behind. He knew which way he had been brought here. He just had to retrace his steps and find a way out before Faisal— and the empty cell—was discovered.

He came to an old-fashioned lift. As he arrived, the gate opened and a chef came out, a man in a grubby white jacket, carrying some sort of skinned animal, perhaps a goat. There was no time to hide, and Alex knew that any hesitation would finish him. He kept his head down. Half his face was concealed. Without breaking his pace, he brushed past the man and went into the lift. As he had hoped, the man had his mind on other things and didn't even notice him. Alex pressed the top button and heaved a sigh of relief as the door slid shut.

He was carried upward. The lift seemed painfully slow, and Alex was already worrying about what he would see when the door opened again. In fact, he came out in an area behind the calutron, and now he was doubly glad that the complicated machine wasn't working. There was nobody in this part of the complex. Alex hurried around the edge. Part of him was already planning what to do next, but at the same time he was also thinking back to the cell. Who had opened the door? Was there something he was missing? It occurred to him that he might have a friend somewhere in Falcon's Edge. After all, someone had opened the cell door. But if so, where were they and what had happened to them?

He was almost back where he had started. The main storage area was still a mass of activity with at least fifty soldiers moving around, going about their duties, all of them armed. The three supply vans had left. Alex sneaked farther into the chamber and hid behind one of the crates. It was attached to a parachute, and he drew the silk fabric toward him, using it to conceal himself. The outdoor platform where he was to be executed was right in front of him. He could actually see two men setting up a camera and a tripod. It made him feel sick that anyone could think of making a film like that, and he certainly had no intention of being its star. But how was he going to get out of here? The portcullis was the only way. If it was open and if he moved fast enough . . . But he still had to cross the plain, twenty miles or more. The moment they knew he was free, they would come after him. Stealing a jeep was out of the question. Even if Alex had known how to drive, he doubted they'd have left the keys in the ignition. Was there another way?

He remembered the horses. They were still tethered to the railing, three of them, sturdy and fast, by the look of them. Alex hated riding, but at least they didn't need keys! The horses already had saddles and bridles. They were ready to go. Crouching beside the crate, measuring distances, Alex tried to work out a plan. He had no doubt that he could reach the horses without being seen. Everyone was too busy to notice him. It was when he mounted up and began to ride that his problems would begin. The alarm would be raised and they would either shoot him or shoot the horse. If they lowered the portcullis—and that would be the first thing they would do—he would be trapped. He needed the element of surprise. But how?

The idea came to him so suddenly that he almost gasped. It was impossible! It couldn't possibly work. But he was alone, surrounded by an entire army. He was going to be executed in a few hours' time. What other choice did he have?

He started at once. If he thought about this, even for a second, he wouldn't go through with it. It was early afternoon and the sun was at its hottest. That helped. A lot of Drake's men were unfocused, wishing they could have a siesta. They didn't notice the extra soldier making his way around the side of the cavern, carrying a bundle in his arms. Nor did they notice when he picked out one of the horses and got to work. The horse protested, snorting and stamping one of its hooves, but nobody came over. Alex was closer to the platform now and took stock of his surroundings. The camera was ready. Three more men were positioning a wooden stake in the ground, right next to the wall. That was for him. But Alex was grimly determined. Whatever happened, whether he lived or died, he wasn't going to play their game. He would go out fighting. He just wished he had been able to grab one of the AK-47 machine guns. Falcon's Edge was jammed with weapons of one sort or another. He was probably the only person in the entire place who was unarmed.

Alex's heart was thumping and there was a hollow in his stomach as his entire being recoiled at the thought of what he was about to do. A group of soldiers walked past and he leaned down, pretending to busy himself with the horse he had chosen, in fact concealing himself behind it. He waited until they had gone. It was now or never. Once he climbed onto the horse, someone would be bound to see him. He couldn't hesitate, not for one second.

And then the alarm went off.

Someone must have discovered the unconscious man—either that or they had come to check on him in the cell and found that it was empty. The alarm was not a bell. It was a siren that tore through the air, screaming its urgency. Well, that might help him too. For a moment everyone was confused, wondering what the fuss was about. Alex untethered the horse. At the last moment, he noticed a riding crop on the floor and snatched it up, knowing he would need it. Even as he steadied himself in the saddle, he felt the horse resisting. That was the whole secret of riding, that sense of understanding between the horse and its rider. Well, this horse would have realized at once that this Rider was not in control. It didn't matter. Alex was desperate. Somehow he would get the animal to do what he wanted.

He jerked on the reins and wheeled around. At the same time, the scarf slipped and somebody cried out. They had seen him! Alex dug in his heels and for good measure lashed out with the crop. If the horse didn't move, they would both get killed. Sure enough, there was a shot and a bullet ricocheted off the stone wall above their heads. The sound of it frightened the horse more than Alex had managed. He was almost thrown off as the animal reared up. Alex heard a second shot and felt a bullet pass inches over his shoulders. Everything was happening at the same time. He felt the cavern spin around him. There were men running toward him. The siren was still blasting at full volume. The horse's front hooves made contact with the ground and then the two of them were off.

They were going the wrong way! The horse had set off at a gallop, but it was heading back into the cavern, toward the jeeps and the helicopter. Alex pulled frantically on the reins and wheeled the horse around. He heard a series of shots and the windows of the jeep right behind him shattered, the glass crashing down. The sunlight was straight ahead of him. There was the stone arch of the cavern, then the stone platform, and then, if he kept going, a drop of three hundred yards to the plain below. The gate with the portcullis was off to the right, but the guards were already ahead of him. At least ten of them had grouped together to block his way. They were all armed, waiting for him to ride toward them.

Alex wasn't stopping now. With a yell, he whipped on the horse, propelling it out of the cavern and into the light. The soldiers were firing at him. He could feel the bullets scorching the air all around him. At this range, they shouldn't have missed, but perhaps they were trying to hit him, not the horse, and anyway, they had miscalculated—he wasn't riding toward them, he was going straight ahead. They stopped firing. There was no need to waste any more bullets. It was clear to them that Alex was committing suicide. He was heading straight toward the edge of the platform and the sheer drop beyond. Ten yards, five yards, three yards . . . Alex covered the ground in no time at all. Out of the corner of his eye he saw the metal gate crashing down to block the archway and, nearer to him, the execution post, the waiting camera. He ignored them. He had made his decision. It was happening now.

The horse sensed what he wanted, but only when it was too late. Alex whipped it one last time, hating what he was doing, knowing there was no other way. The soldiers stared. The horse screamed. The edge came rushing up toward them. And then they had gone, launching themselves into space. At that moment Alex was only aware of a great stillness, the sun blazing, the plain so far below that shrubs and boulders appeared only as tiny specks. He felt the wind in his hair. There was a sense almost of calm and he thought that maybe this was what death is like.

But he wasn't going to die. Not today. When Alex had crossed the cavern, he had been carrying the parachute that had been used to air-drop the crate. He had attached it not to himself, but to the saddle and to each end of the horse, running the cords under its legs. When he had ridden out, he had been trailing the canopy behind him, and despite the alarms and the gunfire, his greatest fear had been that it would catch on something and tear. He had been lucky. The parachute had been intact as he urged the horse over the edge. The moment they cleared the platform, it was dragged upward, opening out. It was above them now. It had formed itself into a fantastic flower, shading them from the sun. And the two of them weren't falling anymore. They were floating down.

It was a fantastic sight. The horse was terrified, its eyes bulging, its legs flailing as if it were galloping through the air. For his part, Alex was clinging on for dear life, too afraid to look down, vaguely aware of the cords stretching past him and the white silk billowing over his head. The parachute had taken their combined weight with ease. They were heading down toward the plain, at the same time being swept ever farther away from Falcon's Edge. Alex risked a glance back and saw the soldiers on the platform, already miniature. One or two of them were shooting at them—he saw the flash of an AK-47—but they were well out of range. Apart from the rush of the breeze in his ears, everything was silent. Even the horse seemed to have stopped panicking. Gently, they wafted down.

The next time Alex looked, the ground was rushing up toward them, far faster than he would have expected. He tensed himself, waiting for the landing—but already he knew that he had been lucky. He had rigged the parachute perfectly. If the cords hadn't been evenly divided, the horse could have tilted backward or forward and the two of them might have hit the ground as a twisting ball of animal and boy. Everything depended on the next few seconds. Alex had taken the horse with him because it wasn't enough to break out of the citadel. He also needed to be moving at speed. He had no doubt that once they had recovered from the surprise, Drake and his men would be after him.

This was the moment of truth. Once again the horse was pedaling as if it understood what was about to happen. Alex tightened his knees and squeezed the reins. There was a thud as the four hooves came into contact with the ground. The horse stumbled and Alex was afraid that it might have injured itself. But then it recovered and suddenly they were chasing across the plain, dragging the parachute behind. Alex couldn't stop himself. Like a cowboy in the Wild West, he whooped with delight. He had done it! When escape had been impossible, he had made the impossible escape.

It wasn't over yet. Behind him, the gates of the citadel opened. Three jeeps, with four men in each, came roaring out in pursuit.

6

THE SHUJA CEMETERY

THE HORSE WAS BEHAVING perfectly, streaking across the plain in a dead straight line. Alex had thought he would have to stop to release the parachute, but rocks and spiky plants had ripped the fabric to shreds in a few seconds so that only the cords were left trailing behind. It seemed to him that everything had changed. After its ordeal, plummeting through the air, the horse had decided that perhaps Alex knew what he was doing after all and was now obeying his every command. Alex felt more comfortable in the saddle. They were going so fast that, when he looked down, the sand and wild grass swept past in little more than a vague green blur, but he no longer had the feeling that he was going to fall off. He had lost the riding crop as they came down, but he had no need of it. He was clutching the reins, keeping his head low, feeling the breeze rush over his shoulders.

He had no real idea where he was going. Back in London, Mrs. Jones had shown him a map with the location of the Shuja cemetery, but at that time he hadn't thought he would need it. He was meant to be arriving there in the back of a van. He remembered her drawing a straight line with her finger, the direction southwest. She had also mentioned a village with a minaret, five miles on the other side. Alex couldn't be certain, but he had seen where the sun had risen and had guessed that he was heading southwest. Also, there was definitely something tall and narrow on the horizon, although he couldn't make it out yet. A minaret? He would know once he got closer.

He risked a glance back over his shoulder. The three jeeps were making their way down the winding track, going as fast as the hairpin bends would allow them. They already seemed a long way behind him, but Alex felt a tightening in his stomach. Once the jeeps reached the bottom, they would accelerate, and it might take them ten or fifteen minutes to catch up with him. And he didn't really have anywhere to go. He doubted that Rafiq and his men would be waiting for him at the cemetery, and it was unlikely that he would find a hiding place among the gravestones. There was always Mrs. Jones's village—but why would anyone there want to help him? The plain that surrounded him could hardly have been more desolate. He had the mountains behind him, an almost empty horizon ahead. He seemed to be pinned down by the sunlight. He could already feel it burning the back of his neck. The horse was doing its best, and it was a miracle that it hadn't been hurt when it came into contact with the land. But it would soon get tired. Alex's earlier euphoria had soon worn off. Things were looking hopeless once again.

He kept going. What other choice did he have? He heard the chime of a bell and turned in time to see a herd of goats scattering as he thundered past. There was no sign of any farmer or goatherd. There wasn't anyone for miles around. He looked back. The jeeps had already left the track and were racing across the plain, sending up clouds of dust behind. He could even hear the engines. They were only a mile away . . . maybe less. He might have overestimated how much time he had left. He kicked in with his heels and felt the horse jolt forward, doing its best. The poor creature had little energy left. Its flanks were shiny with sweat. There was a part of Alex that felt sorry for what he had put it through, and the last thing he wanted was to see it gunned down. Even as the thought flickered through his head, he heard a gunshot. It was too far away to cause him any alarm, but it was a warning. The soldiers had him in their sights and they were getting closer with every second that passed.

He saw the cemetery. As he approached, it waved and shimmered, forming itself out of the heat haze. It was just stuck there, out on its own. No roads led to it. There were no signs, no indication that anyone had even noticed it existed. Alex saw the remains of a low, square wall built out of mud bricks. There were wide gaps where sections of it had collapsed, eaten away by the constant heat. About thirty or forty gravestones stood grouped together on the other side, with clumps of spiky wild grass and shrubs growing between them. Even as he hurtled toward it, Alex saw that there was something terribly sad about the place. These were British soldiers who had been buried here, victims of a war that had long been forgotten. Who were they? How had they died? They had come here in their bright red tunics, their white belts and helmets, marching into a country they couldn't begin to understand, and they had never returned home. This was where they lay, and even their names were gone, fading away, wiped clean off their headstones by the relentless desert sun.

Nobody was waiting for him. He saw that at once. There were no horses, no men. Rafiq and the other Kochis had decided to go home. He glanced back and saw that the jeeps had halved the distance between him and them. If someone took a shot at him now, there was every chance he would be in range. What should he do? He could see the village on the other side of the cemetery, a collection of dusty houses gathered around a crumbling minaret. Was there any point continuing, or should he simply accept his fate and give himself up?

As if to answer the question, the horse stumbled and Alex was thrown off. There was nothing he could do to stop it. He felt his body separating from the saddle, and next he was turning in the air, his arms in front of him, desperately trying to protect himself. He crashed down. Fortunately the ground was soft, a mixture of dust and sand. He rolled over twice and came up spitting and coughing. He knew at once that nothing was broken. The horse wheeled away and continued around the side of the cemetery, and Alex wished it luck. At least it would be out of range when the soldiers arrived.

They were almost onto him. Alex heard the jeep engines and the sound of the wheels bumping over the plain. He saw the faces, bearded and angry, behind the windows. Faisal was with them! Alex saw him sitting in one of the front passenger seats. He must have joined them, wanting to take revenge on Alex for what had happened outside the cell. As the jeep slowed to a halt, he was the first one out, bringing up the pistol—old-fashioned, also Russian-made—that he had carried with him. Bruised and exhausted, Alex backed into the Shuja cemetery. He was surrounded by dead British soldiers. It was somehow fitting that, quite soon, a dead British spy would join them.

Darcus Drake's soldiers came pouring out of the jeeps, moving more slowly now. They had caught up with Alex. They knew he had nowhere to go. Alex had expected Drake to come with them, but he wasn't going to put himself outside the safety of Falcon's Edge. The commanding officer was a wiry, curly-haired man in his twenties. He had a broken nose, and a beard sprouted unevenly on both sides of his face. He was holding a machine gun, and Alex wondered if he had been ordered to finish it here or to bring him back so that they could make their film.

"Alex Rider," he said. He spoke the words as if for the first time, as if he didn't know what they meant.

The gunshot, when it came, was loud and incredibly close. Alex flinched, expecting to feel the pain—in his chest, in his stomach, wherever he had been shot. Then he realized that the bullet had come from behind him. A red hole had appeared in the commanding officer's head. He fell back, dropping the machine gun.

"Get down, Alex!"

The words, in English, were shouted out of nowhere. Instinctively, Alex obeyed. There were more shots. Two more of Drake's men died.

Alex twisted around and looked behind him, staring in amazement as dusty figures rose up like zombies, climbing out of the graves. His first thought was that the ghosts of the nineteenth-century soldiers were rising up to save him, but he knew at once that it was simpler than that. Rafiq and his men had been waiting for him after all. They had used the old graves as hiding places, covering themselves with a thin layer of sand. Now the four of them were revealing themselves, firing at the soldiers with guns they had been clutching all the time. Surprise was on their side. Another six men had been shot and killed before they understood what was happening.

Faisal was not one of them. Alex saw that he had not fired yet, although he too was armed with an AK-47 and could have taken out Rafiq and the others with a single burst. Could it be that he was reluctant to turn on his former friends? There was the click of a gun being loaded. Alex twisted and saw another of Drake's men just a few steps away, pointing a pistol directly at his head. He knew what was about to happen. He saw it in the man's eyes. Somehow the tables had turned. Alex had reached the cemetery and his friends were here, waiting for him. Half of Drake's men had been killed. But whatever happened, the English boy was not going to get away. This man had decided it. He was going to kill him now.

The commanding officer had dropped his machine gun. It was lying on the ground, just inches away. Alex dived for it. But before he could reach it, Faisal stepped forward and Alex saw the white flame as his machine gun spat out its thirty rounds in a matter of seconds. But he wasn't aiming at Alex. He wasn't aiming at Rafiq. Impossibly, he was shooting Drake's men, including the one who had been about to finish Alex. Alex saw him blasted off his feet.

And then it was over, as suddenly as it had begun. All the Kochis—including Rafiq and Faisal—were alive. So was Alex. Only one of Drake's men was moving. Alex turned away as Rafiq finished him with a single shot.

Faisal was on his side?

It couldn't be true. But as Alex got to his feet, Rafiq was embracing him, the two men laughing. The other Kochis had gathered around in a group hug. And Alex had seen it for himself. Faisal had just saved his life. He had taken out half a dozen of Drake's men. What was going on?

"English boy!" Faisal exclaimed, seeing him. He was beaming, which was odd, because the last time they had met, Alex had kicked him hard where it hurt.

"Can someone explain what's happening?" Alex asked.

"Ask no questions, my friend." It was Rafiq who had

spoken. And suddenly he was speaking perfect English. "We have a long journey to the border, and there is a helicopter that waits. Ask your questions when you are home."

Questions. Yes. The more Alex thought about it, the more he had to ask.

7

SPECIAL DELIVERY

THE TORNADO GR4 LOOKED deadly even before it left
the ground. Officially described as a day-or-night, all-
weather attack aircraft, it certainly looked the part with its
sleek fuselage and V-shaped variable-sweep wings. The
plane was waiting for clearance, sitting in the baking sun
at the end of the runway at RAF Akrotiri at the southern-
most tip of Cyprus. The Tornado GR4 is not a new aircraft.
It was actually developed during the cold war with Russia.
But it remains a favorite of the Royal Air Force: fast, quiet,
and easy to fly. It was perhaps significant that normally, it
might have been armed with all manner of missiles: up to five
Pathway 1V smart weapons, for example, or Stormshadow
cruise missiles. But this aircraft carried just two weapons.
They were Brimstone ground attack missiles. They had
been specially primed. There was no chance that they
could miss.

"Go!"

The single word came from the control tower. The
pilot, anonymous in the dark blue Meta-Aramid flight suit
and helmet that would provide thermal, chemical, and
radiation resistance, raised a thumb in acknowledgment.
Seconds later, the two Rolls-Royce 199 Mk 103 turbofan

engines flared and the plane began to roll forward, picking up speed. Each engine provided a thrust of 16,000 pounds. By the time it reached its cruising altitude of 30,000 feet, the Tornado would be traveling at around 1,000 miles per hour.

The sun glinted off the wings. In seconds it was gone, clearing the airport and arcing over the Mediterranean Sea.

It was on its way to Afghanistan.

In London, Alex was sitting opposite Alan Blunt, the chief executive of MI6 Special Operations. Mrs. Jones was with him. Less than twenty-four hours before, he had been facing certain execution in the Herat Mountains. He had broken out of prison and ridden a horse over a ledge with a drop of three hundred yards to the ground. He had been involved in a gunfight at a cemetery. Finally, he had crossed the border into Iran, where a helicopter had been on standby to fly him on the first leg of his journey home. In all that time, nobody had explained to him what had really happened—but Alex had begun to work it out for himself. He knew that, once again, he had been used. He wasn't surprised.

And now, here he was on the sixteenth floor of the building on Liverpool Street with the traffic rumbling past outside. Blunt had welcomed him with tea and choco-late cookies, brought in on a trolley. There was something about the normality of it all that really shocked Alex. He was still waiting for the answers. It was as if he had been invited onto a stage to take part in a play—but no one had remembered to send him his lines.

"I don't want you to blame yourself, Alex," Blunt was saying. "We're very grateful to you. The mission may not have gone quite as we hoped, but you really couldn't have achieved any more."

Alex examined the spymaster who had sent him on three missions. Each time he had been lucky not to get killed. Blunt really did look like a bank manager. He was the sort of man you would forget instantly . . . assuming you had noticed he was there in the first place. He was about fifty years old—maybe older—with gray hair, glasses, thin lips. His eyes gave nothing away. Nor was there anything in his office that said anything about him. There were no photographs on the desk, no personal items. Even the pictures on the walls had been deliberately chosen. A view of a field. A vase of flowers. A ship at sea. They were the sort of art you buy to fill a space, not because it is something you want to see.

"We're very glad you weren't hurt," Blunt continued. "And I understand Brookland is opening again tomorrow. You haven't missed any school, which is excellent. I'm sure you'll be quite pleased to be back."

"What about Darcus Drake?" Alex asked.

"You brought us very useful intelligence, Alex. This calutron of his doesn't seem to be working after all. He's not quite as much of a threat as we thought."

"He's still gathering an army," Alex said. "He still wants to attack the West."

"There are plenty of people who want to attack the

West. We were afraid of a nuclear attack, but thanks to you, we know that's not going to happen."

"Forget about Darcus Drake," Mrs. Jones said. She was sitting with her legs crossed and her hands folded on her knees. There was no expression on her face. Alex guessed that she wanted him out of the room. He had gotten that feeling the moment he walked in. "We'll deal with him in due course. He's got nothing to do with you."

"He nearly killed me," Alex reminded her. "He wanted to execute me by firing squad. He was going to film it and put it on the internet. Jack would have seen it. So would all my friends."

"We're just relieved that you escaped."

"No!" On the two last occasions when he had been in this room, Alex had done what they wanted. He hadn't argued with Blunt or Mrs. Jones. This time was different. He knew something was wrong. There was something he hadn't been told. "It doesn't make any sense," he went on. "The whole thing . . . from start to finish. It doesn't add up."

Blunt twitched his lips in the sort of smile that could have been drawn with a pencil and a single line. "I don't know what you mean, Alex."

"Then let me tell you." Alex took a breath. "First of all, you send me all the way to Afghanistan to take photographs of a machine that isn't even working. I don't believe you didn't know that. You've got spies. You've got satellites. You knew everything about Darcus Drake. You must have known he didn't have the ability to make nuclear weapons."

"That's what we sent you to find out," Blunt said.

"I don't believe you," Alex said. He was surprised how easily the accusation slipped out. "I think you sent me there for another reason. I've gone over what happened. You paid a bunch of Afghan tribesmen to take me up into the mountains, and I crawled through the pipes like you said. But while I was doing that, one of them—a man called Faisal—rode into Falcon's Edge and told Drake I was on the way. That's how I was captured."

"Faisal was bribed," Blunt said. "You can't really trust these people. They'll work for the highest bidder."

"That's what I thought. But here's the funny thing. When I was in my cell, someone came down and unlocked the door. I never found out who it was—but now that I think about it, Faisal was right outside. I saw him in the corridor and I assumed he was going to raise the alarm. I was wrong, wasn't I? It was Faisal who'd unlocked the door. He must have been about to open it and let me out when a group of soldiers came along and he was forced to hide. As soon as they were gone, he came back for me, but by that time I was already on my way, and before he could explain that he was on my side, I knocked him out. That was my mistake, but how was I to know?"

"Are you saying that he changed his mind?" Mrs. Jones asked.

"I don't know, Mrs. Jones. But he certainly helped me when I got to the Shuja cemetery. He shot a whole load of Drake's men. And Rafiq and the others were happy to see him. They didn't think he was a traitor. They were all delighted by what he'd done. And while I'm at it, here's another question. Why were they waiting for me in the cemetery? I'd missed the rendezvous, but they were all there, buried in the graves. They knew I'd be coming eventually and they were there to help me."

"Did they tell you anything?" Blunt asked.

"They wouldn't talk about what had happened," Alex said. "They were very friendly. They got me back over the border, and when I left, we all shook hands like we were the best of friends. Even Faisal embraced me and called me his brother. But they knew something and I think you know it too. So why don't you tell me?"

Alan Blunt coughed. Alex noticed that he and Mrs. Jones were carefully avoiding each other's eyes.

"I'm afraid I can't help you, Alex," he said eventually. "The Kochi people are a law unto themselves, and I don't know what was going on in their minds—although I'd say you're reading too much into it. It sounds like they got paid twice. We paid them to take you to Falcon's Edge and Drake paid them to hand you over. You're just lucky that they decided not to leave you behind."

There was a file on the desk in front of him. He drew it toward himself.

"I can understand that you're disappointed," he went on. "The Stormbreaker business went extremely well, and you followed that by taking out Dr. Grief at the Point Blanc Academy. But if you're going to be a spy, Alex, if you're going to work for us, you've got to learn that you can't be successful every time."

"I don't want to be a spy and I don't want to work for you," Alex said.

Blunt ignored this. "The calutron isn't working. There was no need to penetrate Falcon's Edge in the first place. It's no longer our business." He had a rubber stamp. He pressed it against a red ink pad, then brought it down onto the cover of the file. Alex saw he had printed two words:

MISSION FAIL

"You did extremely well, Alex," he concluded. "The failure is entirely ours, not yours. I'm sure we'll see you again very soon. If we need you, we know where to find you."

"Yes," Alex said gloomily. "You do."

The Tornado was closing in on its target, maintaining a high subsonic cruise speed. Its route had taken it through the airspace of Jordan, Saudi Arabia, and Iran before it had curved up into Afghanistan, but nobody had protested. There are times when governments and intelligence agencies, even the ones that are supposedly hostile to one another, will work together for the common good. This was one of them. It was decided that the mission was so important, the Tornado had been given "invisible" status. As far as the world was concerned, it had never taken off. Its flight path hadn't been recorded. If anyone ever asked, the mission had never taken place.

Inside the cockpit, the pilot prepared to fire the two

missiles. There wasn't even any need to take aim. The Brimstone had originally been developed as part of a system known as "fire and forget." The two weapons had been programmed in Cyprus, before the plane took off. Even if the pilot didn't know the target, they did. The Herat Mountains were coming up ahead of her now. There was white snow glistening on some of the peaks. The great plain stretched out below. The Tornado cast a shadow as it swept forward—but so quickly that it was literally gone in the blink of an eye. The pilot flicked off the safety switch, then made final checks on the computer screen. There was no need for further authorization.

The pilot fired.

The two Brimstone missiles disengaged and at once their independent solid propellant rocket motors fired up, taking them in a matter of seconds to supersonic speed. The millimetric wave radar seekers built into the missiles fed back images of the target and precise information, such as the exact time to detonation, while digital autopilot ensured that they stayed rigidly on course. The missiles weighed just 110 pounds. They were 5.5 feet long. They cost $140,000 each.

The pilot did not wait to see the explosion. Long before the Brimstones hit, she had expertly brought the aircraft around 180 degrees and was on her way home.

Neither Alan Blunt nor Mrs. Jones spoke until Alex was gone. It was only after the door had closed that Blunt turned to his second in command. "That went very well," he said.

"He knows that we used him," Mrs. Jones remarked.

"He's unusually bright for a fourteen-year-old," Blunt agreed. "That's what makes him so valuable. But I don't think he'll guess the whole truth."

"You mean, that you turned him into an assassin?"

"That we entrusted him with what you might call our special delivery. Alex was an excellent postman. It was so unlikely that we'd use a child that Drake didn't ask too many questions . . . not the right ones, anyway."

"You mean, he bought that business about the pipes."

"Well, it was true. No adult would be able to get through." Blunt picked up the file that he had stamped when Alex was sitting in front of him. He tore it up and dropped it in the trash can. Later, it would be shredded. The true file, the actual record of Alex's mission, was on its way to Number 10, Downing Street. "Darcus Drake had to die," he went on. "With or without nuclear weapons, he was a major threat to world security. If he had succeeded in uniting all the different terrorist groups in Afghanistan and elsewhere, there's no way of knowing how dangerous he might have become or how much damage he might have done. He had to be taken out."

"And Alex did that for us."

"Exactly. He delivered the package and he got out of there in one piece. He really is remarkable." Blunt paused.

"Did you know that John Crawley has asked permission to use him?"

"Really?"

"Yes. Something to do with Chinese triads wanting to sabotage the Wimbledon tennis championship. He thinks Alex would make a good ball boy."

"And what did you say?"

Blunt smiled. "I don't see why not . . ."

Darcus Drake was also thinking about Alex Rider. He was smiling, of course. This was the smile that never left his face.

He was sitting at the table in his living quarters, the same room where he and Alex had talked. He still didn't understand quite what had happened. He had sent twelve men out onto the plain following Alex's astonishing escape. None of them had come back. How was that possible? The boy was unarmed. There must have been people waiting for Alex, but even so, Drake was surprised that all his people had been killed.

Well, it didn't matter. Alex had learned that the calutron was useless—but Drake had never pretended otherwise. It made no difference to his plans. Later this afternoon, the leaders of seven terrorist organizations were coming to Falcon's Edge. Only he, Darcus Drake, could have persuaded them to come together. They were the Awakening and they were going to discuss their first operation, an act of violence so shocking that the whole world would sit up and take notice. He had already worked it out. There were just the details to be decided and they would go ahead.

All in all, it wasn't such a bad thing that Alex had come here. Drake had been alerted to the lack of security in the ventilation system, and he had already taken measures to ensure that nobody else would ever break in that way. And there was something else he was grateful for. As he sat at the table, he examined the camera that Alex had brought with him, raising it to his eye and taking a couple of shots. The Leica really was a fabulous piece of equipment. It reminded Drake of his early days in Dublin, when he had worked for the Irish *Times*. Well, it would come in very useful. He would take wonderful photographs of the death and the suffering that he himself would cause. He would even send them to the newspapers. How marvelous it was that MI6 had allowed the camera to fall into his hands.

He didn't know, of course. MI6 needed to deal with him. The RAF needed a precise target. Falcon's Edge was almost impenetrable, and Drake himself was difficult to locate. But Alan Blunt had guessed he would keep a beautiful and expensive camera if it was delivered to him, and so he had built a miniaturized homing beacon into the Leica, a beacon that was even now transmitting a signal to the two Brimstone missiles, which swept down almost joyously, picking out the actual window of the room, closing in at the speed of sound, and then vaporizing their target in two giant balls of flame.

THE MAN WITH ELEVEN FINGERS

51.5074°N,
0.1278°W

BREAKFAST IN CHELSEA

JACK STARBRIGHT WAS MAKING breakfast, carefully cutting the toast into fingers before arranging them around the edge of the plate, leaving room for Alex's egg, which was still bubbling away in a pan. She glanced at her watch. There was no sign of Alex, although it was already eight and they had to be out of the house by eight thirty.

She walked over to the door and called up the stairs. "Alex!"

"I'll be one minute, Jack!" The familiar voice came from the bedroom on the second floor.

Jack smiled and went back into the kitchen. As she lifted the egg out of the boiling water, she asked herself—for the thousandth time—how she had managed to get into this situation. And what would anybody think, looking at her? She was fast approaching her thirties. This Christmas, she would be twenty-nine. When she had first come to London, she had been a law student, helping out in a house in Chelsea to support herself. Now, seven years later, she was still living there, sharing the place with a fourteen-year-old boy. It was an unusual arrangement, to say the least.

When Jack first met him, Alex had been seven, a little

boy with messy fair hair, brown eyes, and plenty of attitude. He had come into the room with his hands in his pockets, his shirt out of his trousers, and one shoelace trailing, and she'd had no idea that he was going to completely change her life.

"This is Alex," Ian Rider had said. "Alex, this is Jack."

Alex had stared at her. "Jack's a man's name." Those were the first words he had ever spoken to her.

"Well, it's my name and you'd better get used to it," Jack had replied.

They had become friends almost immediately.

Jack had been in London to study law. She had a place at the School of Oriental and African Studies, one of the best colleges in London—but what she didn't have was money. She had answered an advertisement in the *Times*.

Room in Chelsea available plus living expenses in return for some housekeeping duties and childcare. Would suit a student or part-time professional. Telephone:

The advertisement had been placed by Ian Rider, Alex's uncle, who had introduced himself as a banker working in the city. She could still see him now, a darkly handsome man dressed in an expensive suit, sitting with his legs crossed and a glass of red wine in his hand.

"Let me explain, Miss Starbright. Alex's parents died when he was young, and I've looked after him pretty much since he was born. Alex's father was in banking . . .

the same as me. The trouble is, I'm having to do more and more travel these days—Zurich, Luxembourg, Singapore. That's the joy of international finance! I don't want Alex to have a nanny or anything like that. I try to spend as much time as I can with him when I'm home. What I really want is for someone to live here part-time and to become a sort of friend to him so he won't notice it so much when I'm away. You'll find that Alex is very good at looking after himself. He goes to school just down the road, and I'm sure the two of you will get along well. You're much closer to his age than I am, and he's a very easygoing kid. What do you say?"

How could she possibly have known that almost everything Ian Rider had told her was untrue? He wasn't in banking. He was a spy. Alex's father had been a spy too. Both of Alex's parents had been killed by a bomb planted on a plane, and Alex would have died with them but for the chance of an ear infection that had forced him to stay at home. Sometimes Jack hated Ian Rider for the way he had deceived her. But that hadn't been the worst of it. He had also lied to Alex just about every day of his life, cold-bloodedly preparing him for a destiny that had been chosen for him the day he was born. How could anyone do that to a child? The climbing trips, the martial arts classes, the trips abroad, the different languages that Alex spoke . . . They had all been nothing more than basic training. Ian Rider had molded Alex into an image of himself.

And then Ian Rider had been killed. The police had said it was a car accident, but Alex had found the car and discovered that it was riddled with bullet holes. Another lie. After that, everything had happened very quickly as the entire construction that had been built around Alex's life had collapsed in on itself. Alex had met Alan Blunt and Mrs. Jones on the day of the funeral, and almost immediately afterward he had been recruited by them and sent for two weeks' intensive training in the Brecon Beacons. It had included assault courses, unarmed combat, forced marches, and survival in the so-called Killing House, a mock-up of an embassy used to practice techniques in hostage release. Alex had half drowned in freezing mud and water, stumbled up and down hills, been shouted at by sergeants in khaki whose entire vocabulary seemed to consist of four-letter words, swallowed down meals out of mess tins, and desperately snatched a few minutes of sleep when the exercises ended in the middle of the night. He was a child! Nobody seemed to have noticed.

Jack had learned all this afterward. Over the years, with Ian Rider away more and more, she had become Alex's closest friend, and there could be no secrets between the two of them. She knew everything about his first mission, when he had been sent to Cornwall, to the headquarters of Sayle Enterprises. This was where the Stormbreaker computer was being mass-produced. Sayle planned to distribute them free to every school in the country, and if he had succeeded, the result would have been mass murder. Alex had discovered that Sayle was a psychopath planning some sort of mad revenge on the UK, and Alex had managed to stop him only at the last minute. Jack had been horrified by the whole story. What made it worse was her knowledge that although Alex had almost gotten killed, it wouldn't end there. She was certain that— soon—MI6 would be back.

What should she do? Jack sighed as she unscrewed the Marmite and searched for a knife. She had questioned Alex about the Stormbreaker business. Of course she had. When Alex had finally gotten home in one piece, the two of them had talked until late in the night. Alex didn't want to be a spy, but the truth was, he had no choice. Ian Rider had already made the decision for him. Jack had considered going to the newspapers. Part of her wanted to stop this madness before it went any further. But she knew that she couldn't protect Alex by exposing him. All she could do was support him and try to stop him from getting into trouble a second time. It had been years now since she had attended college, and she had to accept that her career as a high-flying lawyer was definitely on hold. Ian Rider was to blame for that too.

She smeared each strip of toast with Marmite, then arranged them on the plate. Looking down, she was annoyed with herself. What did she think she was doing? Alex was fourteen, not four—and she was behaving exactly like the nanny she had never wanted to be. She was tempted to throw the whole lot into the trash and start again. At the same time, Alex liked being looked after. And she knew that he wasn't looking forward to this morning, to what lay ahead.

"Hi, Jack." Alex appeared at the door and slouched, bleary-eyed, over to the table. Like every other teenager, he wasn't at his best first thing in the morning. He was wearing his school uniform (the tie was spectacularly crooked) but he wouldn't be in school until after eleven. He had an appointment. It had been in the planner for weeks.

"Good morning, Alex." She examined him. "You look a bit of a mess today."

Alex yawned. "That's what you said yesterday."

"No. Yesterday I said you were a total mess. Today is definitely an improvement." She slid the plate in front of him. "Breakfast!"

"Thanks, Jack."

She went over to the fridge, took out a carton of orange juice, and poured a glass. When she brought it over to the table, she was absurdly pleased to see that he had lopped the top off the egg and dipped the toast in. What had happened in Cornwall hadn't changed him. At heart, he was still just a kid. "We need to leave in fifteen minutes," she said.

"I can go on my own."

"No. I'm coming with you."

Alex hesitated. "Jack," he said. "I've been thinking about this. Do I really need to go today? I mean, couldn't we wait until the holidays? I've missed enough school as it is."

"One more morning won't make any difference, Alex."

"But it's not hurting anymore. Honestly, I think I'm going to be fine. Let's just cancel."

Jack couldn't hide her smile. "You're not afraid, are you?"

"No!"

"Then what's the problem?"

"There is no problem . . ."

"Then forget it, Alex. We were lucky to get an appointment. Have your breakfast and then go and brush your teeth. If you can remember what a comb looks like, you might also think about doing your hair."

"Jack . . ."

"I mean it!"

Jack went over to make a cup of coffee. She wondered what MI6 would have made of it all. Alex hadn't been afraid of the SAS. He'd been dumped in a tank with a giant jellyfish and survived. He'd parachuted out of a helicopter over London and smashed through the roof of the Science Museum.

But he was still scared of the dentist.

A tiny little filling.

Jack flicked on the kettle while, behind her, Alex finished his egg.

CRUNCH TIME

IT HAD BEGUN, LIKE all toothaches do, with a twinge. Alex had tried to ignore it, but very quickly it had gotten worse. Hot drinks were bad. Ice cream was worse. In the end he had been forced to mention it to Jack, and she had called the dentist right away. Alex needed an emergency appointment and that meant missing a few hours of school. He wasn't happy about that either. Thanks to Alan Blunt and Mrs. Jones, he had missed more than enough school already.

The two of them set off together, walking down the King's Road to Sloane Square tube station. The dentist—his name was Wiseman—had offices just off Oxford Circus. Alex had been there only half a dozen times, but he remembered every detail, from the nasty striped wallpaper to the fish tank with its depressed-looking fish and the old magazines on the round table in the waiting room.

"Cheer up," Jack said as they passed through the turnstile and made their way down.

"What's there to be cheerful about?" Alex growled. "You're not the one having a drill in the top of your mouth."

"You should have thought of that before you ate all those sweets."

"I don't eat sweets." Alex glared at her. "And you didn't need to come with me. I could find my way there on my own."

"Of course I had to come with you, Alex. And if you don't stop complaining, I'm going to insist on holding your hand when we go in."

They waited in silence until the train arrived, then climbed on together. Alex didn't feel like talking and snatched one of the free newspapers that someone had left on the seat. He glanced at the headline: FREDDY FINGERS GOES ON TRIAL. It had been on the breakfast news on television too. Freddy Fingers. Everyone knew who he was. There had been enormous publicity about the trial, which was to take place at the Old Bailey. It began today.

His real name was Sir Frederick Meadows. Until recently, he had been the chairman of the Royal National Bank, one of the biggest banks in the country. The Queen was actually one of its customers, and he had often been photographed coming in and out of Buckingham Palace, a small, bald man with a round face and a nervous smile. Everyone trusted him. He had been knighted for services to banking and had frequently appeared on television, talking about the economy. He was always cheerful. He was easy to understand. And so it had come as a real shock when, after a two-year investigation, the police had arrested him for the theft of one hundred million pounds.

It was well known that Meadows had been born with a very unusual condition. He had an extra finger on his left hand—and of course that had been a gift for the journalists. There were plenty of headlines that described him as being "light-fingered" or "having his fingers in the till." He had become known to the whole country as Freddy Fingers.

Alex read the story in the paper he'd picked up.

Meadows used his position in the Royal National to hack into the bank's computers. Every time a payment was made, one pound was transferred to a secret account he'd set up for himself. This went on for ten years, by which time it is estimated that he had stolen at least a hundred million pounds, and maybe more. Last summer, Meadows announced his retirement and was on his way to Heathrow Airport when a sharp-eyed accountant realized what had happened and called the police. He was arrested as he tried to board a flight to Mexico.

Experts have been unable to locate the missing funds, and Sir Frederick has refused to cooperate. It is believed that he concealed the money in secret bank accounts in Switzerland and the Cayman Islands. The trial, which takes place at the Old Bailey, will have maximum security. More than a hundred policemen will surround the court, as there is a real fear that he may try to escape. Somewhere, there's a huge fortune waiting for him. And you can bet that Sir Freddy will want to give justice the finger!

Alex finished the article, then turned to the sports

section. He supported Chelsea and had watched them tie with Barcelona in the International Champions Cup over the weekend. He read the match report, putting everything else out of his head.

They reached Oxford Circus in good time and climbed the escalator back into the daylight. The strange thing was that Alex's tooth wasn't hurting anymore—but he was still feeling a little queasy. It wasn't just the drill. He could see Dr. Wiseman with his huge eyes magnified behind his protective goggles, bending over him. He hated the thought of the man's hand, with its latex-covered fingers, poking around in his mouth. Still, there was no point arguing. It was ten to nine and the intersection where Regent Street met Oxford Street was packed with commuters. The dentist was about a five-minute walk away.

"Free snacks! Try a Cadbury's Crunch Bar. They're free today. Try one now!"

There were half a dozen men and women on the sidewalk, dressed in mauve jackets and jeans, covering all the station entrances. They were handing out little bars of chocolate, and Alex guessed there would be more of them in other parts of London. It was quite common when new products were being launched. The big companies gave away free samples at all the main stations. Almost without thinking, he reached out and took one.

"Forget it, Alex," Jack said. "You can't eat chocolate five minutes before you go to the dentist."

Alex was annoyed. When he had been training with

the SAS, he had been treated almost as an equal. Certainly nobody had made allowances for his age. But here he was in the middle of London with Jack, and she was treating him like a child. "I'm not going to eat it now," he protested. "I'm only taking it for later."

"You may not be able to eat it. Your mouth will be numb."

"Then you can keep it for me." He was about to hand it over when he stopped and looked at it more closely. The chocolate bar was in silver foil with the name in bright red. All around him, people were grabbing their free samples. Even as they stood there, a hundred or more bars were given away. "That's really weird," he said.

"What?"

"The wrapper." He held it out so Jack could see. "Read what it says."

"Cadbury's Crunch Bar." She read the words out loud. She didn't understand what he was getting at.

"It's wrong," Alex explained. "That's not how you spell it. It ought to read 'Cadbury' without the apostrophe and the *s*."

"Are you sure?"

"I think so. It doesn't look right."

Jack shrugged. "They must have made a mistake. New product, new typing error." She took the bar and slipped it into her pocket. "We'd better get a move on, Alex. I don't want to be late."

But Alex was puzzled. He examined the man who had

given him the sample and who was still working his way through the crowd. He was very muscular, his hair cut short, clean shaven. With a slight jolt, Alex noticed that the man was disabled: he had only one hand. Alex turned his attention to the others. There was something quite similar about all of them—and it wasn't just the mauve jackets and jeans. They were all fit. They all had short hair. All of them—the men and the women—carried themselves in a certain way. It was in their body language, the way they stood. And they were nervous, as if they knew something bad was about to happen.

A van pulled in across the road and parked on a yellow line. The driver got out and went around to open the back door. If Alex hadn't been alerted, he would have barely noticed him, but as it was, he felt a sudden shock. He recognized him!

In his twenties with close-cropped hair. Well-built. The cold eyes of a mercenary. Alex couldn't believe what he was seeing. It was impossible that the man should be here, in the middle of London, but he knew he wasn't making a mistake. You never forget the face of someone who has threatened to kill you—and that was just what this man had done in the secret research center under Sayle Enterprises. He had been a guard employed by Herod Sayle, and he had grabbed Alex as he came out of the disused mine.

"If you make any moves, I'll shoot you in the head."
Alex remembered the voice. The guard had been

overconfident. After all, he had a gun in his hand, and this was just a fourteen-year-old boy. He had also been stupid. He had looked away long enough to allow Alex to take him out with a single karate move, an *enpi*, or elbow strike behind the ear.

Why was he here?

Alex watched as the driver took out a cardboard box and walked to the area where the sidewalk widened in front of the Niketown store. There were two distributors here, hard at work. One of them had a black eye patch slanting across his face. They nodded at him, took the box, and began to unload more of the bars. Alex tried to make sense of it all. A hired killer from Sayle Enterprises had now become a delivery boy in central London. Well, that wasn't as unlikely as it sounded. Herod Sayle was dead. Sayle Enterprises had been closed down. He would need another job. But there was something else. The chocolate bars were supposed to be made by Cadbury, but somebody had made an elementary mistake with the spelling.

Perhaps it was something he had inherited from Ian Rider. Or maybe it had been knocked into him when he was with the SAS, moving through the dark and silent passageways of the Killing House. But Alex had learned to trust his instincts, and right now there was a warning bell jangling madly in his head. It might be that he was about to make a complete fool of himself. But that didn't matter. He knew he had to act.

"Jack," he said. "I need you to contact Alan Blunt."

"What?" Jack stared at him. "What are you talking about?"

"Alan Blunt and Mrs. Jones. You need to call them."

"I can't call them. I don't have their telephone number."

"It doesn't matter. Find them somehow. Or call the police. But I think there's something going on."

"Alex. If you're trying to get out of going to the dentist—"

"I'm not. These chocolate bars they're giving out. There's something wrong with them. I'm sure of it."

"Because they made a spelling mistake?"

"Just do it, Jack!"

Alex didn't have time to explain. He already knew what he had to do. The man with the cardboard box, the man who had tried to kill him, was waiting for the distributor to finish emptying it. Without saying another word, Alex ran across the road, weaving between the traffic. There was the scream of a horn, and a bike messenger on a black Kawasaki swerved around him, the driver swearing beneath his helmet. Alex reached the white van. He looked inside. It was empty. This must be the last delivery. There were some old blankets lying on the floor. They were perfect. He took one quick glance around, then climbed in and pulled them over himself.

For Jack, it had all happened too quickly. She had heard what Alex said and watched him race across the street, almost getting mowed down by a motorbike. She had seen him climb into the back of a white van, and now she watched the driver return. Was he going to look inside? No. He casually closed the doors and returned to the front. He climbed in and a moment later the van drove off.

Jack was left there, with the free sample in her pocket, and Alex's words rang in her ears.

"Alan Blunt and Mrs. Jones. You need to call them."

She didn't doubt him. How could she? He had been right before. Once again, Alex had put himself in danger.

MI6. They worked in a building that called itself the Royal & General Bank on Liverpool Street. That was where she would start. She could still see the men and women handing out the chocolate bars, more and more of them. Quickly, she took out her phone and made the first call.

THE MEAT MARKET

A ROUGH WOODEN PANEL DIVIDED the back of the white van from the driver's seat, but fortunately there was a knot in it that provided Alex with an eyehole directly over the driver's shoulder and out the front window. It felt strange to be only inches away from a man who had once held him up at gunpoint, and Alex had to be careful not to shift his weight while the van was standing still. Any movement would have told the driver that he was carrying an uninvited passenger.

In fact, Alex was beginning to question the wisdom of what he was doing. Could it be that he had imagined a danger that didn't exist? The driver had once worked for Herod Sayle. That didn't mean he was involved in anything criminal now. And had there really been a spelling mistake on the chocolate bars? Now that Alex thought about it, he wasn't quite so sure. Cadbury's or Cadbury? There wasn't such a huge difference between the two.

It was too late to back out now. He was in the back of a van being carried across London. Jack would be trying to contact MI6. Quite possibly he was making a complete fool of himself, but he might as well see it through to the end.

They were heading east. They stopped at a red traffic light, and Alex was able to make out another tube station: Holborn. There were more distributors in mauve jackets, more Crunch Bars being handed out. The men and women looked exactly the same as the ones that Alex had seen at Oxford Circus: military haircuts, fit, quite young. And they were just as popular here. Before the lights had gone green, they must have handed out another twenty or thirty bars. Was that so surprising? The truth is that chocolate is one of the few things that unites adults and children. There are very few people who don't like it.

The van continued past the huge building site that Farringdon had become with the construction of all the new office blocks and luxury flats that were springing up around Crossrail. The driver slowed down and turned onto a narrow street that threaded its way between offices and fast-food restaurants. Ahead of him, Alex saw a strange building, almost like a railway station, made out of stone, brick, and iron, decorated with statues of dragons and knights. There was a great archway and the road—which was cobbled—continued straight through it and out the other side. The whole thing looked like something out of Sherlock Holmes, and it took Alex a minute or two to re-member what it was.

Jack had brought him here once. The meat market at Smithfield. He remembered her telling him that there had been a market here for over eight hundred years. It was one of the oldest in London, and unlike the fish market at Billingsgate and the fruit and vegetable market in Covent Garden, it had refused to move out. Huge tractor trailers would arrive in the middle of the night, unloading hundreds of carcasses, whole pigs and sheep, dangling on hooks. They would trundle slowly forward on the next stage of a journey that would finally take them to the restaurants or supermarket freezers.

With his face still pressed against the eyehole, Alex watched as a couple of workers crossed the road, wearing bloodstained white overalls. A huge truck—PETERSFIELD ORGANIC MEAT—pulled away. Several sections of the market had been closed. They stopped in front of an ugly building with a green sliding door. This was one of the storage facilities that had been built just after the war. Jack had told him that they were empty and there were plans to knock them down. It seemed that they were going inside. The driver pressed the button on a remote control and the door slid open. They drove into a wide, empty space that led directly to a solid brick wall. There was absolutely nothing here, just dust and debris, a few planks of wood, rusting oil drums, and scraps of cloth. It was obvious that nobody had been here for years. Alex heard the sound of an electric motor and the door slid shut behind him. The driver didn't move. What the hell was going on?

And then there was another click and, in front of him, the brick wall began to sink into the floor, carried by hidden hydraulics. The whole thing was fake. There was a huge space behind it, brightly lit, spread over several floors and illuminated by powerful spotlights. It was hard to make out very much through the small hole cut in the wood, but Alex was aware of some sort of control center with several television screens, a digital communications system, computers, ticking clocks. Unlike the rest of the meat market, everything was gleaming clean and modern. The white van swung around to the right and parked. As the driver turned off the engine, Alex heard a voice being relayed over a loudspeaker.

"Fourteen minutes until outbreak."

Outbreak? What did that mean? Normally, if you used the word *outbreak*, you'd be talking about a disease. The more Alex saw of this fantastic operation, the less he liked it. He needed to tell Jack where he was and get someone over here . . . ideally in the next fourteen minutes. He began to reach for his phone, then silently cursed. Cell phones weren't allowed at Brookland. He had left his at home.

The driver got out of the van. Alex heard him walk away, then hurried over to the back door. He was lucky— it could be opened from inside. Gently, he eased down the handle and slipped out. He saw at once that the van had been parked next to another vehicle: an ambulance. That was another question. What was it doing here? Being careful to make no sound, Alex moved forward. He was protected here. Nobody could see him. But crouching down between the two vehicles, he could see everything.

There were four men grouped together, surrounded

by metal tables with computers, maps, radio transmitters, and various weapons. Their attention was fixed on a bank of television screens that were showing fuzzy black-and-white images of London streets, the traffic moving slowly in different directions. Alex guessed that they had somehow hacked into the closed-circuit cameras that were all over the city. A fifth man sat in a leather chair with his back to Alex. The driver walked up to them and stood to attention. The chair swiveled around and Alex saw that it was occupied by an enormous man, well over six feet tall, with square shoulders and muscular arms, dressed in loose-fitting combat fatigues. The man had a strangely babyish face with blond hair and blue eyes so intense that even at this distance Alex felt himself being hypnotized. The driver saluted and suddenly Alex understood what he should have known all along. They were all military. He remembered the man he had seen, missing a hand. He must have been wounded in action. Just a short while ago, Jack had been serving him Marmite soldiers for breakfast. Now, somehow, he had stumbled onto the real thing.

"Welcome back, Charlie." The blond man smiled. Somehow Alex wasn't surprised that he had perfectly white teeth too. "Report?"

"Distribution proceeding smoothly, Colonel."

"No interference from the police?"

"No, sir. In fact, a couple of them even came over to ask for some of the samples."

"That's very good."

"Will it kill them?" Another man, dark-skinned, had asked the question.

"Don't worry, Khyber. I've already told you. It's a hallucinogen, not a poison. Extracted from toads in Peru! They're not going to feel well. They may think they've had a heart attack. But they'll be fine."

"That's him!" One of the other soldiers had spoken. The blond man spun around again and looked at one of the other screens.

This television was tuned to Sky News, and there was a report about the banker that Alex had read about on the tube. Sir Frederick Meadows was being taken to the Old Bailey. Alex saw a security van driving into the famous court with a scrum of journalists and photographers firing off their cameras into the blacked-out windows. Was that what this was all about? None of it made any sense.

"Thirteen minutes until outbreak." The amplified voice sounded again.

Alex couldn't hang around any longer. He had to get out of here before he was discovered—or at least find a working telephone so he could contact Jack. The men were all gathered in a group. They had no idea he was here. Keeping close to the ambulance, Alex backed away, then slipped around the side of the chamber, staying in the shadows.

He came to a metal staircase and crept down. The complex—he thought of it as an operations center—was all metal and glass, with just a few of the older brick walls painted white. Once it must have been part of the meat market. Alex could imagine live animals being kept here before they were sold. Someone had come in, hollowed the place out, and then created this modern construction inside. It must have cost millions—but then maybe that's what this was all about. Sir Frederick Meadows had stolen more than one hundred million pounds. The newspaper had said he might try to escape. Alex had just seen him being taken to court. He could have planned this before his arrest.

Alex went through an open doorway into a room that turned out to be a kitchen with a brand-new coffee machine, a gleaming aluminum fridge, a table with six chairs, and a cupboard. His eye was drawn to a photograph on the wall. It was a newspaper clipping that showed a man in a ceremonial uniform, holding up a medal for the cameras. Alex recognized the fair-haired man he had seen upstairs. The headline read MEDAL FOR WOUNDED IRAQ HERO. He read some of the text:

> Colonel Aubrey Sykes, who was badly wounded in Operation Telic in Iraq, today visited Buckingham Palace, where he received the Distinguished Service Order from the Queen. Colonel Sykes saved eleven of his men when he came under fire in an ambush near Mosul—even though he himself had suffered major shrapnel injuries . . .

He was right. They were all soldiers, the whole lot of

them. Or ex-soldiers. And whatever they were up to, they were treating it like a military operation. They saluted each other. They called their senior officer "sir." The whole thing was hard to believe.

He crossed the kitchen to a second door, which led into a larger space. Alex found himself surrounded by machinery: some sort of industrial oven, a conveyor belt, a printing press, a great cylinder of silver paper. The smell of sugar and cocoa still hung heavy in the air. Of course! This was the factory where the chocolate bars had been produced. Alex went over to a metal counter and found one of the samples, discarded with the wrapper torn. Cadbury's Crunch Bar. He couldn't help smiling. All this planning and then someone had made a stupid mistake because they didn't know how to spell.

He continued through a frosted glass door, which slid open to allow him into a third room, this one a laboratory with the usual apparatus spread out across a sanitized work surface. He walked past glass flasks and test tubes. Ahead of him there was a shelf lined with about twenty or thirty identical plastic bottles, most of them empty. He picked one up. This one still had an inch of some sort of colorless liquid. There was a label with the name— BUFOTENINE—and a picture of a crouching frog. Alex unscrewed the bottle and sniffed. The liquid had no smell.

"Eleven minutes until outbreak."

The voice, booming out over the loudspeaker, reminded Alex that time was fast running out. He needed a telephone. He put the bottle down and headed back to the kitchen. Surely there would be one there, although he couldn't remember seeing it. He went through the factory and had reached the door when he heard the clang of footsteps on the metal stairway and ducked back just in time to avoid being seen. It was one of the soldiers from upstairs. He was dressed in the dark green trousers and short-sleeved shirt of a London paramedic. He wore tinted glasses and he had a mustache and thick black hair, neither of which looked quite real.

Alex watched from the doorway as the man opened a cupboard, took out a selection of cups, and filled them with coffee from the machine. He wasn't sure what to do. There was no telephone. He needed to get out of here— but that meant going back upstairs. He was also painfully aware of time running out.

A moment later, the decision was made for him. The soldier twisted around. "Who the hell are you?" he demanded.

Alex froze. How could the man have known he was there? He hadn't made a sound. He glanced left and right, then understood. It was the fridge. He had been given away by his own reflection in the aluminum door. Alex didn't hesitate. Smiling, with his hands raised to show that he was unarmed, he moved into the kitchen. The man didn't move. All he saw was some innocent-looking fourteen-year-old boy who had appeared out of nowhere. It was the same mistake that many of the guards had made at Sayle Enterprises. As soon as he was close enough, Alex twisted around and lashed out with his foot, driving the heel and sole into the man's solar plexus. It was the fastest and easiest way to make sure that he went down and stayed there, but just to be sure, Alex followed through with an elbow strike to the side of the head.

The man collapsed. As he slid to the floor, the wig he had been wearing came loose from his head. The tinted glasses and the mustache were fake too. Alex understood. The man had been in disguise. When this operation was over, he wouldn't want to be recognized. But what exactly was the operation?

Somehow, in the next few seconds, Alex managed to piece it all together. The chocolate bars, the ambulance, the laboratory, Sir Frederick Meadows. Yes. Of course. He remembered what Colonel Sykes had said. *It's a hallucinogen, not a poison.* He must have been talking about the liquid that Alex had just seen. They were planning to poison London! The bufotenine—or whatever it was called—wasn't lethal. They weren't planning mass murder. But there was going to be mass panic as people all over the city thought they were having heart attacks. And they were going to drive an ambulance right through the middle of it all. They would get into the Old Bailey and grab the banker before anyone knew what had happened. One hundred million pounds! It was a huge risk, but the reward made it more than worthwhile.

"Eight minutes until outbreak."

What was he going to do? The soldiers were waiting for their coffee. If it didn't arrive soon, one of them would come down to investigate. Alex searched through the pockets of the unconscious man. There was no phone. Moving quickly and silently, he went over to the cupboard and opened it. It was empty and there was plenty of room inside. He remembered seeing parcel tape in the room where the samples had been manufactured. That provided part of the answer—but the rest of it? He picked up the wig and the glasses. The man was short, only a few inches taller than Alex himself. Yes! If he was lucky, it might work.

"Seven minutes until outbreak."

Three minutes later, dressed as a paramedic, wearing the wig, mustache, and glasses, Alex climbed the metal staircase and went over to the television screens where the men were still waiting. He just hoped they wouldn't look at him too closely. The man he had attacked was still downstairs, stripped to his undershorts, tied up and locked in the cupboard. Keeping his head down, Alex placed the tray with the coffees on one of the tables and moved away.

"You took your time, Sarko," the man, Khyber, muttered.

Sarko. Some sort of nickname. Alex realized this must be the man he had knocked out. Alex grunted and moved to the far corner of the room, trying to keep himself out of sight.

The men drank the coffee. At the same time, they

studied the images on the television screens, the various
roads of London, as if they were searching for a single
vehicle in the endlessly moving traffic. And all the time,
the prerecorded voice continued the countdown until a
red light glowed on the control panel and the announce-
ment came:

"Outbreak commencing . . ."

Colonel Aubrey Sykes, the man who had been given
a medal by the Queen, got to his feet. He towered over
the other men. "Gentlemen," he said, "we are about to
see something that has never happened before in London,
something that has never happened in any European city.
Let's have no illusions. We didn't set out deliberately to kill
anybody, but nonetheless, people are going to die today.
Maybe a lot of people. I understand that you may not be too
happy about that. We're not criminals. We're not killers—
even though all of us have killed for our country.

"What we are today is victims. I don't want any of
you to forget that. Khyber, you were driving a Snatch
Land Rover in Afghanistan when you drove over a land
mine. It wasn't a suitable vehicle and that's why you're
missing a leg. Charlie—you were put on trial, accused of
killing people in Iraq. The judge seemed to forget that was
why you were sent there. Sarko . . ." Alex straightened
up. The Colonel was addressing him. "You watched your
best mate get blown to pieces right next to you, and you
have nightmares every night, but nobody cares about you
anymore. Danny and Gareth"—these were the last men in

the group, also dressed as paramedics—"after you were wounded in Helmand Province, you both spent six weeks in a mixed National Health Service ward. Nobody gave a damn about your dignity . . ."

He paused.

"Today is all about payback. No more. No less. We are going to get what we deserve, and because the British army wouldn't give it to us and the British government forgot about us, we're going to take it for ourselves."

"Colonel. Sir!" Khyber pointed at one of the TV screens.

Alex looked. There had been some sort of accident. Two cars had collided with each other. It was difficult to see exactly what had happened: the image was fuzzy and in black and white. But a bottleneck had already built up. The cars were at different angles to each other. None of them was moving.

Sykes nodded. "We called this Operation London Down," he said. "And as you can see, it's started. So let's get out there and do it!"

EMERGENCY SERVICES

IT HAD BEGUN NEAR Blackfriars Bridge.

Later on, the newspapers would identify the first victim as Frank Smith, a black cabdriver. He had started work at six o'clock and had continued until half past eight, when he stopped for a break. He went into a Starbucks that happened to be next to a tube station, and when he came out, he noticed a couple of young men giving away samples of some sort of chocolate bar. He'd taken one without even thinking about it and had eaten it with his coffee.

Just after ten o'clock, he had been approaching the bridge when it hit him. First, there seemed to be too much saliva in his mouth. He couldn't understand it. He had a pet dog back home, a bulldog, and he had often seen it dribbling when food was about to be served. Now he was doing the same! At the same time, he realized there was something wrong with his eyes. They were hurting and his vision was going in and out of focus. Frank should have stopped driving then and there, but he decided to keep going. He was sure that whatever was wrong with him would pass in a minute—and if it didn't, he could always pull in at St. Thomas's Hospital on the other side of the river. He could feel his heart beating. It was pounding inside his chest as if it was trying to break out. Ahead of him, the lights changed. Thinking about the hospital, he pressed down on the accelerator.

He didn't even make it onto the bridge. In pain, frightened, and out of control, Frank went the wrong way around a traffic circle and didn't even try to stop himself as he smashed headfirst into another car. Neither he nor the other driver was badly hurt, but almost at once a traffic jam built up around them. As it happened, there were two policewomen on foot patrol nearby. They had seen the accident and came running, but before they had reached the scene, one of them clutched her stomach and fell to her knees. On the other side of the road, a newspaper seller collapsed on the sidewalk in front of his kiosk. The wind snatched a newspaper out of his hand, separated it, and blew the pages across the cars that were already backing up all the way to St. Paul's.

The same sort of scene was being repeated all over the city. The free samples had been distributed all around the West End, the City, and the Docklands, and there were hundreds of people who hadn't even waited to get to work before they had tucked in. The sickness, when it came, was sudden and violent. It was like being punched in the stomach. One after another, they found themselves doubling up in pain: secretaries, shop assistants, cleaners, office workers, security guards, construction workers, traffic wardens, police officers . . . even the poor homeless people who had spent the night out on the street and who had thought they were lucky enough to get something for nothing. Soon the streets were filled with people staggering blindly, throwing up, scrambling for their phones and desperately calling the emergency services.

It got worse. Tube trains had come to a halt as the drivers crawled out onto the platforms and waited for help to arrive. Many of the paramedics were themselves out of action. In the hospitals, nurses and doctors staggered into each other, helpless and frightened, more aware than anyone that something terrible had happened, that it was impossible for so many people in the city to fall ill at one time. The ambulances were going nowhere. Half the streets were blocked. Many of the drivers were out of action. Cars were colliding with each other. Smoke was rising in a cloud over Piccadilly: a van had crashed into a shop and burst into flames. Less than a mile away, a semi had swerved into the side of Waterloo Bridge and was hanging, suspended over the Thames.

Although the public knows very little about the exact machinery, there are a number of rules, or "protocols," in place in case London is hit by a terrorist attack. The police, the intelligence services, the army, the fire brigade, and many other organizations have secretly planned exactly what to do. Less than twenty minutes after Frank Smith fell ill, the prime minister, the home secretary, and a dozen other politicians and civil servants were being rushed to a secure room in Whitehall for an emergency meeting.

Soldiers armed with sniper rifles and machine guns were taking up positions at strategic points around the capital. And the BBC was already transmitting a message that had been recorded a long time ago—just in case it was ever needed.

"This is a terrorist alert. Do not panic. If you are driving, stop your car and wait for assistance. Police and medical authorities will be with you shortly. If you are at home, do not leave the house. News will be broadcast as soon as it is available. The government is aware of the situation and is doing everything in its power to make the city safe."

But people were panicking. Rumors were spreading so fast that even the news channels were unable to keep up. London had been the victim of a dirty bomb. Someone had poisoned the water supply. There had been an attack with chemical weapons. Piccadilly had turned radioactive. Nobody remembered the little bar of chocolate they'd eaten an hour ago—or if they did, they failed to put two and two together. Everywhere now there were people writhing on the ground, crying out for help. Huge lines had built up outside hospitals and pharmacies. There were cars everywhere—on the roads and on the sidewalks—many of them empty. Cell phones weren't working and that only added to the sense of fear. So many people had tried to make calls that the entire network had reached capacity.

The enemy was invisible. That was the worst of it.

London was under attack, but it was impossible to say by whom. Nobody knew who had started it. Worse still, they didn't know if they might be next.

Alex Rider was able to glimpse some of this, sitting in the back of the ambulance as it pulled away from the meat market. But it was the sounds all around him that told him more. Helicopters buzzed overhead. Sirens screamed. Car horns blasted uselessly. It was obvious that London was in the grip of something it had never seen before, and their progress was slow, with countless stops and starts.

The six of them had climbed into the vehicle, all dressed as paramedics. Charlie was once again driving. Sykes was next to him. It was interesting that neither of them had bothered with a facial disguise. The other three were in the back with Alex. The man named Danny was short and very muscular, smoking a cigarette. He had a tattoo, a broken heart, on the side of his neck. Gareth was black, watchful, a little older than the others. Khyber was next to him. Alex was terrified that one of them would address him. So far nobody had given him so much as a second glance, but his voice would be certain to give him away. Fortunately, nobody seemed inclined to talk.

He looked out the back window and saw a woman kneeling beside a baby carriage, holding on to it with one hand. A chef in a white hat and apron lay sprawled outside his restaurant. Many of the roads seemed to be blocked. A fire engine, with its complete crew, had come to a halt at a crossroads. A motorcyclist lay, unmoving, trapped beneath his own bike. He could imagine these scenes repeated all over the city and could only stare in silent horror. And to think that only an hour ago he had been on the way to the dentist!

Colonel Sykes had created the perfect conditions for any crime he chose to commit. London had come to a standstill. The police were going to be too sick or too busy to do anything. He and his men could choose any bank or museum and just walk in. There were millions of pounds' worth of paintings waiting to be lifted off the walls at the National Gallery. Or how about the gold bullion kept in the Bank of England? Alex knew that none of these was their target. In fact, they wouldn't be driving far. The meat market was barely half a mile from the Old Bailey—presumably that was why they had chosen it as their base of operations. Sir Frederick Meadows had to be behind this. Get him out of prison and out of the country and the prize would add up to more than a hundred million pounds, more than enough for all of them.

The ambulance passed St. Bartholemew's Hospital, with hundreds of frightened people crowding around the main doors. Next, it turned onto Newgate Street. St. Paul's Cathedral was just behind them. There were more crowds on the steps and Alex could imagine the priests and the congregation cowering inside. After all, what had happened was like some biblical plague. They swung around to the right and for the first time he saw it: a handsome domed building made out of gray stone with, high up, a statue of a woman carrying a sword and scales. The Central Criminal Court. Also known as the Old Bailey.

He was right.

The ambulance stopped outside a thick, modern wall made of reinforced concrete. The bulk of the Old Bailey was many hundreds of years old, but Alex knew that parts of it had been added more recently. They had come around to one of the side entrances.

Charlie turned off the engine. The Colonel twisted around. "All right, gentlemen," he said. "Let's get suited up."

The other soldiers moved into action straightaway. Alex saw guns being taken out, tested, then concealed. He had no weapon himself—Sarko hadn't been carrying one when he was knocked out—and now he hoped that nobody would notice. Both Charlie and Colonel Sykes had put on surgical masks that completely covered the lower halves of their faces. So that was why they hadn't needed disguises! It was perfectly reasonable for paramedics to be protecting themselves against any contagion and there was no chance of their being recognized.

Everyone was ready. Sykes glanced one last time at his men. "You all know what to do," he said. "Good luck. Ten minutes maximum and we'll be on our way."

He nodded. Charlie stayed in the driving seat. The other men threw open the doors and climbed out. Alex hesitated. He hadn't been there when they discussed the plan. He didn't know what to do.

"Get a move on, Sarko," the shorter man—Danny—called to him.

Alex knew he had no choice. Operation London Down had entered its second phase, and like it or not, he was part of it. Gritting his teeth, he climbed out of the ambulance and joined the rest of them in the street.

PHANTOM LADY

ON A NORMAL DAY, the Old Bailey would have been surrounded by security. During high-profile trials it was quite common to see police officers strolling along the sidewalks with gas-operated Heckler & Koch G36 assault rifles cradled in their arms, and even an ambulance would have been unable to park anywhere near any of the main entrances without proper authorization. But there was nothing normal about this day, and as the Colonel had rightly guessed, a working ambulance with a healthy crew would be welcomed with open arms.

Alex followed Sykes, Khyber, Danny, and Gareth across the sidewalk and in through a modern door, complete with metal scanners and security cameras. They found themselves in a bare, brightly lit reception area, where there were two security guards on duty. At least, one of them was. He was about fifty years old, gray-haired, with the name TRAVIS written on a badge on his jacket. He had the look and the manner of a retired policeman. The other guard was sitting on a chair, bent over, with his hands clutched across his stomach. It was instantly obvious which one of them had eaten a chocolate bar on his way to work.

"What took you so long?" Travis demanded. "I called for backup an hour ago." He was exaggerating. An hour ago, the outbreak hadn't even begun.

"I'm sorry—" the Colonel began, speaking from behind his surgical mask.

"It's madness here. We've got lawyers, judges, half the juries . . . They're all sick. Look at Johnson!" He pointed at the other guard. "He doesn't know what to do with himself!"

"I feel bad," Johnson groaned.

"We'll deal with your friend as soon as we can," Sykes responded. "But we've been called here to deal with one of the prisoners. Sir Frederick Meadows. He's had a major heart attack. He's critical."

Travis had been trained never to allow anyone through the doors, no matter what the circumstances. Normally, he would have demanded to see the paramedics' ID and then called the hospital for confirmation. But he had never encountered anything like this. Everyone around him seemed to be dying. Even Johnson, his closest friend in the building, had been brought down. Finally, help had arrived. He was in no mood to argue.

"All right," he said. "But you're not leaving until you've looked after my mate."

A second door, solid with a small glass window, led out of the reception area. The guard used his electronic key card to open it, and the Colonel, followed by his three men and an increasingly uneasy Alex, passed through.

Should he raise the alarm now, while they were inside the building? No. He remembered the various weapons he had seen when they were in the ambulance. Both Travis and Johnson were unarmed. If he started a gunfight inside the Old Bailey, he might end up getting them both killed. He still had no idea where this was going or how he was going to get out of it, but for the time being he had no choice but to play along.

Travis took them down a long, empty corridor with white-tiled walls and a wooden floor, ever farther into the building. They walked down a flight of stairs to another locked door with a third guard outside, slumped in a chair, sweating.

"Are you all right, Jim?" Travis asked.

"No." It was all the guard could manage, to spit out the single word.

"I've brought help. Open the door."

Jim was as unquestioning as Travis had been. This door had a keypad and needed a six-figure combination before it would unlock, but he managed to do it, fighting his pain to focus on the right numbers. Ahead of them, a second corridor stretched out, this one with cell doors spaced out at regular intervals, facing each other on both sides. A fourth and final guard sat at a small table with a number of files in front of him. He was a young man with a neat beard. He looked up as they approached.

"What is it?" he demanded. He looked past Travis at the group of fake paramedics, and Alex saw at once that he was smarter than his colleagues and that if he'd picked up a free chocolate bar, he hadn't eaten it.

"They've come to help," Travis explained. He made it sound obvious. "They want to see Meadows."

"They can't just walk in here!" The younger guard was astonished. "Do they have authorization?"

"Everyone's sick!" Even as Travis tried to explain, Alex understood what had happened. This new guard had been inside the building all morning and he was completely unaware of what was happening outside. "It's crazy out there," Travis concluded. "You've got to let them in!"

"I'm sorry!" The guard was only in his twenties, but he knew what he was doing. "You've got to follow the procedure. Anyway, I saw Meadows five minutes ago. He's fine!"

That was as far as he got. The Colonel stepped forward and Alex saw him slip a handgun out of his pocket. It was a Mauser M2, self-loading and semiautomatic, and Alex knew he had to act even if it meant giving himself away. He couldn't just watch as the guard was shot in front of him. But before he could do anything, the Colonel swung the weapon through the air, using it as a club. The guard grunted and collapsed. At the same time, Khyber brought out his own gun and held it against Travis's neck.

"What . . . ?" Travis began.

"Shut up," Khyber whispered. "Make a move and I'll kill you."

Travis had gone white. Meanwhile, Danny stepped

forward and searched the unconscious man. He found a bunch of keys and tossed them to Alex. Just for a second, Alex hesitated. "Get on with it, Sarko," Danny growled.

Alex nodded then, keeping his head down, and hurried forward, examining the cells. Each one had a number, but there were no names attached, perhaps for reasons of security. Fortunately, the doors had peepholes. The first two cells were empty. The third contained a red-haired woman reading a magazine. The fourth was empty again. Alex found what he was looking for in the fifth.

Sir Frederick Meadows was sitting on the edge of his bunk, his hands resting on his knees. He was dressed in an immaculate charcoal suit with a white shirt and a dark blue tie. His shoes were brightly polished. Alex recognized him from the photograph he had seen that morning. The banker was perhaps a little neater than he had imagined, with a perfectly round head and a prim mustache that could almost have been drawn on with a pencil. He was wearing round, rather schoolboyish glasses. There was a slight smile on his face. Looking at him, it was hard to believe that he was sitting in London's most famous court, about to go on trial for the theft of a hundred million pounds.

Alex's eye was drawn to a gold signet ring on one of Sir Frederick's fingers. One of his six fingers. It was strange but absolutely true. There were five fingers next to the thumb on his left hand. Alex blinked. If he hadn't read about it in the newspaper, he might not have even noticed, because actually—if you didn't bother counting—the hand looked completely normal. The banker hadn't noticed him yet. Quickly, Alex searched through the keys, found the right one, and used it to open the door.

Sir Frederick looked up. He didn't seem surprised to see Alex. "Yes?" he asked.

Alex wasn't sure what to say—and the less said the better. He had, after all, the voice of a fourteen-year-old boy. "Sir Frederick?"

"That's right."

"It's time to go."

"I see . . ."

The banker got up. He pushed past Alex and emerged into the corridor, where Sykes was waiting. It took him only a few seconds to assess the situation. One guard unconscious, the other being held at gunpoint. He nodded briefly. "You've come for me," he said.

"That's right, Sir Frederick," Sykes said. He stepped forward and spoke a few words into the banker's ear, talking quietly so that only the two of them could hear.

Meadows nodded. "Right," he said. "Let's go."

The Colonel gave a signal and Danny led Travis into the cell that the banker had just left. Gareth and Khyber followed, carrying the unconscious guard. Once the two security men were inside, Alex closed the door and locked it, still doing his best to keep his face turned away. Unlike the others, he had no surgical mask. Sir Frederick was standing beside Sykes, waiting patiently, and Alex wondered how the two of them had managed to organize all this. How had they even communicated? Another question occurred to him. When this was all over, how much would Colonel Sykes and his men be paid?

They were already making their way back to street level, the Colonel first, the banker beside him. Nobody challenged them. As they reached the entrance hall, a policeman rushed toward them and for a brief moment Alex thought they were going to be stopped. But the policeman hadn't even seen them. He was making for a toilet. Alex heard the door slam and the sound of retching from the other side.

The ambulance was exactly where they had left it, waiting in the street with Charlie behind the wheel. This time, Alex and Khyber sat in the front. Sir Frederick was loaded into the back with the Colonel, Gareth, and Danny. As they set off, Charlie turned to Alex.

"All okay, Sarko?" he asked.

"Yeah." Alex muttered the single word without looking up. It was the last thing he wanted—a conversation. Fortunately, Charlie turned on the siren a moment later, drowning out any sound the two of them might have made.

The roads of London were still jammed. If anything, they had gotten even worse in the last ten or twenty minutes. Ahead of them, Holborn Viaduct was an unmoving wall of traffic. There were still sirens going off everywhere. But everything had been planned down to the last detail and they didn't have far to go. Charlie steered the ambulance through a series of backstreets, heading toward St. Paul's. Alex had a front-row seat and saw them dipping down between a series of office buildings, which suddenly parted to reveal the wide expanse of the River Thames. They had been driving for less than five minutes, but he saw that they had arrived. Across the river, the Tate Gallery—once a power station—stood out against a clear blue sky. The Millennium Bridge, silver and slender, curved across the water. Charlie stopped the ambulance and they all climbed out, Alex feeling more exposed than ever in the bright, open air. Any minute now, someone would surely see through his disguise and realize that the real Sarko had been left behind. And what would he do when the moment came to remove the wig and shaded glasses?

"This way, Sir Frederick," the Colonel said.

He led the banker down to the water's edge. And here was the final phase of the operation, a ship moored at a private jetty. It was a sixty-foot white motor cruiser with a luxurious drawing room and dining area opening onto the back deck. A wide staircase led down to a lower area. There could have been half a dozen bedrooms below. The ship was called *Phantom Lady,* and Alex noticed that it was equipped with a sophisticated satellite dish and radio mast. Every part of the plan had been thought through. The roads might be snarled up, but the river wasn't. They could transport the banker past Greenwich and out to sea. Before the sun had set, he would be abroad—in Holland,

Belgium, or France. And the next day, presumably with a false passport, he would be on his way to anywhere in the world.

The fake paramedics had already torn off their surgical masks. Alex guessed that they would have a change of clothes on board so that if they were stopped, they would look like wealthy businessmen or maybe members of the crew. Was this the right moment to make a break for it? Once he was on the ship, he would be trapped, with nowhere to run. The moment they discovered that he wasn't Sarko, they would shoot him and drop him overboard. He thought briefly of Jack and wondered if she had managed to contact MI6 yet. She certainly wouldn't be too happy if he was found floating facedown at Greenwich harbor.

He wasn't given the chance. It was almost as if the other men knew what he was thinking. As the group climbed up the gangplank, they were all around him, giving him no room to move. Sir Frederick was sitting down inside the main living area, out of sight. Charlie had taken his place, once again, behind the wheel. Danny and Gareth were on the deck, on either side of Alex, both of them towering over him. Khyber untied the ropes and climbed on board. Almost at once *Phantom Lady* was away, traveling down the river, helped on by a strong tide. Charlie pressed down the throttle. The sound of the engine rose. They headed east, past the Globe Theatre, passing underneath Southwark Bridge.

Alex didn't like this. Nobody had spoken to him since

they had left the Old Bailey. Had he somehow given himself away? He was weighing his options when he realized that, actually, he didn't have any.

Colonel Sykes walked over to him. He really was a huge man, at least a foot taller than Alex. "What's the matter, Sarko?" he demanded. "You've been very quiet."

Alex waited, knowing what was coming. The Colonel reached out and snatched off his wig, then tore the glasses away from his face. Alex didn't wait for the rest of it. He removed the fake mustache himself.

The Colonel stared at him. Then, slowly, he took out his gun. He pointed it straight at Alex. "I'm going to give you three seconds to answer this question," he said. "And if you're lying to me, I'm going to shoot you where you stand. Who are you and what are you doing here?"

"That's two questions," Alex said.

The finger tightened on the trigger. "Then give me two answers," the Colonel said. "And give them to me now."

DOWNRIVER

PHANTOM LADY CONTINUED ITS journey down the Thames, its two 1050 horsepower diesel engines propelling it effortlessly forward. Sir Frederick Meadows was still sitting on his own in the main salon. He had found a bottle of white wine and had poured himself a glass as if this were just a river cruise and he was an invited guest. Charlie was steering, perched on a high stool behind the wheel. Alex was standing in the middle of the deck. Colonel Sykes was in front of him, Khyber, Danny, and Gareth on each side and behind. He was surrounded by men with guns and he was unarmed. Meanwhile, the famous landmarks were flashing by, one after another . . . HMS *Belfast*, City Hall, the Tower of London. It occurred to Alex that tourists would have paid a fortune to be on this boat. He would have happily paid anything to get off it.

"Who are you?" Colonel Sykes repeated the question.

"He's just a kid!" Khyber couldn't believe what he was seeing. Now that Alex's disguise had come off him, the truth was there for all of them to see, and they were shocked. After months of planning, the operation had been a complete success. But at the final moment, something inexplicable had happened. The group had been infiltrated—not by a policeman or an undercover agent, but by a schoolboy!

"My name is Alex Rider," Alex said. Things were bad, and with every second they were getting worse. Southwark Bridge was already far behind him. London was slipping away. It felt like his chances of survival were going with it.

"How did you get here? What happened to Sarko? What do you think you're doing, sticking your nose in our business?" The Colonel seemed to have shrunk. All the confidence and good humor had left his face. His hand tightened on the Mauser. He was aiming it directly between Alex's eyes.

Alex didn't know how to answer the questions. Where was he even supposed to begin? Looking back at the events that had taken place since he'd gotten off the tube train that morning, he saw that any explanation would be too complicated, too unbelievable. It was easier just to remain silent.

But then Charlie answered, twisting around briefly on his stool. "I know who he is!" he exclaimed. "He works for MI6. He's a spy."

"He's only a teenager!"

"I know, Colonel. But he was there when I was working for Sayle Enterprises. He's had special training . . . martial arts. He knocked me out. I swear to you. I recognize him." Charlie was torn between staring at Alex and keeping his eye on the river. "He was responsible for that whole operation going pear-shaped. That's why I ended up

working with you. Nobody believed it. But it's true. MI6
sent him in."

Sykes turned to Alex. "Did MI6 send you after us?"
he demanded.

"No." There was no point lying. "I saw your driver. I
recognized him. He led me to you." He paused. "Also, you
don't know how to spell *Cadbury*."

There was a long silence. Alex felt the breeze whipping over his shoulders, tugging at his hair. Despite the
bright sunshine, it was cold on the stern of the boat. He
looked at the gray water rushing past and wondered if he
could make a break for it. He could dive into the river and
swim for the shore. The trouble was, there were too many
guns. He was surrounded. He knew he would be dead
before he could even reach the side.

The Colonel had been examining him, struggling with
himself. What was it that he had said, back in the meat
market? *"We're not criminals. We're not killers."* Alex
hoped he'd remember that now.

"We've got to get rid of him," Khyber said. "He knows
who we are. He can identify us."

The Colonel nodded slowly. "You're right, Khyber."
The bright blue eyes settled on Alex as if seeing him for
the first time. "You shouldn't have come here, Alex," he
said. "You shouldn't have interfered. I don't like the idea
of killing children, but you're not a child, are you. You're a
child soldier. That's not the same." He was working himself up into a fury, driving himself toward what he had

to do. "I want you to understand something. What we're doing, we're only doing because we had to. Our country wouldn't look after us, so we had to look after ourselves. And I'm not going to let you or anyone else stop us. Not now, when we're so close." His finger tightened on the trigger. "You brought this on yourself, Alex. I'm sorry."

And then the soldier named Danny cried out and jerked forward as if he had been punched in the stomach. His face had gone white. The heart tattoo on his neck seemed to be beating with a life of its own. "Colonel," he gasped. He ran to the side of the boat and threw up.

The other men stared at him.

"What—?" Sykes began.

"Wait!" Khyber stared.

And then it was his turn. One moment he was standing there, utterly confident, waiting for Alex to be gunned down. The next he was twisting on his feet, reaching out for support. He was sweating. A pulse was throbbing on his forehead. His eyes were glazed and out of focus.

"What is it?" Sykes demanded.

"I'm not well." Khyber croaked out the words. Then: "The coffee!"

Sykes stared at Alex. Suddenly he understood.

When Alex had made coffee for the five men back at the meat market, he had come to an instant decision. He had no gun, no gadgets, nothing he could defend himself with. Somehow he had to turn the situation to his advantage, and he had come up with the one option that was available to him. He would attack the men with their own weapon. Leaving the five cups of coffee to cool on the tray, he had rushed back to the laboratory shelves and to the plastic bottle that he had opened, the one with the crouching frog. He knew that it was fast-acting. He knew that the liquid was nonlethal. He had heard the Colonel describing it. Shortly after you drank it, you'd think you were having a heart attack. That was fine. That would give him the opportunity to get away.

Alex had taken the bottle back into the kitchen and added a dose to each of the cups. Then he had carried them upstairs. He had been waiting for the poison to take effect ever since . . . and it had certainly chosen the right moment. Another few seconds and it would have been too late.

Khyber and Danny were out of it. They had completely forgotten Alex. Even if they had wanted to kill him, they would be unable to shoot straight. Colonel Sykes had frozen, taken by surprise. The bufotenine hadn't worked on him yet. He was so huge that presumably it would take longer to work its way through his bloodstream. Alex was already moving. Even as Sykes swung around to take aim at him again, Alex rushed toward him, covering the short distance in a matter of seconds. His left elbow crashed into his stomach. At the same time, his right hand shot out, grabbing hold of the Colonel's wrist, forcing the gun away. The Colonel fired. Charlie screamed and fell off the stool with a bullet in his shoulder. At once, *Phantom Lady* twisted off course as if with a life of its own.

Alex almost lost his balance as the powerful cruiser veered to one side, then swung around in a giant horseshoe, heading back the way it had come. Danny was less fortunate. He was still leaning over the side of the boat and, taken unawares, he tumbled forward. He cried out and then he was gone, his round head bobbing in the water like a buoy, already far behind. Well, at least that reduced the odds. Now it was only four against one.

Or three against one. Charlie was writhing on the deck, blood seeping out of the wound in his shoulder. The older, black soldier—Gareth—was bringing his gun around on Alex. Perhaps he hadn't drunk any of the coffee. He didn't seem to be affected. But it was almost impossible to aim straight with the boat rocking from side to side, and anyway, Colonel Sykes was in the way. Alex was still holding on to him, trying to keep the gun away. But the Colonel was slowly, steadily bringing it around, and Alex knew he didn't have the strength to stop him.

He felt the deck swaying beneath him. Charlie must have had his hand on the throttle when he was hit, and he had dragged it down as he fell. The boat was rocketing forward, doubling its speed with every second that passed. Tower Bridge with its two mighty turrets and sixty-yard span was straight ahead. Would they go under it or crash into one of its massive concrete piers? Right now that was down to luck. *Phantom Lady* would make the decision for herself.

The boat jerked to the right and for a moment Alex

and the Colonel were like dance partners, locked together as they fought for balance. Alex saw the gun out of the corner of his eye. Inch by inch it was edging toward his head. Sykes was much taller and stronger than him, and Alex knew that he was going to have to play dirty if he was going to survive. He made the one play available to him, suddenly dragging the gun down, leaning forward, and sinking his teeth into the man's wrist.

Sykes howled and dropped the gun. Alex kicked it away across the deck, then brought his knee up into the man's groin. *Phantom Lady* was zigzagging wildly along the Thames. Surely someone would see it and realize something was seriously wrong. The water was roaring past. Tower Bridge was looming over them. Alex had to reach the wheel before they smashed into it! And what about Sir Frederick Meadows? What had happened to him? All these thoughts were tiny fragments spinning through Alex's head as the boat surged on.

Gareth had lost interest. He had drunk the coffee after all and now he was slumped on the deck. Charlie was unconscious. Khyber was groaning. Danny had gone over-board. But Sykes hadn't given up. He lashed out and Alex was thrown backward. He felt his shoulders slam into the deck and for a moment everything swam in front of his eyes. Before he could get up, Sykes was on him, his hands around Alex's throat.

"You've ruined everything!" he screamed. He had forgotten all that he had ever said. He was no longer a soldier, a war hero who had received a medal from the Queen. He was a killer. He was going to take his revenge.

His hands tightened. Alex tried to suck in air, but the man was too strong. Nothing was reaching his lungs. The world seemed to shudder and twist all around him. No. That was what was actually happening. *Phantom Lady* was completely out of control. The steering wheel, with no one to hold it, was spinning so fast, it had become a blur. The bridge was shooting toward them. Alex knew that he was about to black out. The Colonel was strangling him. He tried to fight back but he no longer had the strength.

There was the sound of a gunshot. The Colonel's face was inches from his and Alex saw the look of shock and pain in the man's eyes. His hands loosened and he fell to one side. Alex looked past him and saw Sir Frederick Meadows standing in front of the cabin, holding the Colonel's gun in both of his hands, the second of his eleven fingers around the trigger. Smoke was rising from the barrel. The banker looked shocked.

There was no time to talk. Alex dragged himself to his feet, then staggered over to the steering wheel and grabbed it just as the huge bulk of Tower Bridge rose up right in front of him. He wrenched the wheel down with less than a second to spare. *Phantom Lady* spun sideways with water jetting out. Even so, the starboard side hit concrete and there was the terrible sound of splintering wood as the entire length of the luxury cruiser was torn apart. Alex was sure they were going to capsize. The engines were screaming. He reached for the throttle and rammed it up, reducing their speed. And then they were out the other side of the bridge, slowing down, part of the cabin crushed and the gleaming handrail twisted and broken. At the same time, far behind him, Alex heard sirens. The river police had finally arrived.

Sir Frederick Meadows hadn't moved. He was standing there, small and neat, staring at Alex as if he couldn't quite work out what had just happened but disapproved anyway. Alex was equally puzzled. The banker had just shot one of his own men and saved his life. Why?

"Are you all right?" Meadows asked.

"Yes," Alex said, although it wasn't quite true. His throat had been crushed. It still hurt to breathe.

The banker lowered the gun. "Well, that's that," he said. He didn't sound too happy, but then he had no reason to be. The police boats were drawing closer. In just a few minutes, he would be under arrest once again.

"Why did you do it?" Alex asked.

"I'm sorry?"

"You saved me."

"That man was going to strangle you."

"Yes. But didn't you want him to? He was helping you get away."

"Is that what you think?" The banker smiled. Alex got the impression that it was something he didn't do very often. "You think these men were working for me?"

"Weren't they?"

"They kidnapped me. I had never seen them before in my life. At first, I thought you were genuine paramedics. That's why I went with you. But the Colonel told me the moment I came out of my cell. They were going to force me to give them my money. They would have tortured me to find out where it was. So actually, I was quite glad to shoot him."

Alex looked around him—at Charlie, stretched out on the deck. Sykes wasn't moving. He might be dead. Khyber and Gareth were both whimpering, gasping for breath. Two police launches had reached the boat and he saw Danny sitting in one of them, soaking wet and handcuffed. And finally there was Sir Frederick Meadows in his expensive suit, blinking behind his glasses, still holding the gun.

"Did you really take it?" Alex asked. "The money."

"Yes, I did. A hundred and twenty million pounds. More money than you can begin to imagine."

"What were you going to do with it?"

"Well, you probably won't believe me, but I wanted to give it all to charity."

"Really?" Alex was amazed.

"Absolutely. The fun of it was actually stealing it, doing it under everyone's noses without getting caught. I didn't particularly want it for myself." Meadows smiled again, a little sadly this time. "Of course, that won't make any difference. They'll still put me in prison—but it won't be so bad. I was at boarding school for ten years, so I know what it's like."

The first of the policemen climbed on board, followed by several others. Alex watched as the gang was arrested and Sir Frederick was led away. One of the officers came over to him. "You're Alex Rider?"

"Yes."

The policeman shook his head in disbelief. "We were told you might be on board. We're to take you back down-river. You have an urgent meeting."

"With MI6."

"No. With a dentist."

So there was to be no escape after all. Alex climbed down into the police launch and a moment later they were skimming across the water, heading back the way they had come.

SECRET WEAPON

53.4697°N,
1.3260°W

THE MAN WITH THE two missing teeth had thought a great deal about killing Alex Rider. He had imagined it. He had planned it. And quite soon he was going to do it. There was just one problem. At the moment he was locked up in a maximum-security prison in South Yorkshire. He had only been there for three months. He had been sentenced to twenty years.

That would make him forty-eight when he came out. Middle-aged!

His name was Jake Edwards, although it had been a long time since anyone had called him that. Right now he was prisoner A8793WS. His skin had already gone pale from the amount of time he had spent inside: twenty hours a day locked up in a cell with two bunks and a toilet, which left just four hours divided between the prison workshop, the education center, and the exercise yard. The prison food hadn't helped either. He had been thin and unhealthy-looking when he went in, but now his own mother wouldn't have recognized him. Not that she would have anyway. She had walked out when he was three years old.

Jake had been fostered and brought up in the housing projects in Dagenham, east of London. His new parents had done their best for him, but it was as if there was some sort of infection in his blood. At school he had been difficult and disruptive. Though small for his age—smoking hadn't helped—he knew how to use his fists, and the other children were careful to keep their distance. By the time he was ten, he had become the head of a gang of bullies and misfits who enjoyed hurting anyone unlucky enough to get in their way. He had stopped even pretending to do any work. Why did he need school? He had been excluded from two of them and knew that there were plenty of ways to earn a living that didn't involve math or science or reading or any of the dreary things that were thrown at him in class.

He was eleven years old when he first became involved in drugs. There was a gang—a real gang—in the neighborhood where he lived, and Jake was thrilled when he was asked to join them. A small, sickly boy was exactly what they needed. This was how it worked. The customer would draw up in his car and hand over the money to the dealer, paying for a "twenty bag" or a "forty bag" or however many grams he needed. Once the dealer had the money, he would signal to Jake, who was waiting at a corner, usually smoking. The dealer would walk away and only then would Jake come forward with the product. That way, the dealer was protected if there was a police ambush, and because Jake was underage, there was a limit to the amount of time he could spend in jail.

Jake sold drugs. He took drugs. As far as he was

concerned, it would have been stupid not to. By the time
he reached his teens, his two front teeth had rotted away,
his eyes had gone a strange shade of yellow, and he had lost
most of his hair. As if to make up for the collapse in his
appearance, he had become interested in body piercing.
He had five studs in his ear and others on his tongue,
the side of his nose, and his nipples. He really liked this
new image even though to everyone else, including his
horrified foster parents, it simply looked as if his body was
falling to pieces and he had made a desperate attempt to
pin it back together again. He started seeing a girl called
Lucy and had LOOSIE tattooed on his arm. It was a shame
that he had never learned to spell.

Jake did well as a criminal—certainly better than he
had ever done at school—and he was lucky. One summer,
when he was sixteen, all his bosses got wiped out in a gang
war, and this left him free to go into business for himself.
He started selling drugs on his own behalf, although he
was smart enough to keep well clear of his old stomping
grounds, moving his operation to the other side of the city.
He settled in Putney, in the west of London. His customers were the kids in the local schools, the young men and
women on their way to the clubs . . . anyone, actually,
who wanted to sniff, smoke, or inject what he had to sell.
Nobody knew him as Jake anymore. He was known by the
name of the car he drove when he did his rounds.

People called him Skoda.

And Skoda had one remarkable idea that would

serve him well for years to come. He needed a base where he could prepare the drugs he was selling. This meant cutting them down. The various white crystals that came into his hands had been smuggled all the way from South America, and once he had them, he added glucose, baking powder, dried milk, even rat poison . . . anything to make them go farther. By this simple method he could double or triple his profits, and what did he care if he was ripping off his customers, threatening their health at the same time?

His brainwave was to buy a boat, a barge called *Blue Shadow,* that happened to be moored on the River Thames close to Putney Bridge. Working quietly and using suppliers from all over London, he converted it into a floating laboratory with glass flasks, weighing machines, Bunsen burners . . . everything he needed. It was the last place the police would have thought of looking, which was quite ironic, because it was close to a major conference center that they often used. It amused Skoda to think that while they were all gathered there, going on about the "War on Drugs," he was actually continuing the war right under their noses.

Everything went well for Skoda until the day Alex Rider came along. Even now, Skoda wasn't quite sure what had happened. He'd been enjoying a glass of gin with a friend of his—Beckett—the two of them measuring out the next batch of drugs, when suddenly, without warning, the barge had begun to rise out of the water. It had been a moment of complete insanity, with cups and plates, jars and test tubes, pipes and burners all tumbling and smashing on the floor. Desperately, the two men had tried to get out onto the deck, only to find that the door was locked. Skoda's world had been turned upside down— for real. He and Beckett had found themselves tangled together at the bottom of the cabin, screaming in fear as the entire boat was lifted out of the river into the air.

It was only much later, when he was recovering in the hospital, that he found out what had happened. Skoda had been selling drugs at a school in Chelsea, a place called Brookland. It turned out that one of the boys who went there had followed him back to *Blue Shadow* and somehow hooked it to a crane. The boy had climbed up to the control cabin at the top of the crane, started it up, and lifted the five-ton barge sixty yards into the air. And that wasn't the end of it. The chain had snapped. The boat had plunged down—through the roof and into the conference center. The next thing Skoda knew, he was lying on his back with a broken arm, a broken leg, and a fractured pelvis, surrounded by about five hundred police officers lining up to arrest him.

All because of a fourteen-year-old boy!

That was the worst of it. Strangely enough, nothing had been written about it in the newspapers, and the kid's name hadn't been mentioned at all. But in the next couple of months, as he recovered, Skoda used his contacts on the street to begin making inquiries of his own.

Apparently there was a boy at Brookland who had been involved in something strange just a few weeks before, a shoot-out at the Science Museum. Nobody knew who he was, but there was a whisper he was connected in some way to the security service. Skoda pushed a little harder. Someone knew someone who knew someone, and finally a name came up: Alex Rider. Skoda checked. Yes. There was an Alex Rider at Brookland, and he had been absent for a large chunk of the summer term. Skoda managed to get a photograph smuggled into the hospital and found himself examining a good-looking boy with fair hair and dark brown eyes. It was him. Somehow he knew it. And that was the moment he began to plan his revenge.

The story of his humiliation had followed him to HM Prison Doncaster, which was where he was being held. That was how it was in the criminal world. People knew things. It didn't matter how they found out—they just did, and they never forgot. Skoda was mocked from the day he arrived. He wasn't the big-deal drug trafficker that he pretended to be. He was the guy in the boat who had allowed himself to be beaten by a kid. Even the guards laughed at him, and at night, lying in his bunk, Skoda would feel hot tears of anger trickling down his cheeks. It wasn't being in prison that upset him. It was how he'd gotten there.

He also knew how he was going to get out. Skoda wasn't stupid. After all, the *Blue Shadow* idea had worked brilliantly until Alex Rider came along. Breaking out of a maximum-security prison wouldn't be easy—not with steel doors, closed-circuit television cameras, sensors in the walls and the floors, guards patrolling every hour of the day and the night. But he'd worked out a way.

It was four o'clock in the afternoon and Skoda was out in the yard, along with another thirty men, all strolling around in the afternoon air, trying to catch a glimpse of a bird or a plane or anything that might remind them of normal life outside. The walls blocked out any view, and even the blue sky was framed by a twisting coil of razor wire. Armed guards in observation towers looked down on them as they walked aimlessly back and forward with nowhere to go. Prison really was a horrible place, Skoda thought. He would get out even if it killed him.

He glanced up at the nearest tower, then casually reached into his trouser pocket and took out a bright green object about six inches long. It was a makeshift knife—or shiv—that he had created for himself, a horrible-looking thing made up of a toothbrush with the handle melted and the blades from three safety razors embedded in the plastic.

This was going to hurt. But it had to be done. Skoda drew his head back and let out a bloodcurdling scream. Then he drew the knife across his own chest.

2

HE HADN'T CUT HIMSELF deeply, although there was a lot of blood. The moment he had screamed, alarms had gone off all over the yard and guards had come running out, herding the prisoners back to their cells. Skoda had collapsed. His hands were crimson. There was a bright stain spreading on his shirt. The knife lay on the tarmac nearby. Several guards came running over to him and soon he was surrounded.

"Help me!" he screamed. "I've been attacked! I'm dying! I can't breathe! Someone tried to kill me!"

"Who was it?" The first guard to reach him was crouching down, examining the wounds. They didn't look life-threatening at all.

"I didn't see, sir. I was just walking, minding my own business. The next thing I know . . . they hurt me!" Skoda was weeping. Tears were also oozing out of his nose. He was squirming on the ground.

"You must have seen them!"

"No, sir. Honest! I just felt this terrible pain and then there were these horrible cuts in my chest."

There is, of course, a code in prison. No matter what happens, nobody tells the guards anything. Nobody snitches. The guards knew that, so they didn't ask any more questions. They scooped Skoda up and carried him over to the hospital wing.

It was exactly what he wanted. So far, his plan was working.

Two days before, another prisoner had been admitted into the hospital—and this was the man that Skoda wanted to see. His name was Harry Baker, but he was known to everyone as Spider because of the huge tattoo he had on his forehead. Harry had created it himself, using a sharpened paper clip to make the punctures and soot mixed with shampoo for the ink. It was a hideous thing, a great black tarantula that sat between his eyes with the front legs stretching out toward his ears. Harry had killed a policeman during a bank robbery and he was in prison for life, but that life had almost run its course. Only a week before, he'd had a major heart attack and the prison doctor had assured the governor that he would be dead by the end of the week.

Skoda and Spider were not friends. The two men had barely spoken—but as soon as he heard what had happened, Skoda had known what he had to do. He made the shiv out of a toothbrush. He stole a black felt-tip pen from the education center. He bribed a prisoner who worked in the hospital wing to tell him what he needed to know. And now everything was going according to plan.

Skoda was examined by the prison doctor. His cuts were hardly more than scratches that wouldn't even need stitches, but he was given an injection, just to be on the safe side. His chest was wrapped in bandages. And because he was still in hysterics, it was agreed that he should spend the night in the hospital wing. He was placed in the same ward as Spider. There were six beds but only two patients . . . which was exactly what he had expected. The hospital was still part of a maximum-security prison. The windows were barred and the doors kept locked. But there were fewer guards. The atmosphere was more relaxed. After all, sick and dying men are unlikely to try to escape.

At six o'clock, Skoda was seen by the doctor and given a bowl of soup and some bread. The lights in the ward went off two hours later, although a single bulb was left on. It would glow all night. Skoda settled back. His head nestled against a pillow that was much more comfortable than the one in his cell. There was an ugly smile on his face. His smile was always ugly, thanks to his missing teeth. Slowly, he turned his head and examined the other man, who was lying two beds away. He could hear Spider wheezing. His chest was rising and falling but very slowly, with difficulty. He hadn't spoken when Skoda arrived. Nor had he had anything to eat or drink. It was obvious that the end was fast approaching, but Skoda was relieved that he wasn't dead yet. If he had been, it would have been impossible to murder him.

Skoda waited until the night was at its darkest and the silence at its most complete. Then he got out of bed and tiptoed across the ward. He stood looking down at the other man.

"Cheerio, Spider," he muttered. "Forgive me, mate. It's nothing personal."

He had carried his pillow with him. He took one quick glance at the door, then slammed it down on Spider's face, holding it there with all his strength. Spider reacted at once, his body jerking, his hands desperately clawing at the fabric. But there was nothing he could do. He was lying on his back. Skoda was much stronger than him. It was all over very quickly. Skoda stepped back. The man in the bed lay still.

There could be no going back now. Skoda went back to his bed, replaced the pillow, then hit the alarm button set in the wall. There was one beside every bed, connected to the medical office just down the corridor. A few minutes later he heard the rattle of a key in a lock, the lights went on, and the door opened. Two men stood there, one a prison guard, the other a young doctor.

"What is it, Skoda?" the guard demanded. He looked suspiciously at the prisoner. There didn't seem to be anything wrong with him. "I hope you're not wasting our time," he added.

"No, sir!" Skoda jerked a thumb. "It's Spider, sir. Just a moment ago he woke up. He was coughing and spluttering and then he made this horrible gurgling noise and now he's gone quiet. I went over and had a look at him, but I don't think he's breathing . . ."

The doctor hurried over. First he looked into Spider's eyes, then he felt for a pulse at the side of the neck. He knew at once it was over. "He's dead," he muttered.

"Dead?" Skoda's voice was high-pitched and trembling. "Poor old Spider! He was my mate, sir. I can't believe it!"

"You don't need to upset yourself," the guard muttered. "He didn't have much time left anyway."

"You're not going to leave him in here, are you?" Skoda sounded terrified. "I can't share a room with a dead man."

The doctor and the guard exchanged a look. "I'll call for an ambulance," the doctor said.

"I can't bear it!" Skoda climbed back into his bed and pulled the blanket up to his chin. "I don't even want to look."

"You go back to sleep, Skoda," the guard suggested. "We'll get a stretcher and move him out of here."

The doctor and the guard left the room, once again locking the door. Skoda made sure he was alone. Then, at once, he leapt out of bed. It was time to put the second part of his plan into operation. First of all, he grabbed hold of Spider, dragged him out of his bed, and threw him into his own. Then he covered him with the blanket so that none of his face was showing. He took out the black felt-tip pen that he had stolen and went over to the corner of the room. There was a mirror hanging there. As carefully as he could, he drew a spider on his own forehead, placing it right in the middle with the legs pointing at his ears. Finally, he got into Spider's bed, closed his eyes, and waited for his heart to beat a little more slowly. The secret now was to relax. He had to look dead.

Skoda knew exactly what he was doing. He and Spider were both bald, thin, and unhealthy. They were about the same age. They were wearing the same prison pajamas. There wasn't much light in the ward and they looked fairly similar to begin with. But it was the tattoo that actually clinched it. When people looked at Spider, all they saw was the ugly black decoration on his forehead, and they recognized him instantly. The same would have been true if he'd had a peculiar mustache or even a birthmark. When you look for someone in a crowd, you start with what's obvious.

Sure enough, when the guard and two paramedics arrived about half an hour later, they didn't look twice. They simply lifted the man with the tattoo onto a stretcher and carried him out. They didn't need to check that he was dead. The doctor had already done that when he'd first come in. Nor did they glance at the other prisoner, who was still hiding under his covers and seemed to be asleep. They just wanted to get this over with as quickly as possible so they could all get to bed.

The supposedly dead man was taken out of the prison in an ambulance and left on a gurney in the morgue at Doncaster Royal Infirmary. It was well after midnight when a nurse noticed that the gurney was empty and an inquiry began to find out who had moved the body and where it might be. By then, Skoda had stolen the wallet and a complete set of clothes belonging to one of the patients in the hospital along with a car, parked outside, that belonged to a doctor. By the time the alarm was raised, he was already on the M1 motorway, heading for London.

He didn't know where Alex Rider lived.

But he knew where he went to school.

3

ALEX WAS LATE. IT was one of those days when nothing had quite gone right. His alarm hadn't gone off and Jack—who had come into his life long ago as his nanny and still occasionally found herself doing the same job— had to drag him out of bed with the breakfast getting cold on the table. He couldn't find two pages of homework, an essay on renewable energy that had taken him an hour the night before. Then he missed the bus and had to run all the way to Brookland, the local high school, which today wasn't local enough. He was crumpled and sweaty, and even then he might have made it to homeroom on time except, at the last minute, he was stopped in the corridor.

"No running!"

Hearing the voice, he stopped and turned. There was a woman standing behind him and although he hadn't met her yet, Alex knew at once who she was. Everyone had been talking about the new substitute teacher who had turned up just a few days before. She taught chemistry, and suddenly half the boys in the school were saying it was their favorite subject. Miss Maxwell was young, still in her twenties, and incredibly good-looking, with shoulder-length blond hair, blue eyes, and movie-star lips. She dressed like a teacher in a gray tailored jacket, serious shoes, and glasses. But she walked like a model.

She wasn't smiling as she examined Alex. "You're late," she said.

"That's why I was running," Alex replied.

"Mr. Bray has made it clear that he won't tolerate running in the corridors." Henry Bray was the principal at Brookland. Everyone liked him, but it was true that he had his occasional crusades. It could be running, hands in pockets, chewing gum, cell phones. It depended on the time of the year. "You have to understand," she went on. "It's a health and safety issue. If you slipped, you could hurt yourself quite badly."

For a moment, Alex felt a sense of unreality that he knew too well. Only a few weeks before, he had been fighting for his life on Air Force One, the presidential plane, with a mad pop singer trying to strangle him. And now he was being warned that he might hurt himself running down a corridor! Sometimes it was impossible to connect the two worlds he inhabited, one minute a schoolboy, the next a very reluctant spy.

"What's your name?" Miss Maxwell asked him.

"I'm Alex Rider."

"Oh yes!" She'd obviously heard about him. "You've missed some school recently."

"I've been away . . . sick."

"You seem to get sick a lot."

Alex shrugged. He didn't enjoy telling lies. That was

the worst part of what had happened to him. It was easier
to say nothing at all.

"Well, just be careful. This is the only warning
you're going to get, Alex. Remember—I'll be looking out
for you."

Alex wondered how anyone so pretty could be so se-
vere. As a result of his confrontation with Miss Maxwell,
he was late for homeroom and was given a detention. That
was just the start of it. Geography, math, biology . . . Alex
found himself struggling to keep up in every class. The
trouble was, Miss Maxwell was right. He had missed so
much school that he was falling far behind, and the only
bright spot in the day came when he got a gold star for an
essay he'd written on Russian politics and the collapse of
the fleet at Murmansk. Alex couldn't help smiling. What
he'd learned about Murmansk hadn't come out of a book.
If it hadn't been for him, Murmansk—along with half of
Russia—would no longer exist.

He was glad when lunchtime arrived, and after
wolfing down his food, he strolled outside for a breath of
fresh air. He was joined by Tom Harris, who was his best
friend at Brookland. The two of them were almost exactly
the same age—their birthdays were two days apart—and
they had fallen into a friendship on the day they met. Tom
was small and skinny, with messy black hair and freckles.
Most of the teachers had given up on him . . . He was
last in his class in every subject. But at the same time,
everyone liked him. He was good at sports. He was funny.

He'd been brilliant in the school play, and even if he never got a single A, everyone agreed he had a future as an actor.

Tom was in a gloomy mood. "It's not fair," he said as he slouched on a bench at the bottom of the schoolyard.

"What isn't fair?" Alex said.

"This trip we're having to do this afternoon. We won't be back until five thirty. It's like having two extra hours of school. And it's not as if we're going anywhere interesting."

"We're going to the V and A," Alex said.

"Exactly! What's the point?"

It was a history trip to the Victoria and Albert Museum. They were leaving at three o'clock. Alex had been looking forward to it, although he didn't like to say so now.

"I hate museums," Tom went on. "My mom and dad used to take me all the time. Old paintings, old dresses, old bits of stone. They once took me to a museum of knitting. You probably think I'm making it up, but it was there, I swear to you, in Nottingham. I was so bored. It was like having a knitting needle driven into my brain. When they told me they were going to get divorced, you know what my first thought was? No more museums! But then I got worried that it would mean twice as many. They can take me alternate weekends . . ."

"This one may not be so bad," Alex said.

But Tom was still complaining. "They could have taken us in the morning. Or not at all. It makes you think, Alex. Being at school, you have no human rights at all."

The bell rang for the next lesson, and Alex and Tom began to move toward the main door. Alex certainly didn't want to be late a second time. But as they went, something made him look back. There was a man standing close to the gate, on the other side of the fence that surrounded the school. Although Alex couldn't be certain, he was fairly sure that the man had been there twenty minutes ago when they had come out. Why had he noticed him now? Perhaps it was because he was so still, unmoving. His eyes seemed to be fixed on Alex. He was dressed in a shabby coat with his hands in his pockets, but he was too far away for Alex to recognize him, and even as he looked, the man turned and walked away.

Well, you've got all sorts of weirdos hanging outside schools. If the man really was up to something, he would have been spotted on the school's cameras, and security would have come out to move him on. Alex put him out of his mind.

But Skoda had seen him. Skoda had already made inquiries and knew where he was heading. Skoda had decided what he was going to do.

4

THE VICTORIA AND ALBERT Museum in South Kensington is so huge that you could spend a week there and still not see everything it contains. There are about 4.5 million objects on display in an area larger than ten football fields. As Alex followed the long underground passageway that led from the tube station to the museum entrance, he was thinking that this made a welcome break from ordinary school. There were thirty of them in the group, escorted by Mr. Kydd, who taught history, and Miss Maxwell. Alex wondered how she had managed to tag along. After all, she had barely been at the school for forty-eight hours. But at least she hadn't told him off again.

They were here to visit an exhibition called *Seven Hundred Years of War*. It was basically about weapons, and there were hundreds of them on display, from medieval bows to ultra-modern semiautomatic air-burst grenade launch systems. The collection had been drawn from many different cultures. It seemed that there wasn't a country in the world that hadn't gone to war at some time in its history. Japan had provided samurai swords, razor-edged fans, and battle pipes. There were spears from Africa, tomahawks from America, clubs and boomerangs carved by the Aboriginal people of Australia, silk garrotes that the Thugee cult had used to strangle their victims in India. The First and Second World Wars each had a room to themselves, with models and photographs of planes, rockets, tanks, frigates, and destroyers. There were glass cases filled with hand grenades, gas masks, pistols, knives, bayonets, and flamethrowers. It really was incredible how many different ways human beings had thought up to kill each other.

The exhibition was arranged in a warren of rooms, spread out in the basement of the museum. Each room had a different theme, and Alex found himself fascinated as they moved among them. Even Tom seemed to be showing some interest, although he complained that all the weapons were locked away or fastened to the wall and that it would be much more fun to see some of them being demonstrated . . . particularly the flamethrower. They had arrived at three thirty and had a full hour and a half before the exhibition closed for the evening, after which they would return as a group to Brookland before they went home.

Alex particularly liked some of the secret weapons that were on display. These had been designed so that at first sight they didn't look like weapons at all. There was a flashlight from Korea that fired a bullet at the touch of a switch, and an umbrella from Bulgaria that shot a poisoned pellet from the tip. It had famously been used to kill a dissident writer in the middle of London back in the seventies. Back in the nineteenth century, someone had come up with another tiny gun that could actually be worn around a finger, like a ring. It was called the Dyson LePetit Protector Ring Pistol. And there were all sorts of devices invented by the British Special Operations Executive during the war: a spring-loaded cosh that leapt out of the sleeve, a dagger concealed in a pencil, a lipstick that fired tear gas. Alex couldn't help but think of Smithers, who had supplied him with all sorts of bizarre gadgets for his various missions. Would they be on display here one day? he wondered. The exploding ear stud, the book with concealed knockout dart, the stun grenade key ring?

Alex was so wrapped up in his thoughts that he didn't notice that he had lagged behind. He was in a room dedicated to ninja weapons—the ninjas had lived in ancient Japan and were famous for their fighting methods. He looked up just in time to see the last members of his party leaving the room. It was almost five o'clock, and this section of the museum was closing for the day. The last thing he wanted to do was hold everyone up when they were in a hurry to get home, and he moved quickly to catch up, only to find his way blocked by a museum guard.

"What is it?" Alex asked. He had barely looked at the man, who was wearing a white shirt and dark trousers, same as all the other museum staff. There was a radio transmitter hanging from his belt.

"Are you with the Brookland school group?" the man asked.

"Yes."

"I'm afraid I'm going to have to ask you to wait here a minute."

"Why?"

"There's been some damage done in the World War Two gallery. The museum director is on his way down."

"I had nothing to do with it," Alex said.

The guard nodded briefly. "In that case, you've got nothing to worry about. I won't keep you long."

A whole minute went by and Alex was aware that the basement was suddenly very quiet. He was tempted to push past the guard and rejoin the group, but he was nervous about making a bad situation worse. The man might claim he'd been attacked or something . . . and if it came to that, someone in authority versus a schoolboy, who would be believed? At the same time, Alex knew there was something wrong. The guard was looking at him strangely, and now it occurred to Alex that his uniform didn't fit. The shirt and the trousers were both one size too large. His face was also unnaturally pale. It had all the color of a corpse. He was missing two teeth. Alex only noticed because the man's lips had curled into an unpleasant smile. He was enjoying this.

Alex realized he was in danger before he understood why. Suddenly he remembered the man he had seen standing outside the school and knew that this was the same man, and he had been held back on purpose. He was angry with himself. It was something he should have learned by now. Just because someone is wearing a uniform—a policeman, a fireman, a nurse—it doesn't mean that's what they are. He'd seen the clothes. He hadn't examined the person inside them.

It was too late now. The guard was already moving toward him, his face no longer concealing a grimace of pure hatred. Alex didn't hesitate. He kicked out, his right foot lashing through the air. The guard had been expecting it. His hand swung down, catching Alex's ankle. He twisted hard, then jerked upward. Alex lost his balance and was thrown backward. His shoulders slammed into one of the display cases, smashing the glass, which rained down over him. He slipped to the ground and lay there, momentarily dazed. Some of the ninja weapons had tumbled out: a length of chain, a blowpipe, and a handful of *shuriken*, five-pointed stars with razor-sharp edges, designed for throwing. The guard strolled to the other side of the room and drew a curved sword off the wall. Alex watched, fascinated, as the smooth silver blade came clear of its mountings.

The guard weighed it in his hand. He stepped forward so that he stood over Alex, who was lying on his back, surrounded by broken glass. "You don't remember me," he said. His voice was trembling with excitement. There was insanity in his eyes.

"Yes . . ." Alex was fighting for time, trying to work out what to do next. "You were at Madame Tussauds."

"What?" The guard frowned.

"The Chamber of Horrors. Third from the left, next to Jack the Ripper—"

The guard swung the sword in front of him. The blade was so sharp that Alex could almost feel it cutting the air. He knew he had made a stupid joke, but he didn't care. He wanted to annoy his attacker, to throw him off guard. That way, he would be more likely to make a mistake.

"I was at Putney," the guard said. "*The Blue Shadow.*"

The Blue Shadow! Alex remembered the canal boat, the crane, the police conference, and at that moment everything made sense. "Skoda!" he muttered.

"That was what people called me. I had a business. I had money. I had everything going for me—and then you came along! You tipped up the boat. You hooked me on a crane. How did you do that? Why did you do that?" The words were pouring out. "And because of you, I broke bones. I was in the hospital for five weeks. You ruined me."

"You ruined a lot of people . . . the drugs you were selling."

"I gave people what they wanted!" Skoda stopped. His eyes were wide. There was a vein beating in his forehead.

Alex looked around him, wondering why nobody had come. Surely they would have heard the breaking glass. But it was late. The museum was emptying and they were far down in the basement. And what next? What happened now? It seemed to him that Skoda had been so intense, so determined to explain himself, he had forgotten the sword he was holding. He remembered it now.

"This is all I want," he rasped. "This is all I've dreamed about. Alex Rider." He spoke the name with contempt. "I'll go back to prison. I'll be in prison for the rest of my life. But I won't mind, knowing that you're dead."

"You're too late, Skoda," Alex said, and then continued, speaking to someone in the door behind him, "I'm glad you're here. You can take him now."

Skoda turned. It was the oldest trick in the book. There was no one there. He was distracted for just one second, but that was enough time for Alex to make his move, snatching up the chain and rolling to one side. Skoda knew he had been tricked, spun around, and slashed down with the sword. It missed Alex's arm by an inch, the blade thudding into the wooden floor. For another precious few seconds it stuck fast, and by the time Skoda pulled it free, Alex was on his feet.

And armed. The chain was known as a *manriki kusari*, and in the hands of a ninja warrior it was said to have ten thousand uses. The word *man* means "ten thousand" in ancient Japanese. The weapon that Alex was holding had a handle at each end. It was like a steel skipping rope. But Skoda's sword was even more lethal. It had left a deep gouge in the floor. If Alex hadn't rolled away in time, he would have lost his arm.

"That's not going to help you," Skoda said. He was juggling with the sword, looking for an opening. "Put that down and I might make it easier for you."

"Why don't we talk about this?" Alex had no intention

of giving up his weapon. He gripped it more tightly. At the same time, he was still waiting for someone to come. Surely Mr. Kydd or Miss Maxwell would have noticed he was missing?

"We've talked enough!"

Skoda edged forward and then everything happened in a blur. Skoda attacked, jabbing forward with the tip of the sword. Alex avoided it easily. He was fitter, faster, and lighter on his feet than Skoda, who still hadn't completely recovered from his broken bones. Skoda missed. Alex swung the chain. There was a great thud as it made contact with Skoda's hip. Skoda howled and fell to one side. That left the entrance free. Alex made for it. Six steps and he'd be out of the room. He wouldn't stop running until he had reached the ground floor and found someone to help him. But for once in his life he was unlucky. His foot came down on the blowpipe that had fallen out of the case. He felt it roll beneath him, and before he could stop himself, he had lost his balance and once again crashed down to the floor. The chain was knocked out of his hand. The next thing he knew, he was lying on his back, unarmed, and Skoda was standing over him, holding the sword in both hands.

"Not quite so clever anymore, are you?" Skoda giggled. "This is where it ends, Alex Rider. Shall we do it slowly or shall we do it quickly? Which bit of you shall we cut first?"

"Look behind you, Skoda," Alex said. He could taste

blood. He must have bitten his tongue as he fell. "We're not alone."

"You think I'm going to fall for that one again?"

"He's telling the truth."

The voice had come from the door. Skoda spun around, his eyes widening in shock. Miss Maxwell was standing there, her blond hair hanging loose and something deadly in her eyes. Alex realized that she wasn't wearing her glasses anymore. She didn't need them. Perhaps she never had. There was a gun in her hand and Alex was as surprised to see it as Skoda.

"Put the sword down and step aside," she ordered. "I'm telling you now, and I won't give you a second warning." The strange thing was, her voice was exactly the same as when she had been telling him off for running in the corridor.

"Wait a minute, lady—" Skoda's voice was a whine, but he lowered the sword.

"Are you all right, Alex?"

That was her mistake. In the moment that she looked at him, she had taken her eyes off Skoda, and that was when he swung the sword . . . not at Alex, but at her. She fired and Skoda spun around, screaming. He had been hit in the shoulder. But the teacher hadn't escaped injury either. The tip of his sword had cut through her gray jacket, drawing blood. Alex heard her gasp. Skoda barreled forward, shoving her aside. And then he was gone, out of the room, leaving the two of them alone.

5

"I'm SORRY," MISS MAXWELL said. "That was clumsy of me. Mrs. Jones won't be pleased."

She had examined the wound made by the sword. Fortunately, it wasn't very deep. She seemed more annoyed about the damage to her jacket.

"You work for MI6?" Alex asked.

The substitute teacher nodded. She took out her phone and pressed the speed dial. "This is Maxwell. I'm at the V and A. Subject was here but he managed to get away. You'd better hand over to the police." Quickly she added a description of Skoda, what he had been wearing. "Alex is unhurt," she added. "I'm with him now."

"What exactly is going on?" Alex asked when she'd hung up.

"Jake Edwards escaped from jail a few days ago," she explained. Alex had never actually known Skoda's real name. "Mrs. Jones was worried he might come looking for you, so she sent me to keep an eye out."

"That's very nice of her." But Alex knew that being nice had nothing to do with it. He looked around him. Here he was in an exhibition called *Seven Hundred Years of War*, but in a way he wasn't just visiting. He was part of it and had been ever since his uncle had died. MI6 had made him their secret weapon. They had put him into a glass case of their own, and they were the ones with the key. Miss Maxwell had been sent here to protect him because he was valuable to them. That was all it came down to.

"I noticed you weren't with the rest of the group when we reached the exit," she continued. "So I came back to look for you."

"So what happens now?" Alex asked.

"You heard me say on the phone. Edwards has no money and nowhere to go. He has a bullet in him. He's not going to be difficult to find. We need to get you back home. And of course, nobody else from Brookland must know what happened."

Alex understood why that was important. He was only useful to MI6 while nobody knew about him. "Where is everyone?" he asked.

"They're in the reception hall with Mr. Kydd. He's waiting to take everyone back to the tube station."

"Are you going to be all right?"

Miss Maxwell flexed her shoulder. "I'll get the medic to take a look at it when I'm back. I'm still annoyed. I allowed myself to be distracted. And I should have aimed at his head!" She put her jacket back on. "It's such a great pleasure to meet you, Alex," she said. "I've heard so much about you—and that business with Colonel Sarov really was extraordinary."

Alex tried not to think too much about it. Sometimes,

at night, he was woken up by the sound of gunfire, shattering his dreams.

"I know Mr. Blunt thinks very highly of you," she continued. "By the way, I'm sorry I had to tell you off for running in the corridor."

"I'll try not to do it again," Alex said.

His cell phone rang. He took it out and looked at the display. The call was from Tom Harris. "Alex," Tom began.

Even that single word told Alex that, somehow, trouble had returned. There was a gasp at the other end as the phone was torn away and then he heard Skoda's voice, ugly and excited. "I have your friend," he said. "Your best friend."

"What do you want?" Alex demanded.

"You know what I want. Is it going to be you or is it going to be him? If you want to see him again, come back to where we first met. You know where I mean. I'll send you a signal. You'll see where I am. Come alone. Come unarmed. If I see anyone with you or if I believe anyone is with you, your little friend is going to have a horrible time. Do you understand?"

"Yes."

"You have thirty minutes. After that, it'll be too late."

The phone went dead.

"Who was that?" Miss Maxwell asked.

Alex hesitated. He should tell her. If Skoda had snatched Tom, she would find out soon enough anyway. She could summon MI6. They could send in cars, helicopters . . . the works. But at the first sign of trouble, Tom Harris would die. Skoda had nothing to live for. He had said as much already. And would MI6 care too much about the death of an unknown schoolboy? They were interested in Alex. No one else.

"It was Jack," he said. "She was wondering when I'd get back." He leaned down and brushed a piece of broken glass off his sneaker.

"You'd better join the others. I'll wait here and talk to the museum authorities. We're going to have to explain all this damage."

"Thanks, Miss Maxwell."

Alex hurried up the stairs, but he avoided the main reception hall, where Mr. Kydd and the others would be waiting. Instead, he slipped out one of the side doors. It was early evening and the sky was beginning to darken. The rush-hour traffic was heavy, thundering down the main road. Alex didn't wait for the lights to turn red. He dodged between the cars, ignoring the horns as different drivers jammed on their brakes to let him pass. Skoda had given him thirty minutes. He didn't intend to be late.

6

IT WAS SO STRANGE to be back in Putney. It felt as if years had passed since he had sneaked onto the building site close to the River Thames—his first encounter with Skoda. In fact, it had been a matter of weeks. He saw the wooden jetty jutting out into the river. That was where *Blue Shadow* had been moored, but it was empty now, the brown water churning sluggishly past. And there was the brand-new conference center that he had accidentally destroyed when he dropped the boat. It was covered in scaffolding now. They were building a new roof. The building site was exactly as he remembered it. They hadn't done a great deal of building since the last time he was here. Alex guessed that the arrest of Skoda, the police inquiry, and the confusion surrounding what had happened would have slowed things down. The area was still surrounded by a tall wire fence with a gate giving access from Richmond Road. The gate should have been locked. It was hanging open.

Alex had run down from Putney Bridge tube station. He still had five or six minutes in hand, but he moved warily, looking around him. The clouds had closed in and darkness had come quickly. Skoda could be anywhere. There were half-built walls, scaffolding towers, deep trenches, and vehicles parked all over the compound. Alex examined the mechanical diggers, the bulldozers, the compactors. In the hands of a maniac, any one of them could become a weapon as dangerous as those he had seen in the V and A. Where was Skoda? He thought about calling out to Tom but decided against it. He didn't want to put the other boy in any more danger than he was already in.

He saw something out of the corner of his eye. A light had blinked on and off: a flashlight. Where was it? The beam flashed a second time and Alex looked up, his eyes traveling to the control cabin of a crane that loomed high over him, in the very center of the building site. He waited a moment to be sure. Yes. There it was. Skoda knew exactly what he was doing. This was the same crane that Alex had climbed when he had followed the drug dealer to his river hideaway. He had sat in the control cabin and used the two joysticks to hook *Blue Shadow* and lift it out of the water like some fantastic arcade game. Well, Skoda had invited him back. The fight was going to end exactly where it had begun.

Alex knew he was being watched. He was in full view of Skoda and he guessed that Tom would be up there with him too. He hadn't enjoyed climbing the crane the first time: a metal tower with three hundred rungs and nothing to stop you if you lost your grip and fell. This time it was worse. Skoda was waiting and Alex knew exactly what he intended to do. Would he be armed? Alex was fairly sure that Skoda didn't have a gun, but he had taken the samurai sword with him when he escaped from the museum and he would certainly have it with him now. As Alex took hold of the first rung and began to climb up, he found himself thinking of Miss Maxwell. She'd saved his life, but he was still annoyed with her. If only she'd been a better shot!

The ground was disappearing behind him, the vehicles and building equipment getting smaller and smaller. Just to add to his troubles, it had begun to rain, a thin drizzle that stung his face and the backs of his hands and made the rungs slippery. Part of him wondered if he was doing the right thing. Maybe he should have told Miss Maxwell the truth and let MI6 deal with it. No. Tom was his best friend. Skoda must have seen the two of them together when they were in the schoolyard. This was his fault. He would deal with it.

His arms were aching. His clothes were damp. His hair hung down in his eyes. But finally he reached the top, two hundred yards above ground level. He was effectively in the middle of a gigantic T. The cubicle with the controls was right in front of him, but there was no one inside and the door seemed to be locked. Over to the left, he could make out the massive concrete blocks that kept the whole thing balanced. Looking the other way, he saw the operating arm stretching out into the darkness with the hook hanging below. There were two figures waiting for him about halfway down. Tom Harris was on his knees. Skoda was standing over him with the sword pointed at his neck.

Alex looked down. The ground was a long way below, the drizzle hanging, suspended, in the air. Skoda was about four or five yards away. To reach him, Alex would have to walk along the arm, steel struts crisscrossing each other and wide gaps beneath his feet. Worse still, the safety railings along each side only came up to his thigh. It was hardly safe at all. If he slipped, he could all too easily fall over the edge. And that, of course, was exactly what Skoda wanted to happen. Preferably after Alex had been stabbed.

"So you came!" Skoda said. It was as if he couldn't believe his luck.

"That's right, Skoda. I came." Alex examined the other man. He was in a bad way. Miss Maxwell had shot him high up in the shoulder and his shirt was hanging off him, already made damp by the rain and saturated with blood. Shock and pain were distorting his face. His eyes were wide. His skin had no color at all. It was extraordinary, really, that he was still conscious.

Meanwhile, Tom was slumped in front of him, refusing to look up. He was crying. Now that Alex was closer, he could hear the boy gasping for breath. Everything about him suggested that he was terrified.

"I'm here now," Alex said. "So you can let him go."

"I'll let him go when you're dead!" Skoda almost screamed the words. "I want to see you jump. That's how it works. You do what I say or I'll cut off his head . . . I swear to you."

"Alex!" Tom sobbed. "He grabbed me at the museum. He made me come here."

"It's all right, Tom." Alex looked Skoda in the eyes.

"How do I know I can trust you? Let him go first. Then it'll just be you and me."

"I don't care about him. It's you I want. Climb over now. Do it or watch your friend die."

"Alex . . . !" Tom was wailing like a little child.

"Now!" Skoda tightened his grip on the sword.

And then everything happened at once.

Tom suddenly straightened up, slamming his fist hard between Skoda's legs. Skoda gasped and doubled up in pain. Alex knew that Tom had been faking the tears. His friend was a brilliant actor and there was no way he would have allowed a thug like Skoda to humiliate him. And Alex had been waiting for exactly this moment. Even as he had talked, his hand had been behind him, searching in his back pocket for the weapon that he had concealed there. It was one of the five-pointed stars, the ninja *shuriken*, that had fallen out of the display case back at the museum. With a single movement, he took it out and threw it. The star didn't have very far to travel. It spun through the air and buried itself in Skoda's hand. Skoda screamed and dropped the sword. The sword slipped through one of the gaps in the floor and disappeared.

With a noise that was more animal than human, Skoda threw himself at Alex, half tripping over Tom. Somehow his hands found Alex's throat. For a moment the two of them were close together and Alex saw the man grimacing at him with his dark gap where his front teeth should have been. Tom got to his feet and threw himself at

Skoda. At the same time, Alex lashed out and felt Skoda's hands lose their grip. That was when Skoda lost his balance. He let out a final whimper and toppled to one side. The railing wasn't high enough to save him. He plunged into the darkness.

Neither boy watched him as he fell. It seemed to take a long time before the sound of his body thudding into the gravel came from far below. At almost exactly the same moment, they heard police sirens. Tom pointed. There were two police cars tearing across Putney Bridge. They came around the corner and began to follow the road down toward the building site. Alex guessed that Miss Maxwell must have finally noticed that they were missing and called them in.

Tom was soaking wet. His hair was plastered over his forehead. It took him a few moments to recover from what had just happened. "So what was all that about?" he asked.

"I have no idea," Alex said. He had decided at once that he would have to lie. Nobody at Brookland, not even Tom, could know the truth.

"He didn't seem to like you," Tom said.

"He certainly wasn't very friendly," Alex agreed.

The police cars had arrived at the foot of the crane, their lights flashing blue and white across the yard. A few of the policemen were already searching for Tom and Alex. The others were examining the broken doll that had once been Skoda.

The two boys began the climb down.

HIGH TENSION

43.7102°N,
07.2620°E

IT WAS ANOTHER PERFECT day in the South of France. Once again, the mistral—that irritating wind that pokes in from the northwest—had decided to stay away and the sky was a dazzling blue. In London, the summer had gotten off to its usual shaky start. It was pouring with rain, and with Wimbledon just a week away, everyone was watching the forecasts with a mixture of gloom and resignation. But the French Riviera, the famous Côte d'Azur, knew nothing of that. Here the sun rose early, shone all day, and only crept behind the horizon reluctantly and with the promise that it would soon return.

Alex Rider stood on the terrace of the villa at Mont Boron, just outside Nice. From here he had a stunning view of the entire bay, with the beaches of the Promenade des Anglais sweeping around in a great curve that reached all the way to the airport at the far end. Even as he watched, a private jet took off, tiny in the distance, rising steeply before banking left, corkscrewing up into the sky: some billionaire returning home. It was a reminder that tomorrow, he, too, would be on his way back to England. The visit would be over all too quickly.

This had been a stolen weekend. A school friend of his—James Hale—had an incredibly rich uncle and aunt with a villa perched on the rock face: a couple of living rooms, three bedrooms, and a series of terraces, one above the other, with a circular swimming pool at the bottom and a vertical drop to the Mediterranean far below. James had been invited out and he had taken Alex with him— five days of luxury and a welcome break from school.

Andrew and Celestine Hale were pleasant enough, elderly with no children of their own. He was English. She was French. The two of them had made their money running a chain of luxury hotels. The Royale in Nice, the St. Anton in Cannes . . . A few years back they'd sold the whole lot and now they were living in considerable luxury themselves. If there had been one fly in the ointment, it was that Celestine was always worrying about the boys. She had watched in horror as they jumped off the terrace and into the pool. She didn't want them to go out on their own—she was afraid they'd get lost. When they went snorkeling near the old port, she had been hunched up on the beach, certain they'd be run over by one of the ferries heading out to Corsica. She was a real *tantine*, Alex thought. Not so much an aunt as an auntie, with a touch of granny thrown in too.

But she was also a wonderful cook, and in the evenings, after a few glasses of wine, she seemed more relaxed. Most nights they'd eaten at the villa. Andrew Hale insisted that the restaurants in Nice were mainly overpriced and strictly for tourists. And with the views from the balcony—the sea glowing red and the city ablaze with pinpricks of light— there was nowhere else that Alex would rather have been.

"So what are you doing this morning?" Alex hadn't heard Andrew Hale step out onto the terrace behind him.

James's uncle was wearing a white jacket and a Panama hat. He was on his way to visit a relative at Villefranche, just down the coast, and for some reason James had to go with him. Until lunchtime, Alex would be on his own.

"I'm happy staying here," Alex said. "I can hang out by the pool."

"Nonsense!" Andrew came over and stood beside him. "This is your last day. You ought to do something memorable." He thought for a moment, then a gleam came into his eyes. "Have you ever been parasailing?"

"No."

"Well, it's great fun. You're not scared of heights, are you?"

"Not really."

"Then you should give it a go." He called back into the kitchen, "Celestine! Why don't you take Alex down to the Blue Beach?" Celestine appeared in the doorway. She was holding a plate, wiping it dry. "He wants to go parasailing," Andrew explained.

This wasn't quite true. But that was the way with Andrew Hale. Once he had an idea in his head, he always assumed that everyone would agree.

Celestine frowned. "Why do you always have to suggest these dangerous sports?" she scolded. She spoke perfect English but with an accent.

"It's not dangerous. It'll give him a laugh—if it doesn't scare the socks off him first."

Somehow, Alex didn't think that being dragged behind

a motorboat while attached to a half-sized parachute would be particularly frightening . . . not after what he had been through just a couple of months before. He had been forced to launch himself out of a cargo plane, twenty thousand feet above London, crash-landing through the glass roof of the Science Museum. And there had been a second parachute jump here in France—storming the Point Blanc Academy high up in the Alps, near Grenoble. Not that he could tell Andrew or Celestine Hale anything about it, of course. He hadn't even told James . . . or anyone else at Brookland School, for that matter.

At eleven o'clock that morning, Andrew set off with a grumpy-looking James ("Visiting old people I don't even know isn't my idea of a vacation"), and a few minutes later, Celestine drove Alex down the steeply winding Boulevard Carnot that led into the old port of Nice and then around the headland into the city itself. The beaches were already busy. The season had barely begun, but this was a Saturday and the water was unusually warm and clear enough to be inviting.

They parked near the Opera House and crossed the main road with the sea in front of them. Alex had noticed two or three facilities offering parasailing and other water sports. From his balcony, he had watched the miniature figures dangling underneath the wisps of brightly colored silk as they were towed up and down the bay. He was actually looking forward to trying it. It looked fun and he imagined how peaceful it would be, hanging over the water in his own little space between the sea and the sky. At least nobody would be trying to machine-gun him.

It was also going to be expensive—sixty euros for around ten minutes. But Jack had given him plenty of money before he left, and so far the Hales hadn't let him pay for anything. He and Celestine reached a makeshift hut on the beach where two slim and permanently sun-tanned Australians were getting everything ready while a third man, on a speedboat, waited to launch the ride. The parachute that would lift Alex into the air was already spread out on the shingle. A narrow strip of carpet led down to the edge of the water. The runway.

"You gonna give it a try, mate?" The Australian had somehow guessed that he was English.

"Sure. Why not?" Alex handed over three twenty-euro notes.

"Okay. My name's Jake." He pointed at the other man. "That's Gary. Who are you?"

"Alex."

"Good to meet you, Alex. Let's get you set up."

Celestine watched suspiciously as Alex was given a life jacket, which he buckled across his chest. Gary, the younger and quieter of the two men, held up a sort of harness . . . It was nothing more than a strong canvas belt, shaped like a figure eight, with two industrial hooks like the ones used by mountain climbers—carabiners—one on each side. The harness was fastened around his waist.

"This way, Alex." Jake led him across to the carpet. At the same time, Celestine came over to him.

"Alex, you will not mind if I do not watch? This makes me . . . très nerveuse . . . you understand?" She searched for the English. "Very nervous! If you like, I will buy you an ice cream for when you come down." She nodded at some shops on the other side of the Promenade des Anglais.

"Thank you." It made no difference to Alex if she was there or not.

"What flavor would you prefer?"

"Lemon."

"Very good." Celestine took one last glance at the tangle of ropes, the waiting parachute. "Enjoy yourself," she said, but without much conviction.

Jake was in a hurry to get Alex airborne. The sooner he was finished, the sooner he might be able to sell another ride. "When the boat starts, you take three or four steps," he explained as he handed Alex a black metal bar with about a dozen different cords leading back to the parachute. He snapped the two carabiners into place. The parachute was now securely attached to Alex's waist. When he took off, the metal bar would be pulled above his head. A long rope led from the bar to a pole in the motorboat, just behind the driver's seat.

Alex noticed that the driver of the motorboat was smoking. It seemed slightly odd and out-of-sorts with what was meant to be a healthy outdoor activity. The driver was old and overweight. He was hunched over the steering wheel and didn't seem happy at all.

Jake must have seen the look in Alex's eyes. "That's Kristof," he said. "The usual guy's got the day off. But don't worry. He'll give you a good ride." Jake stepped back and took hold of one corner of the parachute. The other Australian, Gary, did the same, the two of them holding it up so that it would catch the wind. Jake gave a signal. Kristof sat down and gunned the engine. Alex saw the boat move forward and the rope began to go taut.

He took three steps and rose effortlessly off the beach. He could barely even feel the parachute pulling him—all the strain was taken by the harness and divided equally between his thighs. As the boat picked up speed, he climbed faster until he was about sixty feet above the water. He noticed the various swimmers watching him go. There must have been forty or fifty people in the sea and maybe a couple of hundred more, some of them spread out on towels on the public beach, others lying sardine-like on the blue-and-white sun loungers on the private Plage Neptune next door. There were children building sand castles and paddling. A couple of them waved at him as he soared above them.

The speedboat was an American-built Tige 21V Fox Racer, twenty feet, six inches long, with a single 315 horse-power outboard engine. It was speeding down a narrow channel between two lines of buoys with the open sea ahead. Alex was quite surprised by how high up he was.

From this height, even Kristof seemed to be doll-sized, Alex watched as the driver flicked his cigarette into the slipstream. That surprised him too. The butt of a cigarette is made of cellulose acetate, a type of plastic, and would take years to biodegrade. It would also leak tiny amounts of lead, formaldehyde, cadmium, and arsenic straight into the Mediterranean. As if dumping plastic in the sea wasn't bad enough!

He put it out of his mind. He was actually enjoying this. They were still heading out to sea, leaving Nice behind them, and Alex felt a strange sense of both calm and exhilaration. He was too high up to hear the Tige's engine. The sun was sparkling off the sea, the wind rushing through his hair. He would be sorry when Kristof turned around and headed back, but he knew that the ride would last ten minutes at most.

And then Kristof stood up. Alex wondered what he was doing. It was as if he had been stung by a wasp. Still standing, he turned as if about to shout out to Alex. Then he clutched at his chest and toppled sideways, landing on the steering wheel.

He lay still. The boat surged on toward the horizon. Dangling high above, Alex couldn't quite believe what he had just seen. From the look of it, Kristof had just suffered some sort of stroke or heart attack. It was hard to say if he was dead or alive, but he certainly wasn't moving. His whole body was crumpled, his hands hanging limply above the deck. Alex almost wanted to laugh.

This could only happen to him! Well, it looked as if he was going to get a rather longer ride than he had bargained for.

He waited a few moments for Kristof to wake up.

Kristof didn't wake up.

Alex took stock of the situation. He was in no real danger. Provided the Tige kept moving forward, he would continue to fly behind it. It wouldn't take very long for the two Australians to realize that something had gone wrong. They would raise the alarm and send another boat after him. Somehow they would have to climb on to the Tige and bring it back to shore, slowing it down so that Alex could descend. Then they would call an ambulance for the unfortunate Kristof. Perhaps, after this, he would think of quitting cigarettes.

The boat, left to itself, was still speeding in a more or less straight line. Alex glanced back. Nice was now a long way away, the sun glinting off the long row of apartment buildings and hotels that were all packed together, facing the sea with the mountains behind. Despite his first thoughts, Alex was getting a little uneasy. He didn't like being out of control, and right now there was absolutely nothing he could do. He really was a puppet on a string.

Should he unhook the carabiners? It might be possible if he shifted some of his weight onto the metal bar, which was now above his head. Then he would be able to let go and drop down into the water. But that would do no good at all. From this height, he would probably break both his legs.

And then the speedboat must have been hit by a little wave. Kristof slid off the steering wheel and fell back, slumping against the rope that connected Alex to the boat. The movement caused the wheel to turn. The Tige cut a complete circle in the water and began to head back the way it had come. Alex felt himself being pulled around. Suddenly he was facing Nice and saw, with a jolt of horror, exactly what was going to happen next.

Unless Kristof recovered consciousness, which seemed unlikely, the boat would keep going until it hit the beach, slamming its way through any swimmers who happened to be in the way. Alex would be all right—he was safe so long as he was up in the air—but other people would be injured or even killed. And what about the dozens of sunbathers on their beach towels? Unless the boat was stopped, it would plow across the shingle and into them too. Alex was four or maybe five minutes away from a bloody catastrophe. Perhaps the most horrible part of it was that he had been given a grandstand seat.

And there was nothing he could do.

Or was there? If Alex could get into the boat, he could take over the controls . . . slow down and stop. But how was that possible when he was sixty feet up in the air? The carabiners! Alex reached up and grasped the metal bar, using both arms to drag his weight upward. That took the strain off the hooks connecting him to the parachute, and with great difficulty, he managed to free one of them, contorting his body and reaching back with one hand. Then he did the same on the other side. This was more difficult because the moment the second hook was unfastened, he would be hanging free, with all his weight transferred to his wrists and hands. If he let go, he would fall.

The beach was getting closer. The boat seemed to be rushing gleefully toward it. Why couldn't another wave hit the damned thing and turn it back again?

The second hook came free. Now Alex was clinging to the bar with the harness hanging uselessly off his thighs. He could imagine the crushing impact if he let go and fell. Even if he managed to save himself, it would be at the expense of everyone else. He would be responsible for the carnage as the boat smashed into the beach.

He had to get down to the level of the water. That was the only reason he had unhooked the carabiners. And he had worked out how to do it. On his first mission, he had been given parachute training by the SAS in the Brecon Beacons, and part of it had involved emergency procedures. He remembered what he had been taught. If he could fold the edge of the parachute in against the wind, he would be able to force a controlled descent. He looked up and caught sight of two colored cords. That was what he was looking for.

It wasn't easy. Having unhooked himself, he was now supporting himself with both hands. He let go with one and immediately felt the strain as his entire body weight transferred itself to the other. There was no time to rest. No time to hesitate. Nice was looming ahead of him. He could already see the swimmers—dots in the distance— bobbing up and down in the water, close to the shingle. The Tige was heading straight for them, almost deliberately, as if it wanted to do as much harm as possible before it crashed into the beach. Alex still hoped that Kristof would regain consciousness, get up, and see what was happening. But he wasn't moving. He was as still as a corpse.

Somehow, Alex's flailing hand caught hold of the rope. With the breeze beating at his face, he transferred some of his weight and pulled with all his strength, expecting the parachute to fold in on itself and then flutter down. But it didn't work. With a sense of dismay, he realized that, as the boat plowed forward, the rush of the wind was too great. He couldn't fight it. He was stuck in midair. He could still save himself. All he had to do was let go and he would fall. He might break a few bones, but the life jacket wouldn't let him drown. The people on the beach would be less fortunate. Alex remembered the two young children he had seen in the water. What if they were hit?

Ahead of him, the buildings were getting closer and closer. He could make out the improbable pink-and-green roof of the exclusive Negresco Hotel . . . He could even read the letters of its name. How much longer did he have? A couple of minutes. Not more. He pulled again. The cord didn't give an inch.

He was saved by the unlikely help of an EasyJet airbus coming in to land at Nice airport. All the parasailing companies were aware of the blowback from the jet engines and the danger they could pose to their clients, but it was far too high up to be any threat to him. In fact, Alex never even saw the plane, but he felt the blast as it hit the parachute. He knew it was now or never and pulled one last time, using all his strength. The silk folded and suddenly he was plunging down, the water rushing up.

He hit it with two feet, not hard enough to do himself damage. Even so, he was shocked by the impact. One moment he had been floating in the air, the next he was soaking wet, being dragged at speed through the sea, salt water lashing into his face. He was blinded. He could barely keep his eyes open. At the very last moment he had let go of the parachute, which had been instantly dragged away behind him, and transferred his grip to the tow rope. This was the critical moment. Time was running out. He only had a few seconds left.

He forced his eyes open. The Tige was in front of him. Fighting against the rush of the water, he began to pull himself forward, one hand over the other, desperately seizing hold of the rope. He was being bounced violently up and down, the water pounding into him. He could hardly breathe. His arms were being torn out of their sockets. He was being tortured a dozen different ways.

He was getting nearer to the boat. Alex didn't have time to congratulate himself. He had become aware of a new, last danger. The Tige's propeller was chopping up the water, turning it into a vicious white froth. If he tried to drag himself over it, his hands and then his arms would be chopped up. Gasping for breath, he hoisted himself above the surface, peering through the curtain of water that hammered into his face.

He'd had one piece of luck. When Kristof had fallen, he had snagged the rope, carrying it slightly over to one side. As Alex drew himself toward the back of the boat, the propeller was horribly close. He could feel it churning inches from his stomach and legs. But it wasn't directly in front of him. By twisting his body to one side, he was just able to avoid it.

There was a duckboard at the back of the boat. Alex reached it and caught hold of a stanchion at the very corner. He had used up almost all his strength. He was choking. He felt he had swallowed half the Mediterranean and the salt water was burning the back of his throat. The roar of the engine was in his ears. He cried out and pulled himself up. Somehow his body came clear. He felt the wooden deck under the life jacket across his chest. He wriggled forward. He was on board!

He looked up and realized with despair that he was too late. The Tige was traveling at about forty miles per hour and the first swimmers were only yards away. Alex could see the horror in their eyes as they took in what was about to happen. On the beach, sunbathers were rising out of their loungers, staring openmouthed, watching the disaster unfolding in front of them. Someone screamed. Alex could pull back the throttle, cut the engine. But even that wouldn't help. Propelled by its own momentum, the boat would still shoot forward, its prow crashing into the swimmers before it hit the beach and stopped. People would die. He had no doubt of it at all.

In the last remaining seconds, Alex threw himself forward. Ignoring Kristof, who was still lying there unconscious, he grabbed hold of the wheel and wrenched it to one side. The prow swung around, missing the first of the swimmers by inches. There were people everywhere. Alex spun the wheel the other way, weaving through them. He heard more screams, rising even above the roar of the outboard motor. Somehow, he managed to avoid them all.

The Tige reached the beach. The shingle was right in front of him. He heard the bottom of the boat grinding against the shallows and knew that the propeller would be next. Alex pulled back on the throttle even as the metal blades came into contact with the ocean floor and shattered. He felt the whole deck shudder.

And then the entire boat had left the water. Alex was in the driving seat, on dry land, sun loungers and umbrellas on one side of him, beach towels on the other, a blur of astonished faces watching him as he shot past. At the very end, he wrenched the steering wheel one last time. There was a narrow gulley with boulders on both sides and, straight ahead, directly underneath the Promenade des Anglais, a dark tunnel with a wire fence blocking the entrance. Some sort of storm drain. The boat was slowing down, dragging against the ground. The prow hit the wire. The boat stopped.

Alex heard shouting behind him—a gabble of French voices. Quickly, he unfastened the life jacket and the harness. Someone else would look after the unconscious driver, and he had no desire to answer any questions. Before anyone could reach him, he dropped out of the boat and ran up a flight of steps leading to the main road.

He had no sooner reached the top than he saw Celestine on the other side, coming out of an ice cream shop with a cone in each hand. Alex was dripping wet. He was only wearing his swimming shorts. Fortunately, in Nice, he didn't look out of place.

Dodging the traffic, he ran over to her.

"Alex!" She was surprised to see him. "What happened? Are you all right?"

"I'm fine." Alex had no intention of telling her what had happened. He looked back. He had moved so fast that nobody had seen where he had gone.

"Where is your T-shirt? And your sandals?"

"They were stolen."

"Stolen? But that is terrible!"

"It doesn't matter. I've got more back at the house." Alex took one of the ice cream cones. He needed something to cool him down. "Can we go home?" he asked.

"Of course. But how was the parasailing? Did you enjoy it?"

Alex glanced back one last time. He could hear the scream of an approaching ambulance. He could imagine the pandemonium on the beach. "Well," he said, "it was certainly quite a ride."

TEA WITH SMITHERS

51.5074°N,
0.1278°W

I'D OFTEN WONDERED WHERE Smithers lived. The truth is, I knew almost nothing about him except that he was massively fat, he was bald with a small, almost comical mustache, and he liked to wear old-fashioned suits. He manufactured gadgets—secret weapons and so on—for MI6. And that was what he provided for me. He wasn't allowed to give me anything lethal. I never got a gun or anything like that. But he seemed to take a great deal of pleasure in thinking up things which a teenager might have in his pockets (apart from his hands), and his inventions saved my life on more than one occasion.

Anyway, the two of us bumped into each other on Liverpool Street and he invited me to tea. He had a funny way of talking, a bit like everyone's favorite uncle or perhaps a principal in a small private school. There were times when I thought that everything about him was a huge act, that it was all fake, but at the same time he was the only person in MI6 whom I actually trusted. He wasn't like Mr. Blunt or Mrs. Jones or any of the others who only ever wanted to use me.

"Alex, my dear fellow!" We were standing face-to-face in the doorway of the building that pretended to be an international bank, but he was talking so loudly, I could have heard him halfway down the road. "What a delightful surprise. I hope we're not using you again. Nobody mentioned anything to me."

In fact, I'd just been in for a debrief. MI6 was closing their files on Dr. Grief and everything that had happened at the Point Blanc Academy, and they'd called me in to give them my version of events. Jack always hated it when I went to their offices. She was sure I wouldn't come back. But it had been an uneventful hour, telling them about my time in Africa. I'd been quite badly burned while I was out there, but that had healed by now and my life was back—more or less—to normal. I'd been on the way to the tube station when Smithers had suddenly appeared. I was quite surprised he used the front door. He was more likely to step into a phone booth that would turn out to be a lift.

"I'm not going anywhere, Mr. Smithers," I said.

"Not another mission?"

"No. They were just asking me about the last one."

"Ah yes. Dr. Grief. I always thought he was a nasty piece of work." He beamed. "In that case, why not come for tea with me? It would be nice to sit down and have a proper chin-wag." It occurred to me that Smithers had several chins with which to do it, but of course I didn't say that. "How about Saturday?"

"All right." I wasn't sure I wanted to have tea with him, but I wasn't doing anything over the weekend, and there was a part of me that wanted to know more. I'd first met Smithers almost a year ago. I'd been involved in eight missions. But I didn't know anything much about him. Where did he live? Did he have a house or an apartment? Did he keep animals? Was he married? Was he gay?

Everyone who worked at MI6 was the same. They spent so much time living in the shadows that in the end they became shadows themselves. I had learned that Mrs. Jones had two children (although somehow she'd lost them). Mr. Blunt was married. Mr. Smithers's first name was Derek. And that was it. That was the full extent of my knowledge.

He gave me an address in Hampstead and said it was a ten-minute walk from the tube station. The following Saturday I arrived on time, walking down through the village and taking one of the narrow lanes that twist their way toward Hampstead Heath. It turned out that Smithers lived in a mews. He had a small pink house with ivy growing up the front. There were three floors and, from the look of it, maybe six rooms. It was the sort of house that might appear in *Mary Poppins*, if you've ever seen that old film. Again, I got the feeling that there was something not quite real about it. There was a gnome standing on the tiny patch of lawn that made up the front garden. I wondered if it was watching me, connected to some sort of surveillance system. And the front doorbell. Would it blow up if I pressed it the wrong way? You never knew, where Smithers was concerned.

In fact, nothing happened for about five seconds after I'd pressed the bell button. I could imagine him heaving himself out of a chair and waddling over to the door. In fact, he didn't appear. There was an intercom set in the brickwork and I heard his voice. "Do come in, old chap! Straight ahead . . . the room at the end." The door opened automatically and I stepped into a home that was as old-fashioned as the outside. There was a hallway with black and white tiles, a ticking grandfather clock, antique paint-ings, a short corridor, a chandelier. I have to say, I was a little disappointed. It was all so ordinary. I closed the door behind me and kept walking. A second door led into a kitchen and living room that ran the full width of the house. Windows looked out onto a small garden behind.

Smithers was sitting in an armchair, tucked away in an alcove. Even on his day off, he liked to wear a suit. It seemed that he hadn't waited for me to arrive. He had a plate with three sandwiches balanced on his knee and he was sipping tea out of a porcelain cup.

"How very good to see you, Alex! Take a seat. Please help yourself. I hope you'll find something that you like."

Egg sandwiches, smoked salmon sandwiches, cheese sandwiches, a chocolate cake, scones and cream, fruit, nuts, freshly made lemonade and tea . . . There was actually enough for half a dozen people, piled up on a table in front of me. I sat down in the seat opposite Smithers and poured myself some tea. Part of me was wishing that I hadn't come. The house was like a theater set. It wasn't like anywhere I imagined Smithers would live. I got the sense that something was wrong, but I couldn't work out quite what it was.

"So how are you?" Smithers asked. "I heard you nearly got killed in France."

"I was lucky," I said. I didn't want to talk about the

chase down the mountain or my near collision with a speeding train.

"Did my exploding ear stud come in useful?"

"I wasn't crazy about the look," I said. "But it got me out of a lot of trouble."

"I'm glad to hear it." Suddenly Smithers was serious. "You know, I do have grave misgivings about MI6 using you," he said. "It's probably illegal and it's certainly immoral. The trouble is, you're too damned useful. You ought to try being less successful."

"If I was less successful, I'd be dead," I said.

"Yes. You have a point. But even so, it was very wrong of your uncle, Ian Rider, to drag you into our world." He glanced at me disapprovingly. "Do please help yourself," he said. "Have an egg sandwich. I used to love egg sandwiches when I was a boy, especially when they were cut into triangles. I'm not quite sure why, but they taste better that shape."

"How did you get into MI6?" I asked. I did as I was told and took a couple of sandwiches.

"You shouldn't ask questions like that, Alex. You know we're not allowed to talk about ourselves." Smithers raised his cup and sipped his tea noisily. His fingers were so plump, they wouldn't fit through the handle. He had to pinch it to keep it in place. "I once asked Alan Blunt what he'd got up to at the weekend and he almost had me arrested as a double agent." Smithers laughed to himself, then set the cup down. "But I can trust you, I suppose.

I got into MI6 because of my grandfather Major Arthur Smithers."

"Was he a spy too?"

"Not exactly. He was in the SOE during the war. I don't suppose you've learned about that in school—"

"The SOE." In fact, we had read about it in history lessons. "The Special Operations Executive."

"That's right. You got it in one!" Smithers was clearly pleased. "Formed in July 1940. It was just after Dunkirk. The French were finished. The Nazis were everywhere. It looked as if we'd pretty much lost the war. So Churchill formed a special unit and famously told them to 'set Europe ablaze.' That was the SOE. A lot of people didn't like them, you know, Alex—because they got up to all sorts of dirty tricks. But Churchill understood. It was a time of crisis. If we were going to win the war, we had to stop behaving like gentlemen.

"Anyway, my grandfather went to work for Station Nine, which specialized in gadgets and secret weapons. One of his earliest ideas was the exploding rat."

I couldn't help smiling. I wasn't sure if Smithers was joking or not.

"I'm absolutely serious! It was a rat with a bomb in it. One of our agents would leave it on the floor in a German factory and someone would come along, pick it up, and throw it in the furnace. And . . . boom!" Smithers gestured with his teacup, sending tea flying onto the arm of his chair. "They also hid bombs in camel droppings. The

Germans would drive over them in their armored vehicles with the same result. The SOE had lots and lots of superb ideas. There was a fountain pen that shot out tear gas. A dagger hidden inside a pencil. A one-man submarine that they tested in the reservoir in Staines. Exploding bicycle pumps, radio transmitters disguised as sewing machines . . . They never stopped!

"After the war, old Arthur used to tell me all these stories and I was absolutely fascinated. Apparently he worked on super-strength itching powder, which he planned to put into the Germans' underpants. I know it sounds ridiculous, but I swear to you, it's absolutely true. You can check the history books! I was quite a small boy, but I began to experiment myself. I had a cousin who used to bully me all the time and the first gadget I ever created was specially for him. It was on his birthday cake. It was rather naughty of me, but I'm afraid I mixed potassium chlorate with the candles. It's a highly efficient oxidizing agent and it reacted with the sugar in the icing. The result was a disaster. Instead of the birthday boy blowing out the candles, the candles blew out the birthday boy. His parents weren't at all amused.

"I also got quite a name for myself at school. I was sent to an absolutely horrible place down on the coast, and I'd only been there one week when I was caught trying to post myself back home. When that didn't work, I started making gadgets just to keep myself amused. I managed to speed up all the clocks so we got shorter lessons, and I was very pleased when I smuggled a mobile telephone into the end-of-term exams."

"I'd have thought anyone could do that," I said.

"Well, yes," Smithers agreed. "But this was ten years before mobile phones were invented. After school I studied physics and chemistry at Cambridge University and I got one hundred percent on my final exams. Unfortunately, the authorities found out that I'd x-rayed the questions a week before."

"What did they do?"

"They recommended me to MI6. That was how I got the job. I've been there ever since, and I have to say, I was getting quite bored until you came along. It's all very well making guns, knives, poison pills, and that sort of thing, but I find it much more fun making gadgets for you. Exploding bubble gum, infared goggles, the motorized yo-yo . . . You must admit, we've had some jolly times together."

Jolly times? Smithers was always smiling when he handed out his latest gadgets, but I wasn't often smiling when I used them. I was too busy trying to stay alive.

"As a matter of fact, there's a brand-new gadget in front of you right now." Smithers leaned forward, challenging me. I could see the reflection of the light dancing in his eyes.

"What do you mean?" I asked.

"Exactly what I say. You've got to remember, Alex, at the end of the day my job is to disguise things. For example, take the Nintendo DS I gave you when you went off to deal with Herod Sayle. It was a smoke bomb. It was a bug finder. It had all sorts of uses, but the main thing was . . . it was invisible. Sayle saw it but he didn't look twice. And that's the point. Not every gadget I make is a weapon, but it's always designed to deceive. Right now you're looking at my latest invention, but you're not seeing it—which is the proof, I suppose, that it works."

What was he talking about? I was looking at something. I thought it was ordinary. But it wasn't. It was a gadget. What could it be?

Very carefully, I examined everything.

The tea. Sandwiches cut into triangles, the scones, the cake. They could all have been drugged or poisoned, although why would Smithers want to do me harm? The cake could have all the ingredients of a bomb. For all I knew, the icing could be plastic explosive.

"It's not the food," Smithers said. He placed his cup on the table beside him. It made no sound. He was watching me closely.

What else? There was a small yellow teapot on the table. I unscrewed the lid. It contained only tea. I widened my search. What about the table itself? It was round, wooden. It looked antique. I reached out and ran a finger along the edge, looking for the telltale hole that might fire a bullet or an anesthetic dart.

"You're not even close," Smithers said.

He was sitting in a high-backed chair with two arms that curved around like scrolls. Press a button and the whole thing might blast off into the air—but he had no-where to go. He had his back to the wall and the ceiling curved over his head. A single spotlight illuminated him, and now that I thought about it, there was something quite theatrical about the way he presented himself. But as far as I could see, the light was ordinary. There was a picture on one wall. It looked like an oil painting, a corn-field, but I remembered visiting Smithers's office on the eleventh floor of MI6. There had been a painting that had started moving even as I examined it . . . It was actually a plasma screen connected to a live satellite somewhere above the Atlantic Ocean. And for that matter, there had been a communications system hidden in the potted plant. I got up and went over to the picture. I ran a finger over the surface.

"It's not the picture."

I was beginning to get annoyed. Smithers was still sitting there. In fact he hadn't left the chair since I had come in. He was looking very smug, one leg crossed over the other. I noticed he was wearing bright red socks. "All right, Mr. Smithers," I said. "You win. Whatever your lat-est invention is, I can't see it."

Smithers laughed. "I owe you an apology, Alex. I really wanted to have tea with you, but in the end it wasn't possible."

"What are you talking about?"

"Mrs. Jones sent me to Singapore. A last-minute assignment. I'm there now."

"Wait . . ."

"Let yourself out, old chap. I'll make it up to you when I get back." Smithers reached out and pressed something I couldn't see. A second later, he flickered and disappeared. So did the chair he'd been sitting in.

That was when I realized he'd never been there. I'd been having tea with a hologram. I wasn't sure whether to be angry or amused. But at least the cake was real. I took it home for Jack.

39.5501°N,
105.782°W

CHRISTMAS AT GUNPOINT

My uncle—Ian Rider—always told me that he worked in international banking. Why did I believe him? Bankers don't usually spend weeks or even months away from home, returning with strange scars and bruises they are reluctant to explain. They don't receive phone calls in the middle of the night from people who refuse to give their name and then disappear at the drop of a hat. And how many of them are proficient in kickboxing and karate, speak three languages, spend hours at the gym, and keep themselves in perfect physical shape?

Ian Rider was a secret agent—a spy. From the day he left Cambridge University with degrees in math and Arabic, he had worked for the Special Operations Division of MI6. Just about everything he ever told me was a lie, but I believed him because I had no parents and had lived with him all my life, and, I suppose, because when you're thirteen years old, you believe what adults say.

But there was one occasion when I came very close to discovering the truth. It happened one Christmas, at the ski resort of Gunpoint, Colorado. Although I didn't know it at the time, this was going to be the last vacation we would have together. By the following spring, Ian would have been killed on a mission in Cornwall, investigating the Stormbreaker computers being manufactured there. That was just a couple of months after my fourteenth birthday. That was when my entire life spun out of control and I became a spy myself.

Gunpoint had been named after the man who first settled there, a gold digger called Jeremiah Gun. He'd had a shack up in the mountains and had cheerfully drunk himself to death, leaving behind a handful of gold nuggets and his name. Gunpoint was about fifty miles north of Aspen, and if you've ever skied in America, you'll know the setup. There was a central village with gas fires burning late into the night, mulled wine and toasted marshmallows, and shops with prices as high as the mountains surrounding them.

We'd booked a hotel, the Granary, which was on the very edge of the village, about a five-minute walk to the main ski lift. The two of us shared a suite of rooms on the second floor. We each had our own bedroom, opening onto a shared living space with a balcony that ran around the side of the building. The Granary was one of those brand-new places designed to look a hundred years old, with big stone fireplaces, woven rugs, and moose heads on the walls. Part of me hoped they were fake, but they probably weren't.

For the first couple of days we were on our own. The snow was excellent. There had been a heavy fall just before we arrived, but at the same time the sun was shining and the weather was unusually warm, so we were talking powder and lifts with no lines. We warmed up with a few gentle runs—greens and blues—but we were soon racing each other down the dizzyingly steep runs high up over Gunpoint itself.

It was on the third day that things changed. It began with two new arrivals who moved into the room next door. A father and a daughter—she was just a couple of years older than me. We met outside the lift—the elevator, she would say—and by the time we reached the ground floor, I already knew quite a bit about her.

Her name was Sahara. Her dad lived and worked in Washington, DC—she told me that he was "something in government," and I guessed she was being vague on purpose. Her mother was a lawyer in New York. The two of them were divorced, and Sahara had to split Christmases between them. She was very pretty, with long black hair and blue eyes, only an inch taller than me despite the age gap. She'd been skiing all her life—and she was completely fearless. And, unlike me, she had her own boots and skis. At the time my feet were growing too fast and, as usual, I'd had to rent.

Sahara Sands. Her father was Cameron Sands, with silver hair, silver glasses, and a laptop computer that never seemed to leave his side. He spent every afternoon in his room, working. Sahara didn't seem to mind. She was used to it, and anyway, now she had Ian and me.

Two more people, both men, came to the Granary on the same day as Sahara and her dad. They were sharing a smaller, twin-bed room across the corridor, and somehow I knew they weren't here for fun. Maybe it would have helped if they'd tried to smile. That was how I noticed them in the first place, sitting in the bar with two glasses of water, neither of them drinking, not even talking. In fact, the two of them never seemed to be far away, although not once did they come over and speak to us. They were both in their late twenties, smartly dressed, and very fit. They could have graduated from the same college. The third time I saw them, they were having breakfast. I asked Ian if he thought they were lawyers. He laughed.

"I don't think so, Alex." Suddenly he was serious. He nodded at them, sitting together on the other side of the restaurant. "Try again."

I looked at them more carefully. They were wearing identical ski jackets. They were two tables away from Sahara and her father, not exactly watching them but keeping them in sight. I remembered seeing them on the slopes, about the same distance away. Suddenly I got it. "Are they bodyguards?"

"Better. At a guess, I'd say they're American Secret Service."

I blinked. "How do you know?"

"Well, their clothes are American. They don't smoke and I haven't seen them touch a drop of alcohol. But more to the point, they're both carrying guns."

"Under their jackets?"

Ian shook his head. "You could never draw a gun out of a ski jacket in time. They've got ankle holsters. Take a look the next time they're in the locker room." He glanced at me over his coffee. "You have to notice these things, Alex. Whenever you meet someone, you have to check them out . . . all the details. People tell a story the moment they walk into a room. You can read them."

He was always saying stuff like that to me. I used to think he was just talking, passing the time. It was only much later that I realized he was preparing me, and it was a full-time job. Just like the skiing and the scuba lessons. He was quietly following a plan that had begun almost the day I was born.

"Are they here with Cameron Sands?" I asked.

"What do you think?"

I nodded. "They're always hanging around. And Sahara says her dad works in government."

"Then maybe he needs protection." Ian smiled. "I'm going to give you a task, Alex. Just for fun. I want you to find out their names by the end of the week." He paused. "And the make of their guns."

But the next day I had forgotten the conversation. It had snowed again. There must have been ten inches on the ground, bulging out over the roofs of the hotel like overstuffed duvets. Sahara and I switched to snowboards and spent about five hours on the chutes, bomb drops, and powder stashes at the bowl area high up over Bear Creek. I never could have guessed that just five months later I'd be using the same skills to avoid being killed by half a dozen thugs on snowmobiles, racing down the side of Point Blanc in southern France. But that's another story.

We had lunch together at a barn-like place high up in the mountains. I had a stew. She ate a salad. It was funny that we'd both been given credit cards by our parents, but in the end she insisted on paying. "Dad won't mind," she said.

"So what exactly does your dad do?" I asked her.

"I told you. He works for the government. You shouldn't ask questions about him. He never talks about his work." She changed the subject. "Where are your mom and dad?"

"I never knew them," I told her. "They died when I was small."

"That's terrible. I'm sorry." She looked genuinely upset. "I miss my mother a lot when she's not around, but at least I get to see her. I see both my parents. I wish they'd stayed together. Divorce is such a stupid idea." She'd bought herself a can of Diet Coke and flicked it open. "You snowboard really well," she went on. "There's a double black diamond we could try after lunch, if you like. It's called Breakneck Pass and it's meant to be wild. My dad told me to keep away, but he doesn't need to know."

"No, thanks." I shook my head. "I don't want a broken leg. Let's take it easy."

"Whatever you say, Alex." She winked at me, but I could tell she was disappointed.

We snowboarded together for the rest of the afternoon, and at half past three, with the sun already dipping behind the mountains, we decided to call it a day. We were both bruised and exhausted, soaked with sweat and melted snow. Sahara hurried off to meet her dad for a hot chocolate. I went back to the Granary on my own. I got changed in the locker room and dropped off my board. Then I had a swim in the hotel pool—twenty lengths without stopping. Even at that age, I tried to keep myself fit. After that I went up to the reception area, thinking that I'd wait for my uncle in front of the fire, but when the lift door opened, I saw he was already there. He was sitting on the corner of a sofa, wearing jeans and a sweater. I was about to call out to him—but then I stopped. I knew at once that something was wrong.

It's not easy to explain, but he had never looked like this before. He was usually laid-back and relaxed, but now he was completely silent and tense in a way that was almost animal. Ian had dark brown eyes—people say I inherited the same from my father—but it was as if a shutter had come down. They were cold and colorless. He hadn't noticed me come in. His attention was focused on the reception desk and the man who was checking in to the hotel.

"People tell a story," Ian had said. *"You can read them."* Looking at the man at the reception desk, I tried to do just that.

He was wearing a black roll-neck jersey with dark trousers and a gold Rolex watch, heavy on his wrist. He had blond hair—an intense yellow, and cut short. It almost looked painted on. I would have said he was thirty years old, with a pockmarked face and a lazy smile. I could hear him talking to the receptionist. He had a Bronx accent. So much for chapter one. What else could I read in him?

His skin was unusually pale. In fact it was almost white, as if he had spent half his life indoors. He worked out; I could see the muscles bulging under his sleeves. And he had very bad teeth. That was strange. Americans wealthy enough to stay in a hotel like this would have taken more care of their dental work.

"You're on the fourth floor, Mr. da Silva," the receptionist said. "Enjoy your stay."

The man had brought a cheap suitcase with him. That was also unusual in the land of Gucci and Louis Vuitton. He picked it up and disappeared into the lift.

I walked farther into the reception area and Ian saw me. At once, he relaxed. But he knew I had been watching him.

"Is everything okay?" I asked.

"Yes."

"Who was that?"

"The man who just checked in? I don't know." Ian shook his head as if trying to dismiss the whole thing. "I thought I knew him from somewhere. How was Bear Creek?"

He obviously didn't want to talk about it, so I went up to the room and watched a DVD before dinner. I'd brought schoolwork with me, but so far I hadn't even looked at it. I was always putting it off until the next day. At half past seven, I made my way back downstairs. As I left my room, I noticed one of the Secret Service men coming out of a doorway across the corridor. He walked toward the lifts without saying anything to me. Sahara and her father weren't around.

Ian and I ate dinner together and everything seemed normal. We talked about school, about skiing, about the news. Ian always wanted me to know about current affairs, which I suppose was also part of my training. He ordered half a bottle of wine for himself and a Coke for me. I must have been more tired than I thought, because at around ten o'clock I found myself yawning. He suggested I go up and get an early night.

"What about you?" I asked.

"Oh . . . I might get a breath of air. I'll follow you up later."

I left him and went back to the room, and that was when I discovered I didn't have the electronic card that would open the door. I must have left it on the table. Annoyed with myself, I went back to the dining room. There was no sign of it, and Ian wasn't there either. Remembering what he had said, I followed him outside.

There was a courtyard around the side of the hotel, covered with snow, a frozen fountain in the middle. It was surrounded by walls on three sides, with the hotel roofs—also snow-covered—slanting steeply. The whole area was lit by a full moon, which shone down like a prison search-light.

And there he was.

Ian Rider and the man who called himself da Silva were locked together, standing like some bizarre statue in the middle of the courtyard. They were fighting for control of a single gun, which was clasped in their hands, high above their heads. I could see the strain on both their faces. But what made the scene even more surreal was that neither of them was making any sound. In fact, they were barely moving. Both were focused on the gun. Whoever brought it down would be able to use it on the other.

I called out. It was a stupid thing to do. I could have gotten my uncle killed. But both men turned to look at me, and it was Ian who took advantage of the interruption. He let go of the gun and slammed his elbow into da Silva's stomach, then bent his arm up, the side of his hand scything the other man's wrist. I had already learned karate for six years and recognized the perfectly executed sideways block.

The gun flew out of the man's hand, slid across the snow, and came to rest just in front of the fountain.

"Get out of here, Alex!" my uncle shouted.

It took him less than two seconds, but it was enough to lose him the advantage. Da Silva lashed out, the ball of his fist pounding into Ian's chest, winding him. He followed through with a vicious roundhouse kick. My uncle tried to avoid it, but the snow and the slippery surface didn't help. He was thrown off his feet and went crashing down. Da Silva stopped and caught his breath. His mouth was twisted in an ugly sneer, his teeth gray in the moonlight. He ran a hand through his blond hair, smoothing it back. He knew the fight was over. He had won.

That was when I acted. I dived forward, throwing myself onto my stomach and sliding across the ice. My own momentum carried me as far as the gun. I snatched it up, noticing for the first time that it was fitted with a silencer. I had never held a handgun before. It was much heavier than I had expected. Da Silva stared at me as I brought it around, aiming it at him.

"No!" My uncle uttered the single word quietly. It didn't matter what the circumstances were. He didn't want me to kill a man.

Da Silva stared at me. Even at that moment, I saw the contempt in his eyes. As far as he was concerned, I was just a kid holding a gun. He didn't think I had the nerve to use it.

I pulled the trigger. I felt the gun jerk in my hand. There was no noise, just a soft ripping sound as the silencer did its work. Even so, the power of the weapon shocked me. I emptied the chamber, one bullet after another, all seven of them. The recoil hurt my wrist. But I wasn't shooting at da Silva. At the last moment I had lifted the gun and fired into the air above him, over his head. At last it was over. The gun was empty. All the bullets were gone.

Da Silva stood where he was, unharmed. Very slowly, he reached behind him and took out a second gun. My uncle was still on the ground; there was nothing he could do. I lay where I was, my breath coming out in white clouds. Da Silva smiled. I could see him trying to make up his mind which one of us he was going to kill first.

There was a gentle rumble and a ton of snow slid off the roof directly above him. It was exactly what I'd hoped for. I had cut a dotted line with the bullets, and the weight of the snow had done the rest for me. Da Silva just had time to look up before the avalanche hit him. I think he opened his mouth—either to swear or to scream—but it was too late. The snow made almost no sound, just a soft *thwump* as it hit. In a second, he was gone. Buried under a huge white curtain.

My uncle got to his feet. I did the same. The two of us looked at each other.

"Alex—" he began.

"Do you think we should dig him up?" I asked.

He shook his head. "No. Let's leave him to chill out."

"Who was he? Why did he have a gun? Why were you fighting him?"

There were so many things I wanted to know when we finally got back to our room. Ian had called the police. They were already on the way, he told me. He would talk to them when they arrived. The gun that he had taken from da Silva was beside him. I could still feel the weight of it in my hand. My wrist was aching from the recoil; I had never fired a handgun before.

"Forget about it, Alex," he said. "He had nothing to do with me. Da Silva—that's not his real name, by the way—is a wanted criminal and I just happened to recognize him when I saw him in the lobby. He's been involved in bank fraud."

"Bank fraud?" I could hardly believe it.

"That's right. I was out for a walk and I met him quite by chance. I challenged him—which was pretty stupid of me, now that I think about it. He pulled out the gun . . . and the rest you saw." Ian smiled. "I expect he'll have frozen solid by now. At least he won't be needing a morgue."

If I'd thought a little more, I'd have realized that none of it added up. When I had come upon the two men, they were fighting for control of a single gun. They had dropped it—and then da Silva had produced a second gun of his own. So logic should have told me that the first gun actually belonged to my uncle. But why would he have brought a gun with him on a skiing vacation? How could he even have gotten it through airport security? It was such an unlikely thought—Ian carrying a firearm—that I accepted his story, because there was no alternative.

Anyway, I was exhausted. It had been a long day and I was glad to crawl into bed. There were all sorts of questions tugging at my mind, but I ignored them and fell asleep almost immediately. Ian was surprisingly quiet the following morning, and it occurred to me that he hadn't even thanked me for what I had done the night before. Over breakfast, he told me he wouldn't be coming skiing. Apparently he'd spoken to the police when they'd finally arrived, and they wanted him to come to their offices in Cale and tell them as much as he could about da Silva and the fight outside the hotel. There was further bad news too. Somehow da Silva had dug his way out of the great mound of snow. He had gotten away.

"I would have thought he'd been flattened," Ian said over boiled eggs and grilled bacon. He never ate anything fried. "But he managed to tunnel his way out like a mole. I'm annoyed with myself, if you want the truth. I should have checked."

"Do you think he'll come back?" I asked. The thought made me a little nervous.

Ian shook his head. "I doubt it. He knows I recognized him, and he's probably out of Colorado by now. Maybe he's even left the States. He won't want to hang around."

"How long do you think you'll be?"

"A few hours. Don't let this spoil the vacation, Alex. Just put it out of your mind. You can ski with Sahara today. From the way you two are getting along, I'd say she'll be glad to have you on your own."

I didn't know what he meant by that, but I didn't argue. In fact, when I knocked on her door an hour later, Sahara wasn't there. It was opened by her father, Cameron Sands.

"I'm sorry, Alex," he said. "You're just too late. She left a few minutes ago; she's got a lesson this morning. But she'll probably call in later—I can ask her to meet you."

"Thanks," I said. "I'll be up at Bear Creek."

He nodded and closed the door, and as he did so, I looked over his shoulder and saw that he wasn't alone. The two young men were with him, one sitting on the sofa, the other standing by the window. The Secret Service men. I could see his desk too. The laptop that I'd noticed before was there, surrounded by a pile of papers. Cameron Sands was meant to be on vacation, but from the look of it, the work never stopped. I wouldn't have been surprised if he'd taken the computer skiing with him.

I went downstairs to the locker room and a few minutes later was clumping out to the ski lift with my skis over my shoulder and my poles dragging behind me. I didn't much like the idea of skiing on my own and wondered if Sahara would even be able to find me . . . if she came looking. There were a lot of people around, and the thing about skiers is that they all look more or less the same. On the other hand, I was wearing a bright green jacket—a North Face Free Thinker. She'd already joked about the color and I was sure she'd recognize it a mile away.

But as it turned out, I saw her before she saw me. The nearest lift to the hotel was a gondola, taking twenty people at a time to an area called Black Ridge, about a half mile higher up. Sahara was right at the front of the line, standing between two men, and I could see at once that something was wrong. She wasn't smiling. There was something like panic in her eyes. I examined the two men. I had never seen them before, but whoever they were, they certainly weren't ski instructors. They were standing very close to her, sandwiching her between them like they didn't want to let her slip away. One of them was round-faced, fat, and white. The other looked Korean. They were both big men—even with the ski suits, I got a sense of overworked muscle. Sahara was scared, I saw that too. And a moment later I saw why.

A third man had gone ahead of them and was waiting inside the gondola. I only glimpsed his face behind the glass, but I recognized it instantly. It was da Silva. His hood was up and he was wearing sunglasses, but his pale skin and bad teeth were unmistakable. He was waiting while the other men joined him with the girl.

I started toward them, but I was already too late. Sahara was inside the gondola. The doors slid shut and the whole thing jerked forward, rising up over the snow. I think Sahara caught sight of me just as she was swept away. Her eyes widened and she jerked her head in the direction of the hotel. The message was obvious. *Get help!*

I didn't need telling twice. Sahara was being kidnapped in broad daylight. It was almost unbelievable, but there could be no doubt about it.

I turned around and began to run.

I was running to get help.

If this had happened six months later, if I'd been older and more experienced, I might have tried to do something myself. After all, the three men didn't know I was there. They weren't expecting trouble. I might have been able to follow them, taking the next gondola and somehow tracking them down. It might even have been possible to stop the gondola, leaving them dangling in midair. But this was before I'd been recruited by MI6 and given training with the SAS. I was thirteen years old and on my own in an American ski resort. I wasn't even certain about what I'd just seen. Was Sahara really being kidnapped? And if so, why? According to what my uncle had told me, the man called da Silva was involved in some sort of bank fraud. What possible interest could he have in her?

But then I remembered. Cameron Sands was her father. He worked for the government and traveled with his own entourage of Secret Service men. This wasn't about Sahara. It was about him—and he was the one I had to find.

I stabbed my skis and poles into a mound of snow and ran back into the hotel as fast as I could—not easy in ski boots. Fortunately, it was only a short distance away. You were meant to take your boots off in the locker room downstairs, but I just clomped right in, through the reception area, into the lift, and up to the second floor. I went to my own room first. It occurred to me that my uncle might not have left yet for the police station, and if he was there, he would know what to do.

I was out of luck. The room was empty. I turned around and was about to go next door, where Sahara and her father were staying, when I heard someone talking. I recognized the voice. It was Cameron Sands, outside on the terrace. Our window was open and I went over and looked out. Cameron was standing there, framed against the mountains, on his cell phone. He had his back to me, but I could tell at once that something was wrong. He was completely still and his whole body was rigid, as if he'd been electrocuted. I heard him speak.

"Where is she? What have you done with her?"

Da Silva. It had to be him. He'd taken the girl and now he was talking to the dad, making his demands. What did he want? Money? Somehow, I didn't think so. The Granary was comfortable, but it wasn't the most expensive hotel in the resort by a long way, and if you were into the money-with-menaces business, there were plenty of billionaires to choose from: movie stars, Russian oligarchs, and so on.

Being careful not to make any sound, I leaned forward so that I could hear more.

"All right." Sands spoke slowly and his voice was ice cold. I could see his breath frosting in the air. "I'll bring it and I'll come alone. But I'm warning you—"

That was as far as he got. Whoever he was talking to cut him off. He lowered the phone, staring at it as if it were somehow responsible.

As far as I was concerned, that should have been it. Cameron Sands had two Secret Service men somewhere in the hotel, and this was none of my business. But I couldn't just leave it there. I liked Sahara, and in a funny way I felt as if this was all my fault. It struck me now that I could have done something more when I saw her being loaded into the gondola. At the very least I could have shouted and raised the alarm. I told myself that I wasn't going to get involved, that I was being stupid. But I still couldn't stop myself. When Cameron Sands came out of his room five minutes later, I was waiting around the corner, watching him go.

I followed him downstairs. He had changed into his ski suit with his goggles around his neck and—here was the weird thing—he was carrying the laptop I had seen on the desk. It was sticking out of a black nylon bag. As he went downstairs, he pushed it inside and fastened the zip. There was no sign of the Secret Service men—but I'd heard what he said on the phone: he wasn't going to involve them. Wherever he was heading, he was going there alone.

I waited outside the boot room, then followed him across the front of the hotel to the gondola, picking up my skis and poles on the way. He had his skis too. The nylon bag with the laptop was hanging across his chest, slightly hidden under one arm. There weren't many people at the gondola now. Afternoon ski school had begun and the various classes were already practicing their snow plows on the lower slopes. I watched Sahara's dad hold his lift pass out to be scanned, waited a few moments, and then did the same. By now I'd pulled up my hood and drawn my goggles down over my face. We got into the same gondola and stood only a few inches apart. Even if he looked in my direction, I knew he wouldn't recognize me, but of course he wasn't taking any notice of the people around him. He looked sick with worry. His eyes were fixed on the mountain peaks high above.

Five minutes later we got out at Black Ridge, a sort of wide shelf in the mountains, with another three lifts climbing in different directions. He put on his skis and I did the same. I knew that Cameron Sands was a strong skier, but I reckoned I could keep up with him no matter where he went.

I didn't need to worry. He only skied as far as the nearest lift—a double chair—and took it up to Gun Hill. There was just one more lift that went up from here. It led to an area called the Needle. It was as high as you could get, so high that even on a bright day like today, the clouds still rubbed against the surface of the snow. Once again I went with him, just a few chairs behind.

Da Silva was waiting for him at the Needle.

I saw Cameron get off his chair and look around him. By the time I arrived, a few seconds later, he had already moved away. I slid over to one side, keeping close to the cabin where the lift attendant sat all day, watching people get on and off. From here I saw Cameron Sands ski down about thirty yards to a flat area with a sign marked by two black diamonds. I knew exactly where we were. This was Breakneck Pass, the run that Sahara had mentioned only the day before. The name tells you everything you need to know. From this point, it was the only way down, a vicious, incredibly steep run of ice and moguls that started with a stomach-churning, zigzagging chute, continued along the edge of a precipice, and then plunged into a wood, with no obvious way between the trees. Not many people took it on and I'd had no hesitation in saying no when Sahara suggested it. My uncle said you'd need nerves of steel to take on Breakneck. Or a death wish.

And there they all were, waiting with da Silva: the fat man and the Korean man I had seen at the gondola, with Sahara trapped between them. She was still scared. Nobody could see me. I was thirty yards higher up, and the clouds and snow flurries chasing along the mountain ridge formed a screen between me and them. I wiped the ice off my goggles and watched as the scene played out. Cameron Sands said something. Sahara started forward, but the two men held her back. Now it was da Silva's turn. He was smiling. I saw him point at the nylon bag with the laptop. Sands hesitated, but not for very long. He lifted it off his shoulder and held it in front of him as if weighing it, then handed it over. Da Silva nodded to his companions. They let Sahara go and she slithered—I wouldn't even call it skiing—across to her dad. He put an arm around her. The business was finished.

Except that it wasn't. I hadn't decided what I was going to do—until I did it. Suddenly I found myself racing down the slope, my legs bent and my shoulders low, my poles tucked under my arms, picking up as much speed as I could. Nobody was looking my way. They had no idea I was there until it was too late. The next moment I was right in the middle of them, moving so fast that I must have been no more than a blur. Da Silva was still holding the laptop. I snatched it out of his hand

and kept going, over the lip and down the first stretch of Breakneck Pass.

The next few seconds were a nightmare as I found myself falling off the edge of the mountain, poling like crazy to avoid the first moguls and at the same time managing to get the strap over my head so that the computer was out of my way, dangling behind my back. I nearly fell three or four times. If I'd had even half a second to think what I was doing, I'd probably have lost control and broken both my legs. But instinct took over. I was twenty yards down the chute and heading for the next segment before da Silva even knew what had happened.

He didn't hang around. I heard a shout and somehow I knew, without looking back, that the three men were after me. Well, that was sort of what I'd expected. Da Silva wanted the computer. Sands had given it to him. So he and his daughter weren't needed anymore. I was the target now. All I had to do was get down to the bottom, which couldn't be more than a couple of thousand yards from here. It was just a pity there was no one else around. If I could get back into a crowd, I'd be safe.

I heard a crack. A bullet slammed into the snow inches from my left ski. Who had fired? The answer was obvious, but even so, I found it hard to believe. Was it really possible to ski in these conditions and bring out guns at the same time? The snow was horrible, wind-packed and hard as metal. My skis were grinding as they carried me over the surface. I was grateful that my uncle had insisted on choosing my equipment for me; I was using Nordica twin tips, wide under the foot and seriously stiff. It had taken me a while to get used to them, but the whole point was that they were built for speed. Right now they seemed to be flying, and as I carved and pivoted around the moguls, I almost wanted to laugh. I didn't think anyone in the world would be able to catch up with me.

I was wrong. Either da Silva and his men had spent a long time training for this or they'd been experts to begin with. I came to a gully and risked a glance back. There were less than thirty yards between us and they were gaining fast. Worse still, they didn't even seem to be exerting themselves. They had that slow, fluid quality you may have seen at the Winter Olympics, when the best skiers in the world take to the slopes, and yet the distance between us was closing all the time. Suddenly I knew that there was nothing to laugh about. I cursed myself for getting involved in the first place. Why had I done it? This had nothing to do with me.

I made it to the woodland and heaved a sigh of relief, my breath frosting in front of my goggles. At least the trunks and branches would make it harder for anyone to take another shot at me. I was lucky I'd done plenty of tree skiing with Ian. I knew that I had to keep the speed up—otherwise I'd lose control. Go too fast, though, and I'd risk impaling myself on a branch. The secret is balance. Or luck. Or something.

I didn't really know where I was going. Everything

was just streaks of green and brown and white. I was
getting tired. Branches were slashing at my face. My legs
were already aching with all the twists and turns. And
the laptop was half strangling me, threatening to pull me
over backward. One of my skis almost snagged on a root.
I shifted my body weight and cried out as my left shoulder slammed into a trunk—it felt like I'd broken a bone. I
almost lost control there and then. One of the men shouted
something. I couldn't see any of them, but it sounded as
if they were right behind me, inches away. That gave me
new strength. I shot forward onto a miniature ramp, and
before I knew it I'd left the ground, propelled up into the
air through a tangle of branches that scratched my face
and tore at my goggles.

I was in the clear. The wood disappeared behind me
and I fell into a wide, empty area. But I knew before I
landed that I'd lost my balance and that this was going to
end badly. Sure enough, my legs were pulled in different
directions, my skis slipped away, and there was a sicken-
ing crash as I found myself diving headlong into the snow.
My entire body shuddered. I couldn't see. I was sliding
helplessly in a blinding white explosion. My skis released
themselves and were torn off my feet. I was aware that the
surface underneath me had changed. It was smoother and
more slippery. I was moving faster. I stretched out a hand
and tried to stop myself, but there was no purchase at all.
Where was I? At last I slowed down and stopped.

I was breathless and confused. I was sure I must have

broken several of my bones. The laptop was around my throat and it almost felt as if the ground was cracking up where I lay. No, it really was cracking up! As I struggled to my feet, I realized what had happened. I had gone spectacularly off-piste. There was a lake on the west side of the mountain—they called it Coldwater Creek. I had landed right next to it and managed to slide in. I was on the surface of the ice. And if that wasn't bad enough, the ice was breaking under my weight.

Da Silva and the two men had stopped on the edge of the lake. All three were facing me. The Korean man and the fat man both had guns. My goggles had come off in the fall and da Silva recognized me.

"You!" He spat out the single word. He didn't sound friendly.

There were about ten yards between us. Nobody moved.

"Give me the laptop," he demanded.

I said nothing. If I gave him the laptop, he would kill me. That much I knew.

"Give me it or I will take it," he continued.

There was the sound of something cracking. A black line appeared, snaking its way toward my foot. I steadied myself, trying not to breathe. Water, as cold as death, welled up around me. I wondered how much longer the ice would hold. If it broke, I would disappear forever. There was no use swimming for safety. Five minutes in this freezing water and I would die.

"Why don't you come and get it," I said.

Da Silva nodded. The Korean man stepped forward. He was meant to come and get me, and I could see he wasn't too happy about the idea. He might have been chosen because he was the lightest of the three, but he was an adult, twice as big as me, and he wasn't light enough. On the third step, the ice broke. One minute he was there, the next he was gone, his arms floundering and his face filling with panic as he tried to grip the sides of the hole. His breath came out as great mushrooms of white steam. He tried to scream but no sound came out. His lungs must have already frozen.

He had taken a gun with him. They only had one other. Da Silva snatched it from the fat man—he had already decided he was going to risk his weight on the ice—and pointed it at me.

"Give me the laptop," he said. "Or I will shoot you where you stand."

"What will you do then?" I shouted back. I took another step, moving away from the edge of the lake. The ice creaked. I could feel it straining underneath my feet. "You can't reach me. You're too heavy."

"Maybe. But the ice will harden in the night. I'll return for the laptop tomorrow."

"You think it'll still be working? A whole day and a night out here?"

"I'll take that risk!" Da Silva didn't want to argue any more. I could almost see his finger tightening on the trigger. I had absolutely no doubt that he was about to kill me. "I'm telling you, you little swine, this is your last chance."

"Alex—get down. Now!"

My uncle's voice came out of the woods. As da Silva spun around, I dropped low, hoping the sudden movement wouldn't crack the ice. At the same time there were two shots. Da Silva fired first and missed. My uncle didn't. Da Silva seemed to throw his own gun away. He had been hit in the shoulder. He sank to his knees, gripping the wound. Blood, bright red in the afternoon sun, seeped through his fingers.

Ian Rider appeared. I had no idea how he'd managed to follow us down from the Needle. I'd never so much as glimpsed him. But that must have been what he'd done. He skied to the very edge of the lake and spoke to me, his eyes never leaving da Silva or the other man.

"Are you all right, Alex?" he asked.

"Yes."

"Come back onto dry land. Don't say anything else. Just give me the laptop, then get your skis back on."

I did as he told me. I'd begun to tremble. I'd like to say it was just the cold, but I'm not sure that would be true.

"Who are you?" da Silva demanded. I'd never heard a voice so full of hate.

"You two can take off your skis. Both of you." My uncle raised the gun. The two men took off their skis while I was putting on mine. Ian gestured. They knew what to do. Da Silva and the fat man threw their skis into the lake. Meanwhile, the Korean man had managed to pull himself out. He was lying there shivering, blue with cold.

Both my skis snapped into place. I was ready to leave.

"Enjoy the rest of the day, gentlemen," my uncle said. He gestured at me and we set off together. Da Silva and the others would have to walk down. It would take them hours—and I had no doubt that the police would be waiting for them when they arrived.

And that was it, really. What you might call my first mission.

Sahara and her dad left that day. I thought I'd never see them again, but I met Sahara a couple of years later, and that was when she told me that her father worked in the office of the Secretary of Defense. His hard drive had contained classified information about an American agent working in the Middle East. If it had leaked, it would have put countless lives in danger—as well as being a huge embarrassment for the US government. Someone must have paid da Silva to steal it, but when that failed, he had engineered the kidnapping and the attempted ransom. Something like that, anyway.

I never did find out how my uncle had arrived just in time to rescue me. He said it was just luck, that he'd seen da Silva on the gondola and followed him up the mountain while I was racing back to the hotel. Maybe that was true. He also said the gun he'd used was the same gun he'd snatched in the fight the night before. That certainly wasn't. The funny thing was, we hardly talked about it again while we were in Colorado. It was as if there was an unspoken agreement between us. Ask me no questions and I'll tell you no lies.

When I look back on it, I wonder how stupid I could have been not to see what Ian Rider really was. A spy. But then again, I didn't know what I was either—what he'd made me. I remember he pretended to be very angry that I'd put myself in danger. But at the same time I could see that secretly he was pleased. He'd been training me all my life to follow in his footsteps, and what happened at Gunpoint had shown him I was ready.

And that was just as well. In a very short while, I'd need to be.

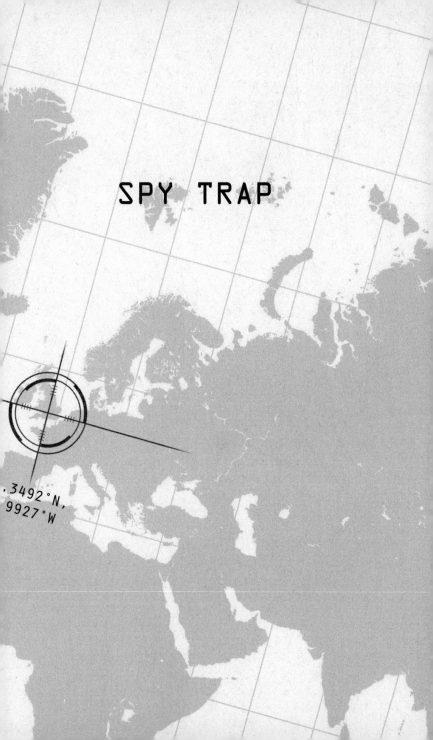

SPY TRAP

.3492°N,
9927°W

THE NURSE

Aᴌᴇx ʀɪᴅᴇʀ ᴏᴘᴇɴᴇᴅ ʜɪs eyes.

He was lying in bed in a room that he didn't recognize. White ceiling. White walls. A single door opposite him. Two windows. A polished wooden floor. No carpet.

How had he gotten here? And where, exactly, was he? He lay completely still for a moment, fighting back the first stirrings of fear, trying to work out what had happened to him. He thought back to the evening before. It must surely have been evening or night when he went to bed but he couldn't remember anything about it. Had Jack been there? Had he been in his room, doing his homework? Looking back into his memory, he saw nothing. It was as if he were standing against a blank screen that was concealing his entire world behind it. His heart was beating faster now. Something was very, very wrong. He didn't even know what day of the week it was. He could have been here for an hour. He could have been here for a year.

He tried to push back the covers and stand up, but that was when he made his next unpleasant discovery. He was too weak to move. He looked down and saw that a needle had been inserted into his arm, kept in place with a neat strip of surgical tape. It was connected to a transparent tube. There was a plastic bag dangling over his head, feeding him with some sort of colorless liquid, drip by drip.

He was in a hospital or a clinic of some sort—but with no knowledge of what had brought him here.

A car accident?

A bullet wound?

This was bad. Very bad.

Forcing himself to keep calm, Alex flexed his fingers and then his toes. He could feel them moving. That was something. Carefully, he shifted himself in the bed, trying to sense if he had any injuries. As far as he could tell, he was in one piece, with no bones broken.

He turned his head and examined his surroundings more carefully—but there was little to add to what he had already seen. The room was perfectly square and very ordinary with no pictures on the wall, nothing to make it more welcoming. There were two wooden chairs and a cupboard but no other furniture. He could make out treetops on the other side of the windows and, to one side, a stretch of water that was a greenish blue. It didn't look like the sea. It must be a lake or reservoir. The sun was shining. There was no sound of any traffic, which suggested that he wasn't in London. But he was in England. He was sure of it. There was something about the quality of the light and the shapes of the leaves that suggested he hadn't left the country. This was August, the end of the summer. At least it had been the last time he looked.

He became aware of something pressing against his head. He managed to lift a hand—the one that wasn't connected to the tube—and felt with his fingertips. There was a bandage running all the way around, under his hairline and over his ears. So he was injured, after all. He wished now that there was a mirror in the room. He badly wanted to look at himself. If he had been in an accident, how seriously had he been hurt?

He lay back, his head sinking into the pillows. Part of him wanted to call out for help, and he might have, except that his mouth was so dry and his heart beating so fast that he doubted he would be able to find his voice. Instead, he looked around for a bell or anything he might use to summon help. There was nothing. A glass and a jug of water stood on a white bedside table. What had happened to his clothes? He was wearing striped pajamas that he had never seen before. Alex never wore pajamas in bed. He preferred shorts and a T-shirt. The material felt heavy against his skin. He was half tied down by the sheets and the blankets. There was an emptiness in his stomach and he wondered how long it had been since he'd had something to eat.

About five minutes passed, although it could have been a lot longer. That was another thing. His watch was no longer on his wrist and there was no clock in the room. Then, quite suddenly, the door opened and a woman came in, dressed in the white uniform and cap of a hospital nurse. She was small and quite elderly, with gray hair tightly packed around her head and a thin nose curving some distance beyond her mouth. The way she walked and the glint in her eyes reminded Alex somehow of a bird. Glancing at her fingers, he saw that they were long and thin too. Like talons or claws.

She beamed, seeing that Alex was awake. "Oh! So you're back with us again!" she exclaimed. She spoke with a heavy Scottish accent and a high-pitched singsong voice. She had a habit of emphasizing some of her words as if they were the ones she most wanted Alex to hear. "The doctor will be pleased. How are you feeling, my dear?"

"Where am I?" Alex demanded.

"Don't you worry now. You're among friends. I know this must all feel a bit strange to you, but the main thing is you've woken up."

"You haven't answered my question." Alex knew he was being rude, but for some reason, the more pleasant the nurse sounded, the angrier he became.

She didn't seem at all put out. She was carrying a tray with a thermometer, a washcloth, and a little plastic cup of water with two pills. She set them all down on a table and reached for Alex's wrist. "You're in Wiltshire," she explained. "On the edge of Salisbury Plain. The building we're in is called Bellhanger Abbey. It really was an abbey once until we took it over. By 'we,' I mean MI6. We took it over and turned it into a hospital and clinic. My name is Wendy McDarling, but you can call me Nurse Wendy." She had been checking his pulse rate. Now she released him. "You're very fit," she said. "I can see you look after yourself, my dear. You're in excellent shape." She paused. "But you don't remember what happened?"

"No." Alex's voice fell. He hated having to admit it. He felt completely helpless.

"You were in an accident," the nurse explained. She reached for the thermometer, gave it a quick shake, then slipped it into Alex's mouth before he could protest. "You were on your way to London, on the motorway. We're not quite sure what happened. There's an investigation going on even as we speak. But we think a truck went out of control and crashed into you. Anyway, your car was forced off the road and you got a nasty bang on your head. That's probably what's affected your memory. You were brought here to Bellhanger Abbey to be looked after. This is a private hospital . . . very private. When MI6 operatives come back from their missions, they often have to spend time here. We look after them and we don't let them leave until they're as good as new!" She drew the thermometer out and checked it. "That's excellent!" she announced. "Your temperature is normal."

"I want my iPhone," Alex said. "I want to call Jack."

"Is Jack a school friend of yours?"

"No. She looks after me."

The nurse sighed. "I'm afraid your phone was destroyed in the car."

"Then can you get me a phone?"

"You'll need to see the doctor first. Meanwhile, I'm going to ask you to take these." She held out the pills.

Alex looked at them suspiciously. They were lying like white maggots in the palm of her hand. "What are they?"

"They'll help you sleep."

"I don't want to sleep. I've only just woken up."

"I'm sure that's what you think, but your body needs all the rest it can get. You've had a terrible shock." Alex still didn't take them, so she added, "If you don't want to take them, I can give you an injection instead."

She was smiling sympathetically, but Alex was sure there was something threatening in her voice, and if she still resembled a bird, it was suddenly a vulture. Her hand was stretched out. He looked at her wrist with the veins showing dark blue beneath her skin as they wormed their way up her arm. Her dark eyes were fixed on him, daring him to challenge her.

Alex was too weak to argue with her, too confused.

He took the pills.

THE DOCTOR WILL SEE YOU NOW

THE NEXT TIME ALEX woke up, it was late afternoon. He could tell from the light. How long had it been since Wendy McDarling had first introduced herself? It could have been that same morning, but Alex no longer trusted himself. He had been drifting in and out of consciousness with the result that he had no idea how much time had passed.

Once again he examined himself. He was still wearing the striped pajamas. That was his first, sour observation. But there was some good news. Turning his arm, he saw that the plastic tube had been removed. A small bandage covered the area where the needle had entered his arm. And somebody had left a plate of sandwiches and a glass of apple juice on the table beside his bed. The sight of them reminded him how hungry he was. Before he knew what he had done, he had wolfed down two of the sandwiches and drunk the juice—which was cold but too sweet. He felt better after that. More in control.

He wanted to get out of bed and stand up, but he was still too weak. He pushed back the covers and examined his legs. The striped pajamas really were horrible . . . the last thing he would have chosen to wear. As far as he could see, apart from the bandage around his head, he was unhurt. The nurse said he had been in a car accident on the way to London. Where had he been coming from? Why had he been out of London in the first place? Alex shivered. However much he tried, he couldn't remember anything. It was strange and scary . . . living inside this empty bubble.

He was actually quite glad when the door opened and the woman came back in, this time accompanied by a young man pushing a wheelchair. He was dressed in shabby jeans with a tight-fitting T-shirt, and Alex could see that his arms were covered in tattoos: butterflies, hearts, flowers . . . but also guns and hand grenades. His hair was cut so short that his scalp showed through. He had piercings in one of his ears and the side of his nose. He hadn't shaved, allowing the stubble to spread over his cheeks and upper lip. All in all, he was the last person Alex would have expected to see working in a hospital.

"How are you feeling, my dear?" the nurse asked, using exactly the same words as last time.

"I want to call Jack," Alex said.

"I know! I know! You told me that this morning." So it was the same day. "Jack knows where you are. We've given her a very full account of what's happened to you. She's very relieved that you're all right." The nurse moved to the side of the bed. "The doctor will see you now."

"So where is he?"

"He's in his office. This is Ivan. He's here to help you,

but don't try talking to him, as he doesn't speak a word of English. We're to bring you to the doctor."

That was good. Alex wanted to get out of the room, if only to see what was on the other side of the door. Even so, he didn't like the idea of being taken in a wheelchair. "I can walk," he said.

"Oh no!" Nurse Wendy frowned and shook her head. "I don't think so, Alex. If you tried to stand up, you'd just fall over!" She gave a signal and Ivan, the man with the tattoos, wheeled the chair forward, then leaned over Alex and scooped him out of the bed. He was surprisingly strong, and Alex could do nothing to prevent what was happening. Inside, he was seething that he was so weak, unable to fight back. "You'll be able to walk in a day or so," the nurse assured him.

"As soon as I can walk, I'm out of here," Alex growled.

That made her frown a second time. "I'm sure the doctor will tell you when you're fit enough to leave," she said.

"What's the doctor's name?" Alex asked.

Nurse Wendy smiled. "Dr. Feng."

DARK GLASSES

THEY WHEELED HIM ALONG a corridor that managed to be both ancient and modern at the same time. The walls were made of stone and looked like the inside of a church—which, Alex reminded himself, they were. But the polished wooden floor and the lighting were brand-new. They passed a lift with gleaming stainless steel doors followed by a stone staircase with wrought iron banisters, sweeping down to what looked like a drawing room. The downstairs windows were barred. Perhaps it was the effects of the drugs he had been given, but Alex couldn't piece it all together. Abbey, hospital, hotel, prison . . . The building had something of all of them. He took a deep breath and tried to focus on his surroundings. Any detail, no matter how small, might help him later on.

Alex's room was number 1. He had seen it written on the door. He was taken past five more rooms, all of them identical to his and empty, but the door of the last one—number 6—was closed.

"Who's in there?" he asked.

"Nobody," Nurse Wendy replied, a little too quickly. Alex made a mental note. There was something in her voice that suggested she might not be telling the truth.

"Am I alone here?"

"I'm not permitted to talk about the other patient." Nurse Wendy scowled, realizing what she had just said. "I mean, if there was another patient, I wouldn't be allowed to talk about him." She was looking angry now, as if Alex had deliberately tricked her. "The doctor will tell you everything you need to know."

They came to the end of the corridor and a plain-looking door with no number or name. The nurse knocked, and in response to a single word—"Come!"—she opened it and they went in.

Dr. Feng was sitting behind his desk. As his name might have suggested, he was Anglo-Chinese. He was also very round and fat, with black hair going gray at the sides and a small beard that began under his lower lip and hung about a centimeter below his chin. He was dressed in an old-fashioned three-piece suit complete with a striped tie and a watch chain that stretched across his stomach. There was a stethoscope hanging around his neck. Although it wasn't particularly bright in the room, he was wearing sunglasses. Alex thought he might remove them as Ivan wheeled him in, but they stayed where they were, completely masking his eyes.

Alex quickly examined the office. It looked somehow fake, like a stage set, with its shelves full of books, the rugs on the floor, the oversized fireplace. A human skeleton stood in a corner, hanging in a frame, with another door just behind it. A large window looked out onto a series of well-kept lawns with hedges that had been cut into precise mathematical shapes: spheres, cubes, and pyramids. Three Roman gods were fighting among themselves as the centerpiece of a huge marble fountain, the water spraying around them. The garden was enclosed by a tall wire fence, and there was a locked gate with two men standing guard. A gravel driveway led out, disappearing into thick woodland that obscured any further view. They could have been anywhere.

"Good afternoon, Alex," the doctor said. When he spoke, he revealed slab-like teeth that might have been false. His voice was soft, slithering over his lips. "I'm Dr. Raymond Feng, and it's a great pleasure to meet you." He pointed at his dark glasses. "You'll forgive me for not taking these off. I don't mean to be rude, but the truth is I have a slight problem. I suffer from photophobia. It means that my eyes do not like the light. My father had the same trouble with his right eye. My mother, as it happened, suffered with her left eye." He spread his hands. "When I was born, it was soon discovered that I was afflicted in both."

Nurse Wendy and Ivan had both left the room. Alex heard the door close behind him. He and the doctor were alone.

"I'm sure you have a lot of questions, Alex," the doctor went on. "The trouble is, you've taken a nasty blow to the head. Your car hit a traffic light and you were thrown forward in your seat. It's lucky you had your seat belt fastened."

"Wait a minute!" There was something the doctor

had just said that didn't add up. Alex's brain still wasn't working properly and he had to struggle to work out what it was, but at last it came. "How could we have hit a traffic light?" he asked. "The nurse said we were on a motorway, and there are no traffic lights on motorways!"

"Did I say traffic light?" The doctor stroked his beard. There was a solid gold signet ring on his fourth finger. "Maybe it was a road sign or another car. To be honest with you, I haven't been given all the details. All I know is that you have a concussion and that's confused you. You may be having issues with your memory. Please don't worry. Everything's going to be fine. You just need a little time."

"Where's my phone?" Alex asked. "Why won't you let me call Jack?"

"Surely Miss McDarling—Nurse Wendy—told you. Your phone was damaged in the accident. In fact, it was completely smashed."

Alex tried to work out how that might have happened. Surely, if it had been in his pocket, he would have been badly bruised too. He could only assume that it had somehow fallen out at the moment of impact.

"You have to trust us," the doctor went on. "Jack will come and visit you as soon as I think you're well enough. Right now, you have to rest. We also have to work out how badly you've been hurt."

"I don't feel as if I've been hurt at all."

"That's often the way with head injuries. The brain,

of course, feels no pain. You can hurt it without knowing you've done so and it's actually very difficult to know how badly damaged it is. Do you remember what happened yesterday?"

"No." Alex hated having to admit it.

"You don't remember coming in the car from the airport?"

An airport! A soon as Feng spoke the word, Alex had a flash of memory. For a brief moment, he heard the sound of a plane touching down, the roar as the engines were put into reverse thrust. He had been abroad. He had just arrived home. And there was somebody waiting for him, standing beside a car on the runway. Alex thought he recognized him. But then the image was gone, snatched away before he had time to work out who it was.

"There were three of you in the car," Dr. Feng added. "The driver and the other passenger were both quite badly hurt . . . worse than you, as a matter of fact."

"Where were we going? Where had I been?"

"I want you to tell me that, Alex . . . when you're ready." The doctor picked a bit of fluff off his sleeve. "Over the next few days, you and I are going to have several sessions together. You see, I'm not just a doctor of medicine. I also specialize in the mind. My job is to piece your memory back together again. You're going to tell me everything you can remember about yourself and the missions you've been sent on. I want you to talk to me about your friends at MI6, the people you work for. It's important you tell me everything you know."

"Why?"

"Because it will help me make you better. As soon as I feel that you're on the road to recovery, I'll arrange for Jack to visit you. You'd like that, wouldn't you?"

"Yes." The word fell heavily from his lips, as if he had been hypnotized. Alex wasn't sure if he was awake or asleep. He felt trapped between the two. Everything he was seeing and hearing could have been real or could have been some sort of dream. "I'm not meant to talk about my work," he added.

"I know. But you can talk to me. You and I are on the same side!"

Dr. Feng pressed a button on his desk. "I'll ask Ivan to take you back to your room. I'm also putting you on a course of vitamins to help you regain your strength. They will be given to you in your apple juice so there won't be an unpleasant taste. Just make sure you drink it with every meal."

An apple a day keeps the doctor away. Alex didn't know why the old saying suddenly popped into his head. He said nothing.

"You and I will have our first session tomorrow," Dr. Feng went on. Alex was clearly going nowhere. "We'll start with how you joined MI6—when you were just four-teen years old! I have to say, Alex, I've heard a lot about you and I'm delighted to finally meet you."

The door opened and Nurse Wendy came back in with Ivan, who took hold of the wheelchair. The doctor smiled, flashing his heavy white teeth.

"You can take him back to his room, thank you, Ivan," the doctor said. He turned to Nurse Wendy. "I'll see him tomorrow at nine o'clock, Miss McDarling. Straight after breakfast. We have a lot of work to do!"

"Yes, Dr. Feng."

As Alex was wheeled out, two thoughts went through his head. The first was that it was odd that the doctor had referred to Nurse Wendy as "Miss McDarling." Shouldn't he have called her "Nurse"? The second thing concerned Ivan: the nurse had said that he didn't speak a word of English, but the doctor had just addressed him in exactly that language and Ivan had seemed to understand.

Whichever way he looked at it, nothing made any sense to Alex. What exactly was going on at Bellhanger Abbey, and why was he here?

He intended to find out.

THE CLOWN

LATER, SOMETIME IN THE middle of the night, Alex woke up. He knew at once that something was wrong. The room was pitch-black. There was no light at all. And yet he could see. There was something strange about the silence too. When he called out for help, he couldn't hear his own voice.

There was a figure standing in the room at the foot of the bed. Alex hadn't heard him come in. He could have been there all the time.

A clown.

He had a bald head, tufts of green hair, a grotesque white-painted grin, and a red rubber ball for a nose. He was wearing ballooning black-and-white trousers, a multicolored jacket with handkerchiefs trailing out of the pockets, and a spinning bow tie. There was an umbrella hooked over his arm. Alex couldn't see his feet but guessed he would have elongated shoes.

Alex had always hated clowns. Jack had taken him to the circus once, shortly after she had come to the house in Chelsea where he lived with his uncle. He would have been only seven years old. He still remembered the big tent, the trapeze artists, the jugglers, the contortionists, the fire eaters. But even then he had found the clowns creepy and almost painfully unfunny. They threw cakes at each other. They squirted soda siphons. They slipped on banana peels. And they drove silly cars. But they never made him laugh.

This clown wasn't even trying to do that. He was just standing there in the weird darkness that wasn't dark, gazing at Alex with eyes that, behind the gaudy makeup, blazed with hatred.

Somehow, without moving, the clown came closer. Alex felt himself being drawn toward him. The clown was growing larger and larger in his vision. Now Alex could see nothing else.

"Who are you? Who are you working for?" The clown had asked the two questions without moving its lips and, stranger still, Alex was certain he recognized the voice. He heard a roaring sound. Something flashed past—but so fast that he couldn't see it.

He just had time to realize that none of this was happening. That it was all a bad dream.

Then he woke up.

It was the morning of the next day.

Dr. Feng's Office: 9:05 A.M. (Session 1)
DR. FENG: Good morning, Alex. Did you sleep well?
ALEX: I slept okay.
DR. FENG: And you've had breakfast?
ALEX: Yes.

DR. FENG: I hope you drank your apple juice.

Subject failed to reply.

DR. FENG: Well, let's get started, shall we? What do you remember about your uncle, Ian Rider?

Silence. Subject appears uncomfortable.

ALEX: I don't like talking about this.

DR. FENG: It's completely confidential, Alex. You have to let me into your mind. Trust me.

ALEX: No.

DR. FENG: You have to, Alex. You have no choice.

A long silence. Finally, subject begins.

ALEX: Okay. It's strange, really. I was so close to him. I mean, he was my closest relative. But I never really knew him. My mom and dad died when I was very small, and Ian brought me up. That's what I always called him, by the way. He hated being called "Uncle Ian." He said it made him sound Victorian.

He was always there for me when I was young. He took me on vacations with him, but they weren't really vacations . . . like when you go to a hotel or sit on a beach. We went camping in the Sahara Desert, canoeing down the Mekong River in Vietnam. He took me skiing, scuba diving, climbing . . . and he was always making me learn new things. When I was eight years old, it was survival techniques in the Amazon jungle! He showed me how to collect water by making a still. It was a hole in the ground with a bowl in it and a sheet over the top. I knew what to do if I got bitten by a snake. Stuff like that. When we went climbing, he taught me how to survive an avalanche. What to do if I got lost. How to make a fire without matches. He always made it sound like a game, but at the same time he was deadly serious. I mean, this was the man who took me to Everest base camp when I was eleven. He wasn't just having a laugh.

And he was the same when we were together in London. He always wanted me to push myself. I never felt he was bullying me or forcing me to do things I didn't want to do. I wanted to please him. And in many ways I was like every other kid. I watched TV. I played computer games. I hung out with my friends. It's just that I was also going down to the gym twice a week. I was learning different sorts of martial arts. Ian encouraged me to speak foreign languages. I spent the whole of one summer in Paris and another in Madrid, and in that whole time I wasn't allowed to speak or read a word of English. I wasn't much looking forward to it, but I was staying with great families. I loved the cities. And in the end I could speak French and Spanish . . . as simple as that.

DR. FENG: You were too afraid to argue?

ALEX: I told you. I was never afraid of Ian. I respected him. And I did argue with him. The only trouble was, he made me do it in Japanese.

DR. FENG: Why do you say you didn't know him?

ALEX: Because it's true. I didn't see him a lot of the time. He was always away on business. I thought he worked in a bank . . . That was what he told me, and why shouldn't I have believed him? I was looked after by a sort of housekeeper he found. I suppose you could say she was like a nanny, except she wasn't. Actually, she was an American student. She'd come to London to study, but she moved in with us. She got free rent and a bit of money in return for looking after me.

DR. FENG: Her name was Jack Starbright.

ALEX: Yes. I don't want to talk about her. Not with you. Not with anyone. The point is that Ian was lying to her. In fact, he was lying to both of us. He didn't work in a bank.

DR. FENG: He was a spy. He worked for the Special Operations Division of MI6.

ALEX: Yes.

DR. FENG: And he wanted you to be a spy too.

ALEX: I only realized that later. All the time we'd spent together, all the trips abroad, all the stuff he'd made me learn . . . He was preparing me. He wanted me to be like him.

DR. FENG: How do you feel about that?

ALEX: I wish he'd talked to me. I know he couldn't tell me about his work, but after he died, after I found out the truth . . . it made me sad. We'd had all these great times together. Sometimes, when he took me away with him, I thought I was the luckiest boy in the world. But in fact he was manipulating me. Why did he get to decide what I was going to be? I suppose all adults—moms and dads—have dreams for their kids. But that doesn't mean they have to trick them and lie to them and hide things from them. I don't even know what Ian really felt about me. Did he like me or did he just want to use me?

Subject breaks off. He seems upset by what he has just said.

DR. FENG: Are you all right, Alex? Do you want to continue?

Subject nods.

DR. FENG: Tell me about the night he died.

ALEX: Do I have to?

DR. FENG: It's important for your therapy. You got a telephone call, didn't you. It was early in the morning.

ALEX: No. I'm not going to talk about that now. Why do I have to stay here? Why won't you let me call Jack?

DR. FENG: You're tired, Alex. You're upset. I'm going to ask Miss McDarling to take you back to your room. We'll talk more in a few days.

Session terminated: 9:40 A.M.

THE CROW

ALEX WAS STILL CONFUSED. He had told Dr. Feng much more than he intended to, but for some reason he had been unable to stop himself from talking. The words had fallen out of his mouth as if they were trying to escape on their own and he couldn't hold them back.

He was also sleeping far too much—more than was healthy—but at least he had managed to recover his strength. He was able to get out of bed and he was allowed to get dressed, though not in his own clothes. Nurse Wendy brought him a gray tracksuit and a pair of sneakers. It was the sort of outfit he might have worn in a soccer training camp, Alex thought. Or a prison.

But slowly, he was getting better—he was certain of it—and sure enough, the following day, he was told that he could leave his room—not in a wheelchair but on his own two feet. The nurse had changed the bandage on his head, assuring him that his wound seemed to be healing nicely. Now she gave him a tour of the abbey, at the same time explaining the rules in her strange Scottish teacher's voice.

"Bellhanger Abbey is a top secret establishment," she said. "It was a real abbey once. It was founded in the twelfth century and it was inhabited by Cistercian monks until the time of Henry the Eighth and the dissolution of the monasteries. I'm sure you learned about that at school, Alex."

"Yes."

Brookland School in Chelsea. His best friend, Tom Harris. Playing soccer for the first team. One by one, the images flashed through Alex's mind, but somehow they seemed far away. It was as if they were memories that belonged to someone else.

"MI6 took it over and turned it into a rest home for agents who had been injured in action," Nurse Wendy continued. She was walking briskly in her white, over-starched uniform, her arms folded across her chest as if she wanted to get this over with as soon as possible. "As a matter of fact, your uncle stayed here once—although that was before my time. I'm sure you'll be comfortable here. And the important thing is to get well as soon as possible."

Alex's room was on the second floor—the same floor as Dr. Feng's office. Once again, he went past Room 6, but as before, the door was closed.

"Who else is here?" Alex asked.

"I told you. I'm not allowed to say."

"You said there was another patient."

"There were three of you in that car, Alex." Her little black eyes blinked rapidly. "I can't give you any names, but I'm sure you'll all meet in time."

They reached the staircase that Alex had seen earlier. The area at the bottom was actually an entrance hall with a heavy oak door leading out. The floor was made out of flagstones with a couple of thick sheepskin rugs. Two huge candlesticks stood on an antique wooden table to one side. As they walked down together, Alex almost felt that he was entering the world of Harry Potter. Add some talking portraits in frames and a few messenger owls and the picture would be complete.

"I don't suppose you'd like to go outside?" Nurse Wendy asked.

"Yes." Alex was pleased. If they let him out of the building, he might get a better idea of where he was. It might also help him find a way to escape.

The door was unlocked. It led out to the front of the abbey with the neatly trimmed hedges and the fountain that Alex had already seen from Dr. Feng's office, and a bell tower looming overhead. Alex was glad to be outside, breathing in the fresh air with the sun on his face, but he knew that he was still a prisoner. He was standing in front of a fence that was fifteen feet high, with searchlights mounted on several of the posts, facing both toward and away from the abbey. The woodland on the other side of the fence looked dark and uninviting—even if he had been able to reach it.

There were two guards standing beside the main gate, both of them dressed in army fatigues with rifles slung over their shoulders. One of them had an enormous dog, a German shepherd, on a lead. Seeing Alex, it pricked up its ears and growled.

"We take security here very seriously," Nurse Wendy exclaimed. She could see what was in Alex's mind.

"There's no way out," Alex muttered.

"There's no way in. We're only thinking of your safety."

"Why would I be in any danger?"

"You're a spy, Alex, my dear. You have enemies. We still don't know if the road accident really was as innocent as it seemed. We're still investigating. And until we find out for sure, we have to look after you."

As if on cue, one of the two guards walked over to them, leaving the other man and the dog behind. As he drew closer, Alex saw that he was very muscular, black, in his thirties, with a snub nose that seemed to have been pushed into his face and black, greasy hair sweeping down over his eyes. There was a wire running behind his ear, connected to a radio receiver and a throat mike.

"This is Karl, our head of security," the nurse said.

The man nodded. "Good to meet you, kid." He had a rough London accent and the sort of voice that sounded permanently angry, on the edge of violence. "I'm sure you want to explore," he went on. "But there are a few things you need to remember. Never come out here at night. Brutus will be loose in the grounds and he can be vicious."

"Is Brutus your friend?" Alex asked, gesturing at the other man.

"No. His name's Vaudrey. Brutus is the dog. You upset him, he'll rip your legs off. And he's easily upset."

"Right."

"Another thing. You don't want to touch the fence. You hear that buzzing sound? I'm sure I don't need to tell you it's electrified, kid. There are ten thousand volts running through it. You even put a finger on it, you can say good-bye to your arm. You try and climb it, there won't be enough of you left to bury."

"I'll remember that," Alex said. He disliked everything about the security man, particularly the way he kept on calling him kid.

"We have half a dozen guards working here, including me and Vaudrey, and we've all been instructed to shoot on sight." Karl smiled unpleasantly. "Don't come out at night. I'd be very upset if there was an accident."

"I'd be upset too," Alex agreed.

"Let's walk around the back," Nurse Wendy suggested. "I'll show you the tennis court and the lake."

Alex was about to follow her when a strange whirring sound made him look up. At first he thought he'd imagined it, but then he saw something small and black hovering above him, silhouetted against the sky. It still took him a moment to work out what it was. A drone!

"Don't worry about that, kid," Karl grunted. "That's also part of our security. We call it the Crow. It's a radar detection system and real-time spectrum analyzer. It's equipped with a high-resolution thermographic camera and gives us three-hundred-sixty-degree views of the surrounding area, day and night. It's controlled from the security center up in the tower."

"Also for my safety?" Alex asked.

"Why else?"

Guard dogs. Guns. Drones. Searchlights. An electrified fence. So why didn't Alex feel safe?

Over the next thirty minutes, Alex got a good idea of the layout of his new home looking for any weaknesses, anything that might offer him a way of escape. Bellhanger Abbey looked huge from the outside, mainly because of the grounds that surrounded it and the single tower that rose up high above it. That was where the bells that gave the place its name would once have been located, but now it was partly ruined. It had been rebuilt with modern plate glass and new bricks, which showed where Karl's security center had been constructed. They passed a tennis court and a croquet lawn, but as they continued around the back of the building, Alex's eye was drawn to the lake that he had glimpsed when he first woke up. It had to be at least half a mile wide. There was a wooden jetty stretching over the water with a wooden dinghy bobbing beside it. An old hoist, a sort of miniature crane used for loading and unloading supplies, stood at the end.

"What's the dinghy for?" Alex asked.

"Dr. Feng likes to go fishing." The nurse sighed. "Unfortunately, all the fish in the lake are either poisonous or inedible."

Somehow, Alex wasn't surprised.

There was a door at the back of the building that led into a common room that Nurse Wendy had mentioned. Sure enough, there were several fishing rods leaning against the wall, as well as ancient fish, stuffed and mounted in glass cabinets. The sofas and chairs were well worn and comfortable-looking. There were newspapers scattered about and some miniature palm trees growing in pots, the sort of thing you might get in an old folks' home. From here, they passed into a library with just a few paperbacks resting on otherwise empty shelves, a dining room with more miniature palms, a snooker room, and a TV room. There were fireplaces everywhere, but they were empty and unused, as if no one had ever thought to make a fire.

As they made their way into the hall, Alex noticed a notebook and a pencil lying on a table, perhaps left there by one of the guards. He waited until Nurse Wendy was looking the other way, then picked them up and slipped them into his pocket. It was a small rebellion, but it made him feel good. He was beginning to fight back.

Later that evening, after he had finished his dinner and been taken back to his room, he took out the notebook and opened it. The pages were blank, but that didn't matter. He needed it to help him set out his thoughts. He sat down and made a list of the people he had encountered so far.

- Dr. Feng

- Wendy McDarling
- Ivan
- Karl—head of security
- Vaudrey (+ Brutus)

Karl had said there were four other guards, but the abbey still seemed deserted. Maybe that was why it felt so creepy. From the moment he had woken up, Alex had felt completely alone. And that reminded him of something. Nurse Wendy had admitted that there was one other patient at Bellhanger Abbey. And yet, Dr. Feng had said quite clearly that there had been three people in the car when the supposed accident had taken place: Alex, a driver, and another passenger. The other two had been hurt worse than him—so why was only one of them here? That was something else that didn't add up.

Something was screaming at Alex inside his head. They were lying to him. He shouldn't be here. Normally, he would have already started working on an escape plan. It didn't matter that he was surrounded by armed guards and an electric fence and that he still had no real idea where he was. He would have found a way out. But his thoughts were scrambled. His head wasn't working properly. It was as if he was seeing the world through a thick fog.

He spent the rest of the evening drawing a detailed map of Bellhanger Abbey—the tower, the fence, the lake, the dinghy—putting in all the details he could remember. Some time later, he fell asleep. He hadn't even gotten undressed.

6

THE CLOWN (PART 2)

A LEX WAS AWAKE AGAIN.

It must have been after midnight. What was this? The third day since his arrival at Bellhanger Abbey, although it felt as if he had been here for weeks. He was lying on the bed, not in it, still fully clothed. There was a crumpled piece of paper in his hand and once again he read the names, at the same time hearing voices.

"I hope you drank your apple juice." Dr. Feng.

"We're only thinking of your safety." Nurse Wendy.

"There won't be enough of you left to bury." Karl.

Had he been drugged? How else could he explain the way he was feeling, the fact that his brain refused to function properly? Alex hated having chemicals in his system. He avoided food with too many additives and preservatives. He would never have been tempted to smoke. Now it occurred to him that he hadn't been feeling like himself ever since the accident—and it wasn't because of what had happened on the motorway. It was because of the treatment he had been receiving, supposedly to make him better.

He looked up, and with a jolt of fear, he saw that the clown was standing in front of him once again, clearly visible in the darkness. The makeup was as hideous as before, the brilliantly colored hair and clothes fighting against each other like paint tins thrown at a wall. Alex tried to tell himself that he was asleep, that this was just a nightmare . . . but at the same time he knew that it was more than that. Something was fighting inside him. His brain was working overtime, desperately trying to make him remember what had really happened.

Once again, he felt himself being carried forward. He heard the blast of something that might have been a car horn and a man's voice echoing around him. "Don't worry, Alex!" The clown opened its mouth. Alex saw yellow teeth and two dark holes that were the back of its throat. As he lay there, staring into the shadows, the mouth grew wider and wider. Now it was bigger than the head that contained it. The mouth had become the size of the room. Alex was staring into an impossible cave, hurtling toward it.

Alex cried out. He wanted to close his eyes but he couldn't.

The clown swallowed him whole.

Dr. Feng's Office: 10:30 A.M. (Session 2)

Subject appears tired and distracted. Eyes not fully focused. Hair untidy. Clearly has no wish to be here.

DR. FENG: Alex, the last time we spoke, you told me how your uncle, Ian Rider, prepared you to be a spy. How were you actually recruited into MI6?

ALEX: I don't want to tell you.

DR. FENG: Why not?

ALEX: It's classified.

DR. FENG: You remember, then.

ALEX: Yes.

DR. FENG: It's important to go over these details. I need to know that your memory is functioning properly . . . that there hasn't been any damage as a result of the injury to your head. And as I've explained to you, I work for MI6 too. Have you forgotten that?

ALEX: Why are you keeping me here? I want to leave.

DR. FENG: Then the sooner we get through this, the sooner we can make that happen.

A long pause. Subject trying to remain silent.

ALEX: All right. I was recruited after Ian died. At first, they told me he had been killed in a car accident. It seems to me that MI6 tells quite a lot of lies about car accidents.

DR. FENG: You think I'm lying to you?

ALEX: I didn't say that.

DR. FENG: Go on.

ALEX: I tried to find out how Ian had been killed and that led me to MI6. I nearly got killed myself . . . twice. The first time, I hid in a car crusher and they started it up. And then I climbed out a window to get into Ian's office.

DR. FENG: And what did you find?

ALEX: Nothing. The whole thing was a waste of time. It was a test. Alan Blunt had already decided he wanted to use me.

DR. FENG: Who is Alan Blunt?

ALEX: He's the chief executive of MI6 Special Operations. If you work for MI6, how come you don't know that?

DR. FENG: I do know that, Alex. I'm just testing your memory.

ALEX: Alan Blunt needed someone to investigate a company called Sayle Enterprises, which had a manufacturing plant down in Cornwall. That was where they were making a brand-new computer—the Stormbreaker—and the owner, Herod Sayle, had offered to give one, free, to every school in the UK. Blunt knew there was something dodgy about him and he asked me to check him out. I went into the plant under a false name. There was a boy who had won some competition to visit the factory and I took his place.

DR. FENG: What happened to Herod Sayle?

ALEX: Somebody shot him. It wasn't me. I never wanted to kill anyone. And when I was sent on my missions, I was never given any weapons, nothing that could seriously hurt someone. Mr. Blunt never let me have a gun and I was glad about that. I'm fourteen. It's bad enough that I have to lie to all my friends about what I do. I didn't want to be a spy and I still don't. If they asked me to kill people, I'd refuse. I'm not sure I'd be able to live with myself if I did that.

To be honest with you, if I had a choice, I'd walk away. A lot of the kids at my school would think it's cool to be a spy and to have adventures and miss class and all the rest of it. But I was never given any choice. So far, I've been lucky, but one day I'm not going to be able to walk away. I'm going to end up in a real hospital . . . or dead.

And what's really sick is that if I get killed, Blunt won't even care. He'll be annoyed. It'll be inconvenient. But in a way, he and Mrs. Jones are as bad as the rest of them. They're using me the same way they'd use a gun or a hand grenade or whatever. I'm just a weapon. A secret weapon. And when the day comes that they can't use me anymore, they'll simply find someone else. They'll forget about me.

DR. FENG: I'm sure that's not true, Alex.

ALEX: I'm tired. I don't want to talk anymore. I want to go back to my room.

DR. FENG: Of course. I'll call the nurse . . .

Session terminated: 12:10 P.M.

7

APPLE JUICE

LYING ON HIS BED, Alex thought about what had taken place.

During the interview with Dr. Feng, Alex had been aware of two quite different thoughts, at war with each other in his head. On the one hand, he felt a need to answer every question that was thrown at him and it was quite difficult to stop talking. He actually wanted to tell the truth. But at the same time, he didn't like the doctor and he didn't trust him. And so, even as he was speaking, he was struggling not to give too much away. He hadn't talked about the SAS training he'd received in the Brecon Beacons before he was sent to Cornwall. He hadn't mentioned the fact that MI6 Special Operations were based in a building on Liverpool Street that pretended to be a bank. He hadn't even intended to mention Alan Blunt's name—and it was interesting that when he had come up with it, Dr. Feng hadn't even known who he was.

Alex was talking too much. He knew it. But at least he could control something of what he said.

So far, he'd had two sessions in the doctor's office. Were they really part of some sort of cure, helping Alex to sort out his memories? Or was something else going on? Sitting on his own in his room, Alex tried desperately to focus on his predicament, but it still wasn't happening.

Being at the abbey was like watching a television program where the picture is distorted and the sound is out of sync.

It was one o'clock. Alex had demanded his watch back and he had been surprised when Nurse Wendy brought it to the room. He was still wearing the gray tracksuit he had been given, and it was as if the watch was the only part of his old identity that remained. He wondered why it hadn't been damaged or broken. After all, the accident had supposedly destroyed his iPhone. But he decided not to ask. He was afraid they might take it away again.

He made his way downstairs to the dining room, where Ivan would be waiting to bring him his lunch. It felt strange, sitting alone at a table big enough to house a banquet, but he had to admit that the food at Bellhanger Abbey was excellent and there was plenty of it. He certainly hadn't lost his appetite. As he sat down, Ivan brought in steak and fries and poured him a glass of the over-sweet apple juice that accompanied every meal.

The apple juice.

Alex had automatically picked up the glass and had been about to drink. It was a little too warm in the abbey and he was always thirsty. But now he had second thoughts. Dr. Feng had told him that he was going to be given a course of vitamins and that it would be mixed with the juice so that there wouldn't be any unpleasant taste. And when they had met, it had been one of the first things he had said. *"I hope you drank your apple juice."* It was always there. Breakfast, lunch, and dinner. Exactly the same amount. Alex found himself staring at the cloudy liquid. Why did you need to add vitamins to apple juice? Wasn't the whole point of the drink that it was full of vitamins, anyway?

He glanced up at Ivan. The tattooed orderly was standing at the door, watching him intently—exactly the same way that Nurse Wendy had watched him when she had given him his pills. She had almost forced him to take them the first time they met, but since then she hadn't ever tried again. Suddenly, Alex was certain. There was something in the apple juice, and whatever it was, it wasn't there to improve his health. There had to be a reason why he wasn't himself, why he couldn't think straight. He was holding it in his hand.

He pretended to take a sip, then set the glass down.

"Can I have some ketchup?" he asked.

"Ketchup?" Ivan repeated the word as if he had no idea what it meant.

Alex mimed squeezing a bottle with his hand. He was still convinced that Ivan understood what he was saying, but he didn't mind playing along. "Ketchup! To go on the fries."

Ivan looked annoyed. He obviously didn't enjoy having to act as a waiter. But he didn't argue. He spun around on his heel and left the room, heading for the kitchen, which was somewhere on the other side of the corridor. The moment he was gone, Alex got up with the glass and looked around him. His eye fell on one of the miniature palm trees, standing in a pot in the corner. He hurried over to it and emptied the liquid into the soil.

He just had time to return to his chair before Ivan returned, carrying a plastic bottle of the condiment. Alex was holding his glass to his lips. As Ivan came over to the table, he pretended to swallow and put the glass down contentedly. Was he imagining it, or did Ivan look relieved?

"Thanks, Ivan," he said.

Ivan did not reply.

Alex had already decided not to eat the ketchup. From now on, he wouldn't put anything in his mouth if he thought it could be tampered with. No soups, no sauces, no juices, nothing that he couldn't examine for himself. It might be that he was imagining all of it. Maybe Dr. Feng, Nurse Wendy, and the rest of them really were trying to help him after a bad car accident on the motorway.

But already Alex felt better. He was making his own decisions. He was taking back control.

Dr. Feng's Office: 4:00 P.M. (Session 3)

DR. FENG: Well, Alex, you've been here for almost a week now. How are you feeling?

ALEX: I'm sort of all right, Doctor. But I'm not sleeping very well. And I'm tired all the time.

DR. FENG: I could ask the nurse to give you some more sleeping pills.

ALEX: Yes. That would be great. I can't think straight at the moment. Do you think it's because of the accident?

DR. FENG: Of course. What other reason could there be?

ALEX: Have you found out what happened yet?

DR. FENG: I'm sorry?

ALEX: The accident. You said it was being investigated.

DR. FENG: I'm still waiting for the report.

ALEX: But it's been almost a week—

DR. FENG: Alex, let's talk about you. You were in Murmansk very recently. I'd like to know what you were doing there.

ALEX: You're talking about Colonel Sarov.

DR. FENG: That's right.

ALEX: I can't talk about it. He had this plan. He was going to start a nuclear war. But everything went wrong, and in the end . . .

DR. FENG: What happened to Colonel Sarov, Alex?

Subject became visibly distressed. Unable to continue. On the edge of tears.

ALEX: Do we have to talk about this now? I'm not feeling well. I want to go to my room.

DR. FENG: Of course. Don't upset yourself, Alex. I'll call for the nurse . . .

Session terminated: 4:07 P.M.

The session had gone exactly as Alex had planned. Another two days had passed, and in that time he hadn't had so much as a sip of the apple juice. It was surprising that the miniature palm tree in the dining room hadn't wilted and died. Every time Ivan left the room, Alex had emptied his glass into it. But he could already feel the difference in his thought processes. Suddenly he was aware of everything around him. He was beginning to put the pieces together: the guards, the German shepherd, the drone, the electric fence, the lake, the jetty. It was still possible that Bellhanger Abbey was exactly what it pretended to be: an MI6 clinic for agents hurt in action. That didn't matter anymore. Alex was going to find a way out of here.

From the moment he had entered Dr. Feng's office, Alex had pretended to be ill and upset—but actually he was neither and he had steered the conversation the way he wanted. He wasn't going to be coaxed into giving any further information about himself or anything else. It had been interesting, challenging Feng once more about the accident. Could a week really have passed without MI6 finding out anything? For that matter, why had neither Blunt nor Mrs. Jones been to the abbey to visit him? They weren't the friendliest of people. It was unlikely that either of them would bring grapes or flowers. But they needed him. If they knew he had been hurt, they would want to make sure that he was all right.

There was something else.

It was the mention of Sarov that had done it. At last, Alex knew why he had been on the motorway. He had just returned to England at the end of a mission that had taken him from the Wimbledon tennis championship to the Caribbean island of Skeleton Key. He had been recruited by the American intelligence service, pretending to be the son of two agents he had never met. The adventure had ended on the very edge of Russia, in an extraordinary ship's graveyard in Murmansk, and from there he had been flown home in a Royal Air Force jet, the Sentinel R1, normally used for intelligence gathering. Very quickly now, piece by piece, his memory was coming back to him. The plane had landed at an RAF base near Newbury. There had been a car waiting for Alex and also a man, someone he knew. But who was it? Alex still couldn't see his face.

It didn't matter. He was getting stronger with every

minute that passed. The memory would come back soon enough.

Half past six was always a quiet time in the abbey, with dinner being prepared and Dr. Feng on his way home . . . or wherever it was he went when he finished work. That was when Alex left his room, determined to make a proper examination of his surroundings. He headed first for the tower that he had seen from the gardens, which was where the main security office seemed to be located. He had already noticed a low, arched doorway with a spiral staircase leading upward. Moving quickly and silently, he passed through the arch and made his way up. If anyone stopped him, he would say he had gotten lost. After all, he was fairly certain he was meant to be drugged. And he had a good excuse: the abbey was a warren of archways and corridors.

The staircase was narrow, lit by a series of narrow windows that had been cut into the thick stone walls. The tower was about the same height as a six-story building, but there was just a single room right at the top. Alex stopped beside the door and stood there, catching his breath. Then, carefully, he poked his head around and looked into a square chamber with windows on three sides, surrounded by a balcony. The abbey might be centuries old, but this room, the security center, was brand-new.

Two men were sitting at a console, surrounded by computers, television screens, and security apparatus. They were younger than anyone Alex had met so far, maybe in their early thirties. One of them was smoking a cigarette, the other sipping a can of Coke, with his legs stretched out and his heels hooked onto the surface in front of him. They didn't look at all like MI6 agents. In fact, they reminded Alex of the sort of hired hands he had seen both at Sayle Enterprises and at Sarov's villa in Skeleton Key. He took in the rest of the room: a couple of filing cabinets, a solid-looking metal cupboard, a dartboard with six darts scattered across its face. The whole place stank of sweat and cigarette smoke.

Suddenly, one of the men turned, and before Alex could duck out of sight, he had been seen.

"What do you want?" the man demanded. He had a scar that zigzagged across his upper and lower lip. It had the effect of twisting his mouth into two pieces, as if he were being reflected in a broken mirror.

"I'm sorry." Alex stepped into view, trying to look lost and innocent. "Dr. Feng said I could come up here. I want to look at the view."

The two men exchanged a glance. Then the man with the scar shrugged. As far as he was concerned, Alex was just a kid with nothing better to do. "Sure. If that's what the doctor said."

There was a glass door leading out onto the balcony. Alex stepped outside and found himself standing behind a barrier that consisted of a stone wall with a series of columns rising up to his waist. If he leaned too far forward, he would topple over. The sky was getting darker and not just with the coming night. Alex was sure there was going to be a storm. He could feel the closeness in the air. He stood there, examining the lawns far below with the marble fountain and the gate on one side and the tennis court on the other. The electric fence curved around in an almost perfect circle, separating the abbey from the lake with its jetty and crane. From this height, Alex got a sense of the woodland, which continued, uninterrupted, all the way to the horizon. He had been told that he was in Wiltshire, but the truth was that this was a world of its own, utterly enclosed and with no obvious way out.

A car—a bright orange Lada—pulled out from the side of the building and drove toward the gate. Alex could see Dr. Feng in the front seat, sitting behind the wheel like an overstuffed cushion. The two guards, Karl and Vaudrey, examined him briefly before they allowed him to pass. The German shepherd dog sniffed around the wheels, and Alex realized that even if he managed to hide in the back of the car, the animal would know he was there. Anyway, he had tried exactly the same thing when he was a prisoner of Colonel Sarov, and that hadn't ended at all well. He would have to find another way.

He had the beginnings of an idea. Standing there, with the first angry gusts of wind tugging at his hair, he began to measure the distances: the height of the fence, the position of the gate, the distance to the first trees and the edge of the lake.

Could it work?

No.

It would be suicide. There had to be another way.

He went back into the security room, and this time he noticed the drone—the Crow—that he had seen hovering over him when he was outside. It was lying on a work surface with the joystick control beside it. Looked at more closely, it was an ugly-looking thing with four arms stretching out more like a spider than a crow, each one mounted with a black propeller. There was a sophisticated camera attached to its belly, staring across the room with its single eye. That was something else to consider. If Alex did manage to break out of the abbey, he would be tracked every inch of the way. What was the range of the device? He had heard of drones that could fly for up to three miles. The trees would provide him with cover, but Karl had told him that the camera was thermographic, meaning that it didn't even need to see him. His own body heat would give him away.

The two security men were becoming uneasy. "That's enough!" one of them said. "You should get back to your room."

"Sure!" Alex smiled as if he didn't care either way. "Thanks!"

He went back the way he had come. He hated having to sound so meek, but it was important not to raise their suspicions. He had no intention of going back to his room. He had seen Dr. Feng leaving. The entire building seemed to be quiet. He was feeling strong and clear-headed. This was too good an opportunity to miss.

He reached the bottom of the staircase and followed the corridor back the way he had come.

Alex was quite certain that he wasn't the only "patient" being treated at Bellhanger Abbey. Dr. Feng had said that there were two other people in the car when it crashed, and later on, Nurse Wendy had more or less admitted that one of them was here. They had to be in Room 6. It was the only door on Alex's corridor that was permanently closed, and he remembered how uneasy the nurse had been when they walked past. That was where he was heading now. If there was someone else in the room, perhaps they might be able to tell him what was really going on.

There was nobody around. Alex stopped outside the room and rested his hand against the handle. He pressed down. The door wasn't locked, but that wasn't so surprising. There was no need to keep anyone a prisoner in their own room when the entire abbey was little more than a giant prison. Very gently, he opened the door, checking that there was no sound coming from inside. There was nothing. He slipped inside, closing the door behind him.

Room 6 was identical to his own except that it looked out onto the other side of the abbey, with a view of the main gate. Alex saw the same furniture, the same lack of pictures or mirrors, the same white ceiling and wooden floor, the same bed. There was a man lying on the bed. He was partly concealed by shadow, but as Alex drew closer, he was certain that he knew who the man was. An older man dressed in the same striped pajamas that Alex had been given. Hair that was thinning out and a lined, weathered face. His features were slack because he was so soundly asleep, but Alex recognized him at once.

John Crawley. The man who described himself as the office manager at MI6 but who was actually much more. It was he who had first introduced himself to Alex at Ian Rider's funeral, at the same time opening the door into the dark world of espionage. More recently, he had invited Alex to become a ball boy at Wimbledon, pitching him into a confrontation with the Chinese triads that had nearly cost Alex his life. Crawley had once been an effective field agent himself. Alex had always thought of him as one of Blunt's toughest and most capable operatives. And now he was here.

The sight of him lying helplessly in the bed smashed the final barriers in Alex's memory. It was like a falling deck of cards. One after another, Alex saw the images and remembered what had happened.

John Crawley had met him at the air base near Newbury. He had been standing on the tarmac as Alex climbed down from the RAF Sentinel R1. Alex had been exhausted, still drained by what had happened at Murmansk.

"Alex! Good morning. I thought I should come and collect you. How are you?"

"I want to go home."

"I have a car waiting. Mrs. Jones wants to see you."

"I don't want to see her. Just take me home, Mr. Crawley."

"*Of course, Alex. Straightaway . . .*"

The car was a silver Jaguar XJ. It was exactly the sort of car that Crawley would drive, only this time he was going to be a passenger, along with Alex. There was a uniformed chauffeur waiting, and as the two of them approached, he opened the back door and stood back respectfully. At the time, Alex had barely registered him. He was too tired. But now, as the images tumbled through his mind, he saw him more clearly.

Karl! The snub-nosed security man from the gate. How was that possible?

Standing in the bedroom, Alex wanted to shout at himself not to get into the car. But he and Crawley had gotten in. He heard the clunk of the closing door and a moment later they were on their way, swinging out of the airfield and following a series of country lanes to the motorway. There was a blue sign. He saw it now as he had seen it then. LONDON 64 MILES.

"*Would you like some air-conditioning, sir?*" That was Karl's voice, coming from the front.

"*Are you all right, Alex?*" Crawley asked.

Alex hadn't replied, his head resting against the window, staring out.

The motorway was tedious, the cars whipping past. The driver seemed to be in no hurry to get them home.

There was a semi in the road ahead of them. It was moving quite slowly, hogging the middle lane, but for some reason the driver made no attempt to overtake it. Slowly,

Alex became aware of it. The whole thing was covered in pictures and there were words in bright red letters.

DR. FENG'S TOURING CIRCUS.
FUN FOR ALL THE FAMILY.

A clown stared at him, plastered across the two doors at the back. Green hair. White painted face. Red lips. Now the driver was getting closer and closer to the semi. It was almost as if he wanted to cause a deliberate crash.

"Driver, what are you doing?" That was Crawley again, snapping out the words.

The driver ignored him. The distance between the car and the semi was narrowing with every second that passed.

Alex saw Crawley's hand disappear into his jacket. He wasn't reaching for a wallet or a pen. He knew they were in danger. He brought out a gun.

He was too late.

It all happened very quickly. The doors of the semi flew open, revealing two men standing in an interior that was otherwise completely empty. A metal ramp shot out, slanting down toward the road. Both vehicles were traveling at about forty miles per hour but now the chauffeur stomped down on the accelerator and the Jaguar leapt forward, onto the ramp and then up into the truck. The clown doors slammed shut behind them, swallowing them up.

Crawley had his gun trained on the driver's neck. "Who are you? Who are you working for?"

The two men had positioned themselves one on each

side of the car. The car must have missed them by inches as it rocketed in. They were both armed, two guns to Crawley's one, but then Karl turned and Alex saw that the total had gone up to three. He and Crawley were trapped in a doubly enclosed space. Inside a car inside a truck. They were outnumbered. He knew he had no chance.

Crawley had come to the same conclusion. He lowered his gun, turned, and spoke quietly to Alex. "It's me they want, not you. Don't worry, Alex. I'm sure they'll let you go."

Karl was leaning over the front seat, still holding the gun. There was something that looked like a grenade in his other hand. He dropped it onto the floor between Alex and Crowley. There was a hiss and a cloud of gray smoke was released, billowing upward. Karl climbed out of the car, closing the door behind him. It was the last thing Alex remembered. The fumes were choking him. He felt his head spinning. Then he passed out.

Crawley had been wrong. Whoever was behind this had wanted both of them. They had both woken up in Bellhanger Abbey. But why? What was the point?

That didn't matter now. The two of them had to get out of here. Alex hurried over to the bed, grabbed Crawley by the shoulder, and shook him. "Mr. Crawley!" he whispered as loudly as he could. He didn't want to bring in anyone from outside the room. "Wake up! This is Alex."

Nothing. Alex shook him harder.

"Mr. Crawley! Wake up!"

It still wasn't working, and Alex was afraid someone

might come in at any moment. He looked around and saw a glass of water on a bedside table. Without a second thought, he picked it up and threw the contents into the agent's face.

Crawley's eye blinked open. "Alex . . . ?"

"Wake up, Mr. Crawley. You've got to wake up now."

"Where are we?" Crawley was still struggling, trying to fight his way back to consciousness.

"We're prisoners. We were grabbed on the motorway. You have to help me get out of here."

"What?" Water was dripping out of Crawley's hair. The pillow behind him was damp.

"You have to get out of bed," Alex insisted. "I need your help!"

"Help . . . ?"

But it was no good. Crawley was too heavily drugged. His head fell back and he said nothing more.

Alex was on his own.

JACK

IT WAS DARK OUTSIDE. The clouds were heavy and close. Alex knew that Karl would be waiting for him in the dining room, but he was determined to keep moving, to use the silence and the fact that Dr. Feng was away. That was where he was heading now. He'd had four meetings in the doctor's office, and although he hadn't seen a computer or a telephone there, surely there must be one. He'd also noticed a second door, behind the skeleton. That might lead somewhere interesting. The most important thing was to get a message out to MI6 or to Jack. They'd told him that his iPhone had been smashed in the accident, but since he now knew there had been no accident, it was always possible he might find it, and Feng's office was the obvious place to begin.

The office—like Room 6—was unlocked. Alex went in quickly, flicked the light on, and closed the door behind him. The first thing he saw was the human skeleton dangling on its wire frame in the corner. A warning? Alex briefly examined the different bones. A thought occurred to him. He was alone and he was unarmed. The skeleton might just come in useful . . .

It took him less than a minute to do what he had in

mind. After that, he went over to the second door and opened it. To his annoyance, it only led into a small bathroom, and although there was a cabinet above the sink, it didn't contain anything apart from a toothbrush, a bar of soap, and a small pair of nail scissors. He took the scissors anyway.

He was about to leave when he caught sight of himself in a mirror above the sink—it was the first time he had seen himself since he had arrived at the abbey. He looked drawn and thin, probably a result of the drugs he had been given. The bandage was still wrapped around his head. He had forgotten all about it. On an impulse, he tore it off. There was no wound, no mark of any sort under his hairline or anywhere else. Alex wasn't even surprised. The bandage had only been placed there as part of the charade.

He went back into the office and examined the desk. Dr. Feng liked to keep the place neat. There was almost nothing on the surface. Just two pencils and a notepad. No computer and no phone. Quickly, he rummaged through the drawers. He found more papers, including a typed-up transcript of his own three sessions in the room. Alex was wasting time, and he was about to leave when, quite suddenly, a phone began to buzz. The ringer had been turned off but it was still making enough of a sound for him to know that it was somewhere near.

Quickly, he threw open the drawers, trying to find it. He couldn't see it. He pulled out a whole stack of letters. Photographs. Then a clinical report, "On the Use of Sodium

Pentathol in Advanced Interrogation." He took it out,
meaning to glance through the pages but in doing so had
revealed an iPhone, concealed underneath. It was his own.
He recognized it instantly, sitting in its protective silicone
case with his own initials written in blue pen. There was
a large slab of chocolate next to it and Alex remembered
that Crawley had brought the chocolate with him to the air
base. At the time, he had been amazed at the way the MI6
man thought. *You've just saved the world . . . I've brought
you some sweets.* But that didn't matter now. He snatched
the phone and answered just in time.

"Hello?" he said, hardly daring to believe that he
might finally have made contact with the outside world.

"Alex? Is that you?"

He knew the voice at once. "Jack!"

"My God, Alex. I've been trying to reach you all week.
I've been so worried about you. Mrs. Jones told me that you
were back safely from Russia or somewhere and that she'd
sent someone to collect you. When you didn't show up,
I called her, but she wouldn't tell me anything. I knew
something was wrong, but . . . honestly! Those people!"

"I'm safe, Jack. But I need help."

"Where are you?"

"Don't say another word. Put the phone down. If you
speak one more word, I will shoot you."

Alex turned around. Karl, the security man who had
also driven the car into the circus truck, was standing a
short distance away, holding an ugly semiautomatic pistol,

trained on Alex. Alex hadn't heard him come into the room. He was still holding his phone. It was inches away from his mouth. He desperately wanted to say the two words—Bellhanger Abbey—that would lead Jack to him, but he knew he didn't dare. Karl meant business. There was an ugly glimmer in his eyes and he was holding the gun very still, prepared to shoot. Alex cursed himself. He shouldn't have let Jack speak so long. Of course she had been surprised to hear from him. And he'd been overjoyed to hear her voice. But he should have told her where he was straightaway.

Now it was too late. He clicked the phone off and placed it on the desk. Karl took two steps forward, closer to Alex. He was smiling unpleasantly. "That was sensible, kid. Now step away from the desk."

Alex did as he was told.

Karl took a step forward and brought his gun slamming down onto Alex's phone, smashing it. "They should have done that from the start," he said. He examined Alex. "It looks to me like someone hasn't been taking their medicine," he sneered. "What happened to your bandage? Dr. Feng's not going to be very happy with you. My guess is that very soon you're going to be transferred to intensive care."

"Who are you?" Alex demanded. "I know this place isn't a hospital. It's got nothing to do with MI6. And you owe me a new iPhone."

"You can take that up with the doctor!" Karl was mocking him. "He'll be here any minute. Right now I'm going to take you back to your room." He gestured with the gun. "After you, kid."

Alex walked toward the door, at the same time reaching behind him with his right hand. Karl didn't see the movement. Nor had he noticed that before he'd come in, Alex had removed one of the bones from the skeleton—the tibia, which ran from the knee to the foot. It was solid and heavy and had been tucked into the waistband of his tracksuit. As he passed the security man, he withdrew it, then turned and, in a single movement, smashed it into the side of his neck. Karl cried out. Alex hit him a second time, harder. He felt the bone shudder in his hand. It was enough. Karl slumped to the floor and stayed there.

Alex snatched up the gun. He didn't like firearms, but there was no way he was going to leave it behind. Dr. Feng was on his way back. Karl wouldn't stay unconscious long. He had to get out of Bellhanger Abbey fast, and although he'd figured out a way, he was still fairly certain he was committing suicide.

There was only one way to find out. Alex ran out of the room, making for the stairs.

The first thing he needed was a fishing rod.

10

IN THE RAIN

FIFTEEN MINUTES LATER, DR. Feng arrived back in his orange Lada. It had begun to rain, lightly at first, but now the clouds had opened and it was pouring down. Karl had recovered and had made his way out to meet him. The two of them stood there, getting wetter and wetter, shouting above the noise of the falling water.

"What happened?" Feng demanded.

"I found him in your office. He hit me." There was a huge bruise on Karl's forehead. Blood was trickling down over one eye.

"Where is he now?"

"We're searching the building. He has to be inside. The gate has been locked and the electric fence is in operation. The dog is out here. There's no way he can get away."

There was a flash of lightning and Dr. Feng howled, bringing up his fists to cover his eyes. He didn't wear his dark glasses at night and the brilliant light had caught him unawares. "This entire operation is a catastrophe!" he screamed. Rain dripped down the sides of his face and off his beard. There was something frog-like about him, standing there, drenched. "The boy must have guessed—and he's stopped taking the drug! Somehow he's managed to escape. This is your fault, Karl. You'll pay for this."

A third figure joined them, fighting her way through the downpour under an umbrella. It was the woman who called herself Nurse Wendy. "There's no sign of him anywhere," she screeched, fighting against the clamor of the storm.

"What about the agent—Crawley?"

"Still asleep. I told you the dose was too high! He can't even talk."

"This is a disaster." Dr. Feng might have been crying. It was hard to tell with so much water streaming down his face. He collected himself. "All right! Change of plan! Find the boy and kill him. That's all that matters now. Tell the guards to shoot on sight."

"I've already told them that," Karl exclaimed.

"Did he say anything to the woman on the phone?"

"No."

"There's still a chance that MI6 will manage to trace the call. We're moving out of here. We'll take Crawley with us and begin his interrogation in one of our other locations. But we can't do anything until the boy has been neutralized. Find him. Kill him. Tell me when it's done!"

There was an explosion of thunder and another brilliant flash of lightning. Dr. Feng screamed and, covering his eyes, staggered blindly into the building, leaving the others to continue the search.

11

OVER AND OUT

ALEX HAD FOUND WHAT he wanted in the common room.

When Nurse Wendy had shown him around the abbey, she told him that Dr. Feng liked to go fishing, and there were actually three rods ready for use, each one of them brand-new and state-of-the-art, with graphite bodies and titanium oxide guides. These were specialist bass and catfish rods, for use in the lake . . . but fishing was the last thing Alex had in mind. It had taken him only a moment to loosen and then remove the aluminum spools. Each one of them came complete with at least three hundred feet of line. He had taken all of them, racing back up to the first floor and along to the spiral staircase.

He knew that Feng and the others were looking for him. He could hear the guards shouting at each other somewhere in the distance. As he continued forward, he caught sight of someone coming toward him and ducked into a doorway just as Ivan, the orderly who had always brought his food, came rushing past. Alex was lucky that the corridor was dark. The two of them missed each other by inches.

Alex pressed on, through the archway and up the

stone stairs. The security office would be manned, of course. The two men that he had met earlier would be on full alert. But he had a gun . . . even if he was reluctant to use it. Hopefully, showing it to them would be enough.

In fact, only one of the men—the one with the twisted lips—was in the security office. He looked up as Alex came bursting in, the three fishing reels grasped in one hand, the gun in the other.

"Get out of your chair," Alex said. "Keep both your hands in sight. If you try anything, I'll shoot you. I mean it."

The man got up slowly. "You're wasting your time," he said. "You should give yourself up before you get hurt."

Alex looked around him. His eyes settled on the metal cupboard. He opened it. There were a couple of jackets hanging there and about a dozen wire hangers but nothing else. It was perfect. "I want you to get in here," he said.

"You might have to shoot me first."

Very casually, Alex brought the gun around and fired, knowing that the thick walls and the height of the tower would muffle most of the sound. He had intended merely to hit the floor, but quite by accident, the bullet found its target barely an inch from the man's foot. A splinter of wood stabbed into his ankle. The guard leapt up, all the color draining from his face. "All right! All right!" he exclaimed. "No need to get nasty!"

He hurried into the cupboard.

Alex slammed the door. He had taken out several of the wire coat hangers and he used one to secure the handles, twisting it around. The guard might be able to force his way out, but by then, Alex would be long gone. Fortunately, he had seen what he was looking for, the second part of his plan. It was sitting on the console, with the joystick beside it.

The Crow.

Alex's best friend, Tom Harris, had a drone and the two of them had often played with it in Battersea Park, flying it over the Peace Pagoda and the River Thames. They'd always been nervous about getting into trouble, as drones were increasingly prohibited all over London, particularly near airports, and the Battersea Helipad was only a short distance away. The moment Alex had seen the Crow, he'd had a vision of using it to fly himself out of here. He couldn't cling on to it, of course. The maximum weight that a drone like this could carry (he had read about Amazon using drones to deliver packages) was about five pounds. But if he was careful, if he took his time, he could use it nonetheless.

First of all, he pulled out the ends of the fishing lines from all three aluminum spools and tied them to the camera underneath the Crow. Then he took everything outside to the balcony where he had stood only a short time before. He saw that the searchlights had been turned on. The entire area between the abbey and the perimeter fence had been floodlit. It was still raining, but for now the thunder and the lightning had stopped. Dressed only in the tracksuit he had been given, Alex was quickly soaked and he wished he had thought to take the guard's jacket before he had locked him up.

Ignoring the muffled thumping and the shouts coming from the cupboard, he went back for the joystick. He guessed it would work exactly the same way as Tom's—weren't all drones more or less identical?—with one switch to go up and down, the other to go left and right. Of course, he would have preferred a bit of time to get used to the machine's sensitivity, to work out how quickly it responded to his commands. Unfortunately, time was something he didn't have. He heard Brutus barking. The searchlights were crisscrossing the grass. Any moment now, Feng's people would notice that the security office had become completely silent and would be running up to find out what was going on. He had to do this now.

He had set the drone down on the edge of the stone banister. Now he lifted the joystick and activated it. At once, the propellers began to turn. So far, so good. Alex did his best to put everything out of his mind: the lights blazing, the men searching for him all over the abbey, the security guard locked in the cupboard, trying to break out, the possibility that one or more of his colleagues might arrive at any time. All that mattered was the dark black metal and plastic machine in front of him. He pressed on one of the controls, accelerating the propellers, and the Crow lurched into the air, more like a drunken animal than a bird. Alex gritted his teeth as it toppled to one side, seemingly about to crash into the wall of the tower, but at the last moment, desperately manipulating with his thumbs, he was able to hold it steady. The Crow continued upward, carrying the three nylon fishing lines with it. When it was a couple of yards above his head, he paused, examining the lines that glinted in the light and the rain. Taking a deep breath, he guided the drone away from the tower. The three lines had somehow woven themselves together into one. They stretched out, high above the ground.

Now came the difficult bit. The drone had crossed the electric fence, still trailing the triple fishing line. It hovered over the jetty. Alex pressed down, lowering it, then cursed as it dipped too far, briefly out of control. Forcing himself not to panic, not to try and rush things, he steadied it, then guided it around the hoist that stood at the water's edge, effectively looping the line around it. Behind him, he could hear the guard pounding at the metal cupboard, but the twisted metal coat hanger seemed to be holding up. Far below and out of sight, the dog was barking frantically as if it alone knew what was going on. The lights were fanning out left and right, desperately searching for any movement but not looking in the one direction that would have revealed all. Alex had steered the drone over the L shape formed by the top of the hoist and its outstretched arm. It was hard to be certain, with the rain driving into his face. With one sodden sleeve, he wiped water away from his eyes. Had he done it? He was about to find out.

He stabbed sideways with his thumb, pressing the control on the joystick and bringing the drone back to him, the three reels still emptying their load. Effortlessly, the drone soared up and across toward the tower, a good Crow returning to its master. Drops of rain splattered off the black plastic. Now there were no fewer than six lines trailing behind it: three going out, three coming back. He would need that extra strength. The drone hovered in front of him. Alex brought it gently down. All three spools were empty. Alex saw that he had used almost all the line; there couldn't have been more than a few inches left. But he had achieved what he wanted. He had connected the tower and the jetty, using what must have been the thinnest bridge in the world.

Would it hold his weight? Again, Alex remembered his uncle. Ian Rider had often gone fishing and had done his best to persuade Alex to come with him, although Alex had never seen the point of killing any animals in the name of sport. Even so, Ian had talked about his equipment. Alex knew that fishing lines were given test ratings that could be as low as two or as much as four hundred pounds. He didn't know if these lines were monofilament or braided, and they probably had a diameter of no more than 0.015 inches. But he was fairly sure they'd been designed for big fish . . . Nurse Wendy had mentioned catfish, which might weigh up to twenty pounds.

At the end of the day it was all guesswork, but the last time Alex had stood on a set of scales, he had weighed in at 110 pounds. He was probably quite a bit thinner after a week at the abbey. There were effectively six lines stretching out from the tower to the lake. Suppose each one was capable of holding twenty pounds. Six times twenty equals 120. It wasn't a huge margin, but surely, together, the lines would be strong enough to take his weight.

He was about to find out. He was going to slide out of here, over the electric fence. If he didn't actually clear it, if his foot touched the wire, he would die. If the fishing lines broke, he would die. If the guards looked up and saw him, he would die. But if he simply waited for them to find him, the result would be exactly the same. He had no choice. He couldn't think of any other way.

He cut the lines off the drone, using the scissors he had taken from Feng's bathroom, then tied them around one of the stone columns of the banister, ensuring that they were as tight as possible. Finally, he grabbed hold of two of the wire hangers he had taken from the cupboard and bent them into an upside-down U shape, curving over the line. He held one end in each hand. Taking a deep breath, he looked down.

He still couldn't bring himself to go. It was raining harder again and he was half blinded. It was a very long way to the ground. It suddenly struck him that this whole scheme was madness, and he was about to give up and find another way when he heard the door of the security office burst open and somebody shouted.

Alex heaved himself over the edge of the tower and jumped.

He fell, incredibly fast, as if he had simply leapt to his

death. He was certain that the lines—all six of them—would break. But then he lurched back upward and felt a jolt in his arms that told him the fishing lines were holding and that he was actually dangling in the air like an over-sized puppet. Or a fish. His hands were hooked into the bent wire, barely able to keep their grip. He couldn't feel his fingers. The rain whipped into his face. The electric fence rushed toward him in a blur.

He was too low! His feet were going to plow straight into it. Crying out, Alex curled his legs up, putting more strain on his stomach and arms. He folded his knees into his stomach, desperately aware that his feet were still too low. The wire was suddenly very close. He saw the rain hitting it and imagined the current running through it. He closed his eyes, waiting for the shock.

But then, somehow, he passed over it, missing it by less than an inch. He wasn't going to be electrocuted. But there were other ways to die. He was traveling too fast. In about one second's time he would hit the wooden hoist and that would smash every bone in his body. Alex felt the wind and the rain slamming against him. He could hardly see at all. At the last moment, hoping he had judged it right, he swung himself sideways and let go.

Briefly, he hurtled downward. He must have been traveling at forty or fifty miles per hour, faster than a speeding car. For a horrible fraction of a second, he felt himself twisting through the air, falling into nothing. Then his feet hit water. He had missed the jetty and plunged into the lake. Was it deep enough? The thought hadn't even reached Alex's mind before he was sinking into utter darkness, bubbles erupting from his nose and mouth, drowning. He floundered with his arms, kicked out with his legs. Everything was confused.

Then he broke the surface. He was on the other side of the fence, outside the abbey. But the guards had seen him. They knew what he had done and they were already shouting for the gate to be opened. Alex was soaked, he was terrified, he was half frozen. And he still hadn't gotten away.

THE FOREST

THEY WERE COMING AFTER him.

Dr. Feng, Karl, Vaudrey, Ivan, Brutus . . . Alex didn't know how many of them there were. Perhaps Nurse Wendy had even joined them too. He could hear the dog barking, not far behind, and only hoped that the rainfall would deaden his scent and, for that matter, the noise he was making as he fought his way through the woods.

There was a flash of lightning, a vast wall of it, blocking the way forward and briefly illuminating the ancient trees snarled together in knots, thick leaves shaking in the wind, endless raindrops hanging in spider's webs all around, paths that led nowhere, moss, toadstools, grass . . . everything frozen in black and white, as bad as any nightmare Alex had ever endured. He had absolutely no idea where he was going. The forest might continue for miles. He couldn't even be sure that he was still running away from the abbey. He had lost all sense of direction and it was only the sounds of his pursuers, always behind him but getting closer, that told him which way to run.

His foot caught in a root and he was sent flying forward, crashing into the ground. Fortunately, soft mud broke his fall, but when he stood up again, he was even more disoriented than before and, worse, he found that he had twisted his ankle. As he pressed on, every footstep brought with it a jolt of pain that traveled up his leg, into his knee and thigh. He was still drenched from the lake but, impossibly, the rain was making him wetter. He could feel the strength draining out of him.

Should he continue or perhaps climb a tree and hide? He could lose himself in the branches and wait for daylight. Would he survive a night in this storm, and did he even have the strength to pull himself up out of sight? He was still trying to make up his mind when he stumbled through a tangle of bushes, thorns tearing at his clothes, and found himself in a large, circular clearing.

There was a little more light here, the moon somehow penetrating the dense gray clouds. It gave Alex hope. Perhaps, if the trees were thinning out, he might actually have made it to the other side. Could there be a road nearby? He listened for any traffic but there was nothing. He was in the middle of the countryside and it was half past eight at night. Even if there was a road, nobody would be out in this weather. Still, he pressed on with new strength, ignoring the pain in his ankle. Bellhanger Abbey must have been built near a community. Surely he would find it.

He was halfway across when Brutus found him.

The German shepherd came bounding out from the tree line and stopped for a moment, barking furiously. Alex turned and saw it, a dripping ball of fur, blazing eyes and white teeth. It barely looked like a dog at all, more like a wild beast out of one of those medieval paintings . . . a vision of hell. Three men emerged behind it. Alex couldn't make out their faces. It didn't matter. He was fully exposed, in the middle of the clearing. They had seen him. Slowly, knowing the chase was over, they began to move toward him.

There was nothing more Alex could do. The men were armed with rifles. Even if he turned and tried to run, they could shoot him down. Brutus could reach him in seconds. He had done everything he could. But it was over.

The men drew closer. Alex could hear the dog growling.

Alex recognized Karl. Without saying a word, determined to get this over with, the head of security lifted his rifle. He took aim.

There was a shot.

Karl toppled backward, dropping his own weapon. At the same time, the German shepherd launched itself toward Alex. There was a second shot. The dog yelped, tumbled over, then limped away.

The shots had come from behind Alex.

Alex turned and saw half a dozen figures—men and women all dressed in black—emerging from the forest. One of them shouted, "Get down!"

Alex wasn't sure if the words were meant for him or for the men from the abbey. He didn't care. He fell to his knees anyway, taking himself out of the line of fire. Dr.

Feng's people had given up the fight. They were standing with their hands raised, and Alex knew that somehow MI6 had found him.

Someone Alex didn't know came over to him. "Are you all right, Alex?" the man asked.

Alex got to his feet. He was soaking wet, scratched, and exhausted. His ankle was on fire. The drugs he had been fed at the abbey still hadn't left his system. He drew a breath.

"Never felt better," he said, then collapsed, unconscious, to the ground.

LONDON—A WEEK LATER

"I thought you might like to know about Bellhanger Abbey," Mrs. Jones said.

"Actually, I'm doing my best to forget about it," Alex replied.

"I'm sure."

The deputy head of MI6 Special Operations was sitting on the sofa in Alex's front room. Alex was opposite her, with Jack Starbright next to him. This conversation was supposed to be classified, top secret, but she would never have left him alone when this woman was in the house.

Jack was afraid that if she even blinked, Alex would be spirited away to Russia or Cuba or anywhere else MI6 needed him. It worried her. MI6 never left him alone.

"How did you find me?" Alex asked.

"That was easy. We'd been looking for you and

Crawley ever since the two of you had disappeared, and we had agents all over the southwest of England. But it was the moment you answered your iPhone that did it. We were able to lock in to the signal, and we put together an assault team straightaway. They were moving in when they found you."

"Lucky I called," Jack muttered.

"Lucky I answered," Alex agreed.

"But what was it all about?" Jack demanded. "Why had they kidnapped Alex and Mr. Crawley in the first place?"

"The whole thing was an information-gathering exercise," Mrs. Jones explained. "Dr. Feng—if that's his real name—was working for a foreign intelligence service, and his job was to find out as much as possible about MI6 Special Operations. He was particularly interested in you, Alex. The idea of a fourteen-year-old boy volunteering to be a spy is a very unusual idea—"

"I never volunteered," Alex reminded her.

"And they wanted to know who you were and how much you'd achieved," Mrs. Jones went on, ignoring him. "Somehow they found out you were on your way back from Murmansk and set up a trap. They snatched you and John Crawley just after you landed. Both of you were drugged. You were given a cocktail of Rohypnol, which made you sleep and confused you, and Sodium Pentothal, which is also known as the truth drug. I'd be interested to know how much you told them, incidentally."

"I didn't tell them anything," Alex growled. That wasn't

quite true, but he hadn't told them anything that was important. Anyway, the question had annoyed him. Mrs. Jones always put her own interests first. "So which foreign intelligence service were they working for?" he asked.

"We still don't know," Mrs. Jones replied. "The man called Karl was killed in the crossfire. McDarling, Vaudrey, and the rest were ordinary criminals who had been hired by Feng. As for Feng himself, we're interrogating him. He's not talking, but he may have been paid by the Chinese or the Russians. They're both extremely aggressive when it comes to intelligence. It might even be the Americans. Under their new president, I wouldn't put anything past them."

"Well, it was nice of you to call in," Jack said. "But if you don't mind, we have to be moving on. Alex is heading off on vacation for a couple of weeks and we need to leave for the airport."

"Oh." Mrs. Jones got to her feet. "Anywhere nice?"

"Just somewhere in the sun." Jack was determined not to tell her—although she knew that MI6 could find out in seconds.

"You certainly deserve a break, Alex. Enjoy yourself!"

In fact, Alex was heading for the South of France. He had been invited by his friend Sabina Pleasure. He was going to be spending a couple of weeks with her parents in an area known as the Camargue. Upstairs, his bags were already packed.

What Alex didn't know was that a Russian assassin